BLOOD IS
THE SKY

Also by Steve Hamilton

North of Nowhere
The Hunting Wind
Winter of the Wolf Moon
A Cold Day in Paradise

BLOOD IS THE SKY

Steve Hamilton

THOMAS DUNNE BOOKS
ST. MARTIN'S MINOTAUR ☎ NEW YORK

Ham

THOMAS DUNNE BOOKS.
An imprint of St. Martin's Press.

www.minotaurbooks.com

Library of Congress Cataloging-in-Publication Data

Hamilton, Steve.
    Blood is the sky / Steve Hamilton.—1st ed.
        p.   cm.
    ISBN 0-312-30115-4
    1. McKnight, Alex (Fictitious character)—Fiction.   2. Private investigators—Michigan—Upper Peninsula—Fiction.   3. Upper Peninsula (Mich.)—Fiction.   4. Missing persons—Fiction.
    5. Hunting guides—Fiction.   6. Ontario—Fiction.   I. Title.

PS3558.A44363B57   2003
813'.54—dc21
                                                              2002037199

First Edition: June 2003

10   9   8   7   6   5   4   3   2   1

To Jamie

Acknowledgments

Yet again, I need to thank Donna Pine from the Garden River First Nation. You are truly one of my heroes. This time around, I also need to thank Richard Pellarin, Rob Brenner, Laura Lippman, and Mitchell Willis of the Bay Mills Indian Community.

Thanks as always to the "usual suspects"—Bill Keller and Frank Hayes, Liz and Taylor Brugman, Bob Kozak and everyone at IBM, Bob Randisi and the Private Eye Writers of America, Ruth Cavin (another hero) and everyone at St. Martin's Press, Jane Chelius, Jeff Allen, Larry Queipo, former Chief of Police, Town of Kingston, New York, and Dr. Glenn Hamilton from the Department of Emergency Medicine, Wright State University.

As always, I end by thanking my wife, Julia, who makes everything possible, Nicholas, who could teach us all how to live in the moment, and Antonia, the Supreme Ruler of the Universe.

BLOOD IS
THE SKY

Chapter One

I saw a lot of fires when I was a cop in Detroit. I was supposed to help secure the scene and then get the hell out of the way, but sometimes I'd stick around and watch the firefighters doing their work. I saw some real battles, but when they were done, the building would always be standing. That was the thing that got to me. The windows would be blown out, and maybe there'd be a big hole in the roof, but the building would still be there.

Years later, I watched a Lake Superior storm taking down a boathouse. When the storm let up, there was nothing left but a concrete slab covered with sand. It wasn't surprising. Anyone who lives up here knows that water is stronger than fire. Water wins that one going away. But at least water cleans up after itself. It does the job all the way. When water destroys, it makes everything look new. It can even be beautiful.

Fire doesn't do that. When a fire is done, what's left is only half destroyed. It is charred and brittle. It is obscene. There is nothing so ugly in all the world as what a fire leaves behind, covered in ashes and smoke and a smell you'll think about every day for the rest of your life.

That's why I had to start rebuilding the cabin. Maybe I was fooling myself, but it was something I had to do. Even though the days were getting shorter. Even though the pine trees were bending in the cold October wind. No man in his right mind would have started rebuilding then. So of course I did.

I had already taken away most of the old wood, those logs that would have lasted another three hundred years if they hadn't burned. I had hauled them away along with the pipes burned black and the bed frames twisted by the heat. There was nothing now but the stone foundation, stripped of the wooden floor, and the chimney, the last thing my father had made with his bare hands before he died. I knew that the snow would come, and it would cover the black stains on the ground, and the chimney would stand alone in the cold silence like a grave marker. I wasn't going to let that happen.

The rebuilding didn't start well. The man who said he'd be there on Monday with my white pine logs rolled up on Wednesday morning, acting like he had nothing to apologize for. He had one of those long flatbeds with a crane on it, with enough lifting power to set every last log down as gently as a teacup. But it took him all morning to clear the truck, and he damn near knocked over the chimney in the process. Then he stood around for a while, trying to tell me about his own cabin down in Traverse City. "The cabins I passed on the way in," he finally said. "You built those?"

"My father did."

"Looks like you had a big one here," he said. He hitched his pants up as he looked around the clearing. "What happened? Did it burn down?"

"It did."

"Hell of a thing," he said. "You gotta be careful with those wood stoves."

"I can't argue with that."

"Looks like you learned the hard way."

I let a few seconds tick by. "It wasn't a wood stove," I finally said. "Somebody burned it down."

"You're shittin' me."

"This gentleman and I, we had a little disagreement."

It took a moment for that one to sink in. "Are you shittin' me, man? You gotta be shittin' me."

"You don't have to believe it."

"I suppose you're gonna rebuild this all by yourself, too."

"I'm gonna try."

"Seriously, where's all your help at?"

"If I need help, I'll get it."

"It's October," he said. "You're not thinking of starting this now, are you?"

"I'd have to be crazy, you mean."

"Is what I'm saying, yeah. Unless you're just shittin' me some more."

"Well, I appreciate your concern," I said. "And I appreciate you bringing up my logs. You were only two days late. Have a good trip back home."

He was still shaking his head as he drove away. I listened to the distant sound of his truck as he rumbled onto the main road and headed south. When he was gone, there was nothing left to hear but a steady wind coming off the lake.

"Well, Pops," I said to the wind, "let's see if I remember how to do this."

This was the cabin he had built in the summers of 1980 and 1981. I helped him for a few weeks in that second year. I was already out of baseball and working as a police officer in Detroit, and this was my last attempt to make peace with him. The days were hot. I

3

remember that. And as I helped him peel and scribe the logs, it brought back yet another summer, back in 1968, the first time I had ever been up here in Paradise, Michigan. I was only seventeen then, with one more year of school ahead of me before heading off to single-A ball in Sarasota. He wanted me to go to college, but I had my own ideas. Thirteen years later, he finished this cabin, his biggest and best. His masterpiece. Six months after that he was dead.

The cabin may have burned to the ground, but at least we had those summers.

Twenty years later, on a cold October day, I started all over again. I cut the sill logs first, the logs that would run along the bottom of each wall, then secured them to the foundation with j bolts. I cut a groove along the outside edge with the chain saw, just as he had taught me. When it rained, the water would collect in the groove and drip away instead of running down the foundation. Then I cut the grooves for the floor joists. I put rough plywood down for the time being—I'd put the nice hardwood floorboards down when the outside was finished.

That was the first day.

When the light was gone, I went down to the Glasgow Inn for dinner. My friend Jackie owns the place. If you ever find yourself in Paradise, just go to the one blinking light in the center of town, then go north another hundred yards or so. It'll be there on the right. When you step into the place, you won't see a typical American bar—there are no mirrors to stare into while you drink, no smoky dark corners to nurse a bad mood in. The chairs are comfortable, there's a fire going in the hearth every night, regardless of the weather, and there's a man there named Jackie Connery who looks like an old Scottish golf caddie. If you ask him the right way, Jackie will even risk his liquor license and give you a cold Canadian beer.

I take that last part back. Those Canadian beers are just for me.

I felt like hell the next morning. My hands were sore, my arms were sore, my legs were sore, and my back was sore. Aside from that I was fine.

I had my coffee and looked up at the dark clouds. Rain was the last thing I needed, because today was the day I'd start building the walls.

I scribed each log the way my father had done. I did most of the heavy cutting with the chain saw, stopping every half hour to sharpen it. I used an ax to cut the notches, keeping both hands together as I swung it, like a baseball bat. That much he didn't have to teach me. You can't be accurate with your hands apart.

Of course, cutting the scarf just right is the hard part. Or as the old man liked to say, this is where you separated the men from the boys. The idea is to cut it so perfectly that one log will rest on top of the other with no daylight in between. If you do it right, you don't need any chinking. If you don't do it right, then God help you. You've got no business building a cabin in the first place.

The first log I tried cutting that morning, I didn't get right. The second log was worse. The third log you could have put in a carnival and charged people five dollars a head to come laugh at it.

The wind picked up. It looked like rain was coming. I kept working. I was halfway through the fourth log when the hornets attacked me.

The nest was hanging from one of the birch trees. They had already been smoked out the night of the fire, the nest partially caved in by the spray of the fire hoses. They were trying to rebuild,

5

just like I was, but they had run out of time. Now half-crazed by the cold weather, most of them near the end of their natural lives, they saw me moving around below them, rattling around with my chain saw. They decided to go down fighting.

I slapped two off the back of my neck, another off my arm. "Crazy fucking things! Get away from me!" The next one caught me right on the cheek and that was it for me. The day was already going bad enough.

I had my extension ladder there, figuring I'd need it eventually, so I braced it up against the birch tree and climbed up with my ax. I was just about to swing at the branch. I was going to take the whole thing down with one good whack, and then I was going to soak the nest with gasoline and set it on fire. Knowing me, I would have emptied the can, a full two gallons of gasoline, and then I would have thrown a lit match right in the middle of it. All the leaves on the ground would have gone up at once and I'd be running around with my pants on fire and both eyebrows singed right off my face.

I stopped myself just in time.

I took a deep breath and climbed back down the ladder. I dropped the ax.

It wasn't worth it. Watching the nest burn, sending the rest of those hornets to hell. They'd all be dead in another week, anyway.

It was a lesson I had taken most of my life to learn. Sometimes you have to let things go.

The rain came. The dark clouds stayed in the sky. I went back to work.

I had come back up here in 1987. My marriage was over and I was off the police force, with a dead partner in the ground and a bullet in my chest. I came up here intending to sell off the land and the six cabins my father had built, but I didn't do it. Somehow the Upper Peninsula was just what I needed. It was cold and unforgiving, even in the heart of summer. There was a terrible beauty to the place, and I could be alone up here in a part of the world where being alone was the rule and not the exception. I moved into the first cabin, the cabin I had helped him build myself, back when I was seventeen years old. I stayed up here and lived day to day and never thought I'd have to face my past again.

That didn't work. It never does.

Hours after I called it a day, I could still feel the buzz of the chain saw in my hands. There was a deep ache in my shoulder, right where they had taken the other two bullets out.

"What was it this time?" Jackie said. He slid a cold Canadian my way.

He was talking about my face, of course. There was a nice little swollen knot under my eye. Whenever something goes wrong, I end up wearing it on my face.

"Hornets," I said.

"How's the cabin going?"

"It's a little slow."

He nodded his head. He didn't say a word about how late it was in the season or how much of a fool I was. Jackie understood why I needed to do this.

"You know who could help you," he said.

I knew. I took a long pull off the bottle and then set it back down on the bar. "I've got to get some sleep," I said. Then I left.

I was just as sore the next morning, but somehow everything felt different. It was all coming back to me, the way you let the chain saw and the ax do the work, the way you work with the grain of the log instead of fighting against it. The logs started fitting together the way they were supposed to. I had the walls two logs high by lunchtime. Of course, that meant it was getting harder and harder to wrestle the logs into position. I'd have to start using the ramps soon, and eventually I'd have to set up some kind of skyline. That would slow me down.

Hell, maybe Jackie was right. There was one man who could really help me.

But I'd be damned if I was going to go ask him.

My father had bought all the land on both sides of this old logging road, nearly a hundred acres in all. He built the six cabins and lived in each one of them off and on over the years, renting out the others to tourists in the summer, hunters in the fall, and snowmobilers in the winter. When I came up here and moved into the first cabin, I kept renting out the rest of them. It was a good way to stay busy without having to go anywhere.

A few years after I moved in, somebody bought the couple of acres between my father's land and the main road. I was a little worried about what the new owner might do to that land. I had visions of a triple-decker summer home, with every tree knocked down so they could maybe get a view of the lake. But it didn't happen that way. It was one man, and I watched him build his own cabin by hand. If my father had been around to see it, he would have approved of this man's work.

I got to know him eventually. You don't live on the same road up here with one other person without running into each other. I'd plow the road for him. He'd give me some of the venison from his hunts. He didn't drink, so we never did that together, but we did share an adventure or two. I even played in goal one night for his hockey team. The fact that he was an Ojibwa Indian never got in the way of our friendship.

Until one day he had to make a choice.

I didn't hear his truck pull up. With the chain saw roaring away, I wouldn't have heard a tank battalion. I happened to glance at the road and saw his truck parked there. Vinnie Red Sky LeBlanc was standing next to it, watching me. He was wearing his denim jacket with the fur around the collar. I had no idea how long he'd been there.

I shut the chain saw down and wiped my forehead with my sleeve.

"You're gonna go deaf," he said. "Where's your ear protection?"

"I left them around here someplace. Just can't find them."

He shook his head at that, then walked right past me to the stacks of logs. Like many Bay Mills Ojibwa, you had to look twice to see the Indian in him. There was a little extra width to his high cheekbones, and a certain calmness in his eyes when he looked at you. You always got the feeling he was thinking carefully about what to say before he said it.

"White pine," he said.

"Of course."

"Where'd it come from?"

"Place down near Traverse City."

"I thought I saw a truck going by," he said. "That was what, Wednesday?"

"He was supposed to be here Monday."

"Couple of these logs I wouldn't use on a doghouse," he said. "Like this one right here."

"I know. I was gonna put that one aside."

He slipped his hands under the log and lifted it. He was maybe three inches shorter than me, and thirty pounds lighter, but I wouldn't have wanted to fight the man, on the ice or off. He carried the log a few steps and tossed it in the brush.

"That'll be your waste pile," he said. "I see another one right down here."

"You don't have to do that, Vinnie. I know which ones are bad."

He went over to the cabin, knelt down, and ran his hand along one of the logs. "You know which ones are bad," he said, "and yet this one right here seems to be part of your wall already."

"When did you become the county inspector?" I said. "I didn't see it in the newspaper."

He let that one go. "Can I ask why you're doing this by yourself?"

"My father did it by himself."

"Did he start building in October?"

"I know I'm not going to finish it," I said. "I just had to start. I couldn't wait until spring."

He smiled at me as he stood up. "Patience was never your strong suit."

"Vinnie, you always loved this cabin. You told me once you'd buy it off me for a million dollars. You remember?"

"I do," he said. "This was the best cabin I've ever seen."

"Put yourself in my place," I said. "If somebody burned this down, what would you do?"

"First of all, I'd kill whoever did it." He thought about it for a moment. "Did you kill him?"

"No," I said.

"But he's dead."

"Yes."

"Okay, then. The next thing I'd do is rebuild the thing, as close as I could to the original."

"Exactly."

"But I wouldn't do it alone," he said. "Not with a friend down the road who knows twice as much about building cabins as I do."

"Excuse me, twice as much? Since when?"

"Make that three times as much. I was trying to be kind."

"Yeah, well, if you'll excuse me, I've got work to do."

"You'll never even get to the roof," he said. "You want the snow to pile up in here all winter?"

"What are you saying? You really want to help me?"

"Your father's spirit sent me," he said. "He knows what this thing would look like if you did it yourself."

"Ah, Indian humor," I said. "I've really been missing that."

"Let me go get my stuff," he said. "I'll see if I have an extra pair of earmuffs, too."

"Yeah, get me those earmuffs," I said. "I have a feeling I'll be needing them now."

That's how I got my help. That's how we started being friends again.

We worked until the sun went down. I offered to buy him dinner at the Glasgow, but he took a pass. He said he was going over to the reservation to see his mother. The next morning, he was on the site before I was. He was spot-peeling logs with his drawknife.

"Let me ask you something," I said when I pulled up. "Aren't you supposed to be out in the woods this month?" Vinnie's regular job was dealing blackjack over at the Bay Mills Casino, but every fall he'd make extra money working as a guide for hunters.

"I'd rather be doing this," he said.

"And your day job?" I said. "You're still dealing, right?"

"I asked for some time off."

"Vinnie, you don't have to do this."

"I needed a break anyway, Alex. Okay? Don't worry about it. Just help me peel these things."

"Those are already peeled, Vinnie."

"By what, a machine? Here, let me show you the right way to do it."

Somehow, I managed not to kill him that day. When we got to work, we found a good rhythm and added three more rows to the walls. We didn't talk much about anything except what log came next, and where it should go. There was not a word said about what had happened between us.

When we had run out of daylight, I invited him to have dinner at the Glasgow again. He seemed to hesitate for a second before saying yes. "If you've got a hot date or something, just tell me," I said. "I won't be offended."

"I've been over on the rez a lot lately," he said. "They can do without me for one night."

There was a whole story behind that one—Vinnie moving off the Bay Mills Reservation and buying his own land. I knew it didn't sit well with the rest of his family, even though he made a point of spending most of his free time there.

"Come on," I said, "I'll buy you a steak."

Jackie did a double take when we walked into the Glasgow together. "Well, look at this," he said.

"Two steaks," I said. "Medium rare. You know the rest."

"Good evening to you, too," he said. "I'm just fine, thanks for asking." If he was genuinely mad at me, it didn't stop him from opening a cold Canadian and sliding it my way.

"It's good to see you," Vinnie said. "It's been a while."

"Don't tell me," Jackie said. "You're showing Alex how to build his cabin. Am I right?"

"It was too painful to watch," Vinnie said. "I had to step in."

"You guys are hilarious," I said. "Just keep it up."

That's the way it went, on a cold October night. It had been another cold night, not that long ago, when the woman had come to me. She was an Ojibwa, someone Vinnie knew, someone he had grown up with on the reservation. She was in trouble and I did what I could to help her. In the end, Vinnie was involved, and that's when he had to make his choice—whether to trust me or his own people. I had no good reason to blame him, but the choice hurt me just the same. And it had stayed there between us ever since.

Until this night. We sat by the fire and talked about the cabin and what we would work on the next day. We pretended that nothing had ever changed. Maybe that's how you get past it. You pretend until it's real.

He was there to help me the next day, the day after that, and then the next. I bought him dinner every night. Hell, it was the least I could do. We were putting those walls up so fast, we actually had a shot at getting the roof on before it snowed. That's what I thought, anyway. And then, of course, it did snow. It wasn't much, just a few flurries overnight that turned to rain in the morning, but it was enough to knock us out of the game for the rest of the day. Vinnie ran off to do something on the rez, and I checked on the renters in the other cabins. It was bow season in Michigan, so I had all the usual men from downstate, the men who appreciated the fact that my land was right next to the state land, and that I'd leave them a cord of firewood outside their door and otherwise leave them alone. Bow season was easy, because bow hunters are the true gentlemen of the sport. They don't make a racket, and they keep the cabins clean. Firearm hunters were usually okay, although I'd still get my share of drunken clowns.

Snowmobilers, of course, were the worst of all. Just one more reason to dread the winter, and to hope like hell that the snow wasn't coming for good.

It wasn't. Not yet, anyway. The next morning the sun came out and melted away the thin traces of snow on the ground. When I got to the cabin site, I was surprised to see he wasn't there yet. An hour later, I started wondering. I was doing as much of the work as I could on my own, but it was getting harder and harder to set the logs. Without Vinnie to help me, I'd have to set up the skyline. Of course I wasn't even paying him, so what right did I have to complain?

By lunchtime I thought I'd head down the road and check on him. His truck was gone. I couldn't help but think of another day, when I had sat in this exact same spot, looking at his empty drive-way, wondering where he was. It turned out he had spent the night in jail, having taken a hockey stick to the face of a Sault Ste. Marie police officer. That was the beginning of a very bad week.

Good God, Vinnie, I said to myself. I hope to hell you weren't out finding trouble last night.

I went down to the Glasgow for some of Jackie's beef stew and a Canadian. "Where's your man?" Jackie said as he served me.

"You got me. He didn't show up today."

He gave me a look. "Whattsa matter, trouble in Paradise?"

"No trouble. I just don't know where he is."

"Last time, you ended up in the hospital."

"Jackie, he's been helping me all week, okay? Don't you think he deserves a day off?"

"If that's all it is, fine," he said. "I'm just saying, the last time Vinnie got in trouble, you're the one who ended up almost getting killed."

"Okay, I hear you."

"Okay, then."

"Okay."

Vinnie walked in just then and saved us. He came to the bar and sat down next to me.

"Give the man some beef stew," I said.

"No thanks," he said. That's when I knew something was wrong. If you have any appetite at all, you don't turn down Jackie's beef stew.

"What's going on?" I said.

"I'm sorry I wasn't around today. Something sort of came up."

"You don't have to apologize," I said. "Hell, it's not like I'm paying you anything."

Vinnie thought about it. "You realize," he said, "that I'm the one paying you. For what happened. This is how I'm settling my debt to you."

"You don't owe me anything," I said. "We've been through this, remember?"

I sure as hell didn't want to go through it again. Not when we both seemed to be finally getting over it.

"I remember," he said. "But still—"

"For God's sake," I said, "are you gonna tell me what's wrong?"

He sat there for a long moment, while Jackie looked back and forth between us, clearly expecting the worst.

"It's Tom," he finally said.

"Your brother."

"Yeah."

I didn't know a hell of a lot about Tom LeBlanc. I knew he was a few years younger than Vinnie, and that he had caused his family enough trouble to make Vinnie look like the golden boy. There was one incident at the Canadian border that Vinnie never wanted to talk about. I had to read about it in the Soo *Evening News*. That was the last time I had seen Tom, in fact, right before he had gone off to serve his two years at Kincheloe.

"What's the problem?" I said. I knew he was out on parole now, and saying all the right things about staying straight. But hell, if he was in trouble again, it wouldn't exactly shock me.

"He was on a hunting trip in Ontario. He was supposed to be back a couple of days ago."

"And he didn't make it back?"

"No."

"You don't think—"

"What, that he's passed out in some bar in Canada? Is that what you mean?"

"Vinnie, come on."

"It's different this time, Alex."

Here it comes, I thought. He's been going to the meetings; he's a changed man. The whole speech. That's what I expected.

That's not what I got.

"This time," Vinnie said, "he's me."

15

Chapter Two

"He took my place," Vinnie said. "Don't you see what I'm saying? Tommy was up there pretending to be me."

I didn't get it at first. Then it hit me.

"Wait a minute," I said. "Are you telling me he was up there on a hunt?"

"Yes."

"And he was pretending to be you."

Vinnie looked down at his hands. "Yes."

"Because you couldn't go. On account of you helping me with the cabin."

"No, that's not it, Alex."

"Vinnie—"

"It was his job, not mine. They called him."

"So why did he have to pretend to be you?"

"It's kind of a long story," Vinnie said. "Bottom line, I'm the one who let him do this. It's all on me."

"When was he due back?"

"Couple of days ago."

"Who else went?" I said. "Did anyone else get back yet?"

"No, not yet."

"Who was it, Vinnie? Who did he go with?"

"Look, can we talk about this on the way? I've got to get over to the rez."

"We're both going?"

"Yeah, I need you to go with me," he said. "If you don't mind."

"You gonna tell me why?"

"I need you for protection."

"Protection?" Jackie looked at me and then threw his towel in the sink.

"It's my mother," Vinnie said. "I figure if you're there, she'll be less likely to kill me."

I knew that was just a line, but I went with him anyway. I figured I owed him that much. We took my truck, and he sat there on the passenger's side, looking out at the trees. After a few minutes of silence, he gave me the rest of the story.

"This man called him," he said. "From Detroit. He said he had heard he was a good guide, that he knew how to turn a hunt into a real party. You know, not just the usual slog through the woods. Tom told him that he wasn't really doing too many hunts anymore. He recommended me, instead. He told them I was the real deal."

I knew that was Vinnie's first love. There were other hunting guides who could track animals for you, and then field-dress and tag them if you were lucky enough to bag one. Vinnie would do all that and then tell you the stories his grandmother had told him, about the land and the sky, the animals and the seasons. The four points on the compass and how they got their names. The *manitous,* which were the great mysteries, the spirits of Ojibwa mythology. If it was a dark, windy night, he'd tell you about the *windingo,* which was an evil, flesh-eating monster. Vinnie could take an ordinary hunting trip and turn it into summer camp for grown-ups.

Of course, he used his Ojibwa name on these hunts—Misquo-geezhig, which in English is "Red Sky." It just doesn't work when your Indian guide is named Vinnie.

"So why didn't they take you?" I said. We were going along Lakeshore Road, curling around the southern shore of Whitefish Bay to the reservation in Brimley. It was my favorite road in the world, and I figured I'd take it while I still could. In a couple of months, it would be obliterated by ice and snow.

"They told him he was the guy they wanted, and then they said something about him and peace pipes."

"Peace pipes? Oh no, wait a minute—"

"Yeah. He got the idea. He told them he didn't do that kind of thing anymore. This is what got him into so much trouble in the first place."

"Did he tell them he just got out of prison?"

"No, I don't think so. He just told them he was out of that business."

"Okay, so then what?"

"They say they really want him and they'll pay him a thousand dollars."

"A thousand dollars for a week in the woods?"

"And Tom says no. He really can't do it. So they say okay, we'll pay you two thousand dollars."

"Two thousand?"

"So Tom says no, and why are they even asking him to do a hunt in Canada, anyway? He's never led a hunt up there. They have their own guides. In fact, the Canucks would have a cow if they found out these guys from America were bringing their own guide with them. They probably wouldn't even let them go out."

"What did this guy say about that?"

"He said, don't worry, we'll take care of it. And then he offered him three thousand dollars."

"Good God."

"And Tom said, where do you want to pick me up?"

"Vinnie, who is this guy?"

He shook his head. "Tom said his name was Albright. He didn't say what he did for a living, but it sounded like he was some kind of heavy hitter in Detroit. The kind of guy who usually gets what he wants. He said he had four other guys who wanted to get away for a few days. You know, just cut loose in the woods."

"I know that one," I said. "I get the 'cut-loose' type staying in the cabins during firearm season. They stay up all night drinking and then they go out the next morning and shoot anything that moves. They all want that big buck so they can mount his head on the wall."

"Actually, this was a moose hunt. That's why they were going to Canada. They said they'd already done the deer thing. They wanted the big game."

"Moose. Even better. What do those things weigh, like eight hundred pounds?"

"A bull can weigh over twelve hundred."

"Is it firearm season up there already?"

"Yeah, it's a lot earlier in Canada."

"Okay, so for three thousand dollars he said yes. When did they pick him up?"

"Saturday before last."

I did the math in my head. "That was before I even started working on the cabin."

"Yeah, it was."

I looked over at him. "So it really wasn't about you sticking around to help me."

"No," he said. "I told you that."

"Okay, okay. So you let Tom go. Why did he have to pretend to be you?"

Vinnie didn't say anything. He watched the trees go by.

"Oh, wait a minute," I said. "Don't tell me."

"It would have violated his parole."

I just about drove into the lake right there. "Oh, that's beautiful," I said. "This is getting better by the minute."

"He's not supposed to leave the country."

"Yeah, no kidding. When they've already caught you bringing a twenty-pound bag over the bridge, they kinda like you to stay off it for a while."

He looked at me, and then back out the window. "I know it doesn't look like such a good idea right now," he said. "The rest of my family sure doesn't think so."

Lakeshore Road took us away from the bay, onto the Bay Mills Reservation. If there wasn't a sign there to tell you, you wouldn't even know you were on Indian land. It looked just like any other middle-class housing development. There were raised ranches on either side of the road, with well-kept lawns dying off in the cold weather. The road to Mission Hill, with the old burial ground at the top, would have been the first clue that you were in a different kind of place. Then, of course, there were the two casinos—the little King's Club, the first Indian casino in the state, and then the bigger Bay Mills Casino, with its great cedar walls rising against the backdrop of Waishkey Bay.

"So he was due back when?" I said as I turned off the main road. "A couple of days ago?"

"Yeah, they should have dropped him off on their way back."

"Do you have this guy's phone number?"

"Tom left me Albright's cell phone number. I've left a couple of messages, but haven't heard back yet."

"So maybe he hasn't gotten them yet," I said. "Maybe they're just still up there."

"It's a fly-in hunt, Alex. They take you to the cabin, then come back for you a week later. By then you're ready to come home, believe me."

"You're up there all by yourselves for a week?"

"They usually come back once during the week to check on you, fly out any animals you've taken. But aside from that, yeah, you're up there all alone. Depending on where you go, it's usually a long way from anywhere."

"So where did they go? Isn't there a lodge there or somewhere they take off from?"

"I've been trying," he said. "Nobody's answering. I know the phone service is kind of unpredictable up there, but damn, it just gives me a bad feeling."

"But not bad enough to call the police?"

He thought about it for a moment. "You know what'll happen if I do that. If they find out he's up there, he'll go back to prison."

The driveway had four cars in it already, so I pulled off onto the edge of the road.

"More cousins," he said as he got out. "This will be fun."

I followed him around to the back door. There were toys everywhere—a red car, a big plastic yellow house with green shutters, even a wooden fort like something out of the Old West. "What do they do in this fort?" I said. "Play cowboys and Indians?"

"You're funny," he said. "Are you ready?"

"With all your family in there, we're gonna play that game right now. I'll be General Custer."

He shot me a look. "Don't bring any of those jokes inside," he said. "Okay?"

"Lead the way."

As he opened the door, the heat and noise hit us. There were at least twenty people in the kitchen, some men sitting at the table, some women holding young children. Two other children raced into the room, stopped to stare at us for a split second, and then raced out even faster.

One of the men stood up and put his hand on Vinnie's shoulder.

"You've met my cousin Buck," he said to me.

The man shook my hand. As he looked at me, his face told me absolutely nothing.

"I seem to remember," I said.

Vinnie introduced me around to the rest of the room. It was all a blur after the first three or four names. There was a pot of coffee brewing in one of those big machines you see in restaurants. Another half-empty pot was keeping warm on the top burner. Without saying a word, one of Vinnie's uncles poured me a cup.

"Your mother is in the bedroom," Buck said to Vinnie. "She wants to see you."

Vinnie asked me to wait out here in the kitchen. He went down the hallway like a man walking his last mile.

A couple more kids ran into the room and around the table. A woman yelled at them, while another woman right next to her gently rocked a baby in her arms. That baby could obviously sleep through anything.

One man broke open a pack of cigarettes and passed them around. Soon the air was filling up with smoke. Nobody looked at me. Not once.

I shifted back and forth on my feet, looked out the window at the cold, hard ground in the backyard. The telephone rang. A man picked it up. One of Vinnie's cousins—not Buck, but some other cousin whose name I wouldn't have remembered for a million dollars. He turned his back to me and talked in a low voice.

This is what Vinnie left, I thought. A house like this, on land owned by the tribe. All this family around him. Even if he lived in another house on the reservation, the family would be there.

Maybe not all at once like this, but they'd come, one by one, every single day. That's the way it works here. Your door is always open. Some days, I thought it was a great thing. It was something I envied. Today it was making me dizzy.

Vinnie moved off the rez, and his family still hadn't accepted it. Hell, maybe they blamed me for it, like I was the one who kept him there. Move up to Paradise, Vinnie, away from your family. Buy your own land, build your own cabin. Live there all by yourself like a lonely white man.

I stood there for another few uncomfortable minutes, until Vinnie finally poked his head back in the room and beckoned me down the hallway. I sidestepped a couple of the kids to get to him. "What's going on?" I said.

"She wants to talk to you."

"Why does it feel like I'm going to see the principal?"

"Don't be ridiculous. She just wants to ask you a couple of questions." He led me down to the master bedroom and opened the door. The room was empty.

"Where is she?"

"She's in the bathroom," he said. "You're company, so she had to get fixed up."

"Yeah, well, thanks for leaving me out there with the rest of your family. We had a great time together."

"They don't dislike you, Alex. They just don't understand you. In fact, they worry about you."

"They worry about me?"

"Sure, you should hear them talk about you. My mother especially. She thinks you walk around carrying too much pain."

"If your cousins ever get me alone in a dark alley, then I'll be carrying some pain."

He shook his head. "Alex, Alex . . ."

Vinnie's mother came in before I could say anything else. She was wiping her hands on a towel.

"Mrs. LeBlanc," I said, taking her hand. She was a large woman, round and soft around the edges, with big brown eyes. She was the epicenter of the whole family—hell, probably the entire reservation. She carried herself like she had long ago accepted the responsibility.

"Alex," she said. "It's good to see you. Please sit down."

She steered me into the one chair in the room, and then sat herself down on the edge of the bed. Vinnie stood in the doorway.

"I appreciate your coming down here," she said. "I hope it wasn't too much trouble." Whenever she talked about Paradise, this town not even thirty miles away, she made it sound like it was in the Arctic Circle.

"No trouble at all, ma'am."

"You know my son Thomas is missing."

"I wouldn't say he's missing yet, ma'am. Vinnie says he's just a couple of days overdue."

"Yes, from this hunting trip," she said. "With these men we don't know. This trip with my one son pretending to be the other."

"You know that Vinnie's been helping me," I said. "I mean, this is why—"

"He's my youngest child, you know. And he's already had his share of trouble."

"I know," I said. "But there could be so many explanations for why he's not back yet. I don't think there's any reason to be worried yet."

She waved that away like so much smoke in the air. "You know," she said, "when my oldest son was born, my husband's mother asked me to call him Misquogeezhig. You know what that means."

"Red Sky."

"Yes. It's actually a very peculiar name."

I was about to make some remark about that, but held my tongue.

"It comes from the Waubunowin, the Society of the Dawn. That's what the Red Sky is, you know—the eastern sky when the sun comes up at dawn. The Waubunowin, they were outcasts, and most of the tribe were afraid of them. They thought the members of this society had strange powers. My mother-in-law, I knew she had always been interested in the Waubunowin, but when she asked me to give this name to my firstborn, I was not happy. I thought it meant that my son would grow up one day to be an outcast himself."

I looked up at Vinnie. He did not move, or make the slightest sound.

"My mother-in-law said to trust her. So I did. That is how Vincent was given the name Misquogeezhig."

"For what it's worth," I said, "I think it's a good name."

"Yes, well, then I had two daughters. My mother-in-law had no interest in naming them. So I thought to myself, this is good. She is done with the naming of my children. But then I had my other son, Thomas. And she said to me, you must name him Minoonigeezhig, which means Pleasing Sky."

From the other side of the house, I could barely hear the murmur of the men and women talking, punctuated now and then by an outburst from one of the children. It all seemed to fade into silence as she leaned closer to me.

"Pleasing Sky is the sky of the west," she said. "It is the end of the day. The end of life. I always thought it was an unlucky name, Alex. I never should have given it to him."

"Mrs. LeBlanc—"

"No, don't tell me I'm being a silly old woman."

"I wasn't going to say that."

"Perhaps not. But you think that."

"Please," I said. "I don't understand why you're telling me all this."

"I'm asking you to go with Vincent," she said.

26

It took a moment to sink in. When it did, I knew I was com-
mitted. There was no way I could sit in that room with that
woman and have it turn out any other way.

"I want the two of you to find him," she said. "Prove me
wrong. Go find my son with the unlucky name and bring him
back home."

Chapter Three

It was still dark when Vinnie knocked on the door. I let him in and poured him a cup of coffee while I finished dressing. He sat there and drank it without saying anything.

"You know where we're going?" I said when I was ready.

"I think so."

"We'll take my truck."

"We can take mine."

"If we take yours," I said, "we'll never make it back. I saw the tread on those tires."

"They have paved roads in Canada, Alex."

"We'll take my truck."

A few minutes later, we were on our way. The trip started on Lakeshore Drive again, bending around Whitefish Bay, just as we had done the day before. But this time we didn't stop on the reservation. At this hour the only signs of life came from the two casinos. I couldn't imagine anyone wanting to gamble before dawn on a cold October morning, but there were enough cars in the parking lots to prove me wrong.

When we left the reservation, it was a straight shot down Three Mile Road into Sault Ste. Marie—or the "Soo," as the natives call it. We got onto I-75 and headed over the International Bridge, passing over the Soo Locks, and then over the Algoma Steel Foundry Works. With the sun just starting to come up, and the fires burning in the sintering furnaces, the whole scene was like one of the outer rings of hell.

"Get your license ready," I said as we came up to the Canadian Customs booth.

"Little problem," Vinnie said.

I looked over at him. "What is it?"

"Tom's got my license."

"You're kidding me."

"We decided he might need it, just in case. He looks enough like me—"

"This is beautiful," I said. I pulled up to the waiting line. There was one car in front of us. Going through customs can be a breeze, or it can be a pain in the ass, depending on who you've got in the booth and how they happen to be feeling that day. With the amount of time this guy was spending with the driver ahead of me, it didn't look good.

"You got another ID, right?"

"No, Alex."

"A credit card?"

He just looked at me.

"You gave Tom your credit cards?"

"Yes."

"You got anything?"

"I gave him my wallet, Alex. The whole thing."

The car in front of me finally pulled away.

"Pretend you're sleeping," I said.

"What?"

"You heard me. Go to sleep. Right now."

"I'm not doing that."

I started to pull forward. "We're going in, Vinnie. For God's sake, do your dead man act or we'll be stuck here all day."

He said a few unkind words and then did what he was told, dropping his head against the far side of the car and closing his eyes. As I pulled in front of the booth, the man looked at me, then at Vinnie, and then back at me. The man had razor burns all over his neck, and he was not happy. If I'd been sitting in his booth with a scraped-up neck on a cold morning, I don't imagine I would have been happy, either.

"Identification, sir?"

I pulled out my license. He gave it a quick glance.

"And your friend?"

"He's down for good," I said.

The man narrowed his eyes. "Your business in Canada this morning, sir?"

"Just taking him home," I said.

"He's Canadian?"

"I'm afraid so. He's one of yours."

"Think you could slip his wallet out from underneath him, sir?"

"His wallet's long gone," I said. "Lost it. Or had it stolen. He's had kind of a rough night. When I closed the bar, I thought maybe I'd do the right thing, make sure he got back where he belonged."

"You own a bar, sir?"

"Don't I wish," I said. "I just work there a few nights a week."

"Which bar would that be, sir?"

"Glasgow Inn. You ever been there?"

"No, sir. Don't believe so. Apparently, this is part of the service, eh?"

The man was loosening up a little bit. He was even starting to sound like a Canadian.

31

"Like I said, just trying to do the right thing."

"Any alcohol or firearms in your vehicle?"

"No," I said. It felt good to say one thing to the man that wasn't a lie.

"Have a good morning," he said.

Vinnie waited until we were a hundred yards past the booth. "That was real cute," he finally said. "You had fun with that one."

"Matter of fact."

I could tell he was about to say something else. He stopped himself and just shook his head. He didn't say a word as we made our way through the quiet streets of Soo Canada. It's a large city by Canadian standards, about four times bigger than Soo Michigan. But there's something about the place, something I could never put my finger on. It always seemed a little forlorn to me. This cold, gray morning seemed like a permanent part of the city itself.

"You need a donut?" I said.

He shook his head.

"You gonna be this way all the way up there?"

He closed his eyes and leaned his head back against the seat. "You know how it is with us Indians," he said. "One bad night and we're down for the count."

We took 17 north, out of the city and up the Lake Superior coastline. The fog was still heavy on the water as we rounded Batchawana Bay. An hour later, we passed through a small town called Montreal River, and then it was another hour to make our way through the Lake Superior Provincial Park. There was nothing but trees and an occasional glimpse of the lake, stretching out beyond the fog.

"Anytime you want to speak up," I said. "Telling me where we're going, for instance."

Vinnie opened his eyes. "Go to White River," he said. "Then take a right."

"White River's another two hours away."

"What time is it?" he said.

"Little after nine."

He picked up my cell phone. "We still get a signal up here?"

"I imagine," I said. "On this road, anyway. Try it."

He turned it on and dialed a number. "I'm gonna try Albright's number again." He listened for a short while, then he hung up.

"No dice?"

"He's not picking up."

"You said you left a message last time?"

"Yeah, I asked him to call my mother's number. I said I was a member of Vinnie's family, and was wondering why he hadn't come back home yet."

"You don't think this has gotten to the point where you should come clean?"

"Does it really matter who they think he is? Either way, they should have brought him back three days ago."

"I just don't see how this lie is gonna help."

He didn't say anything.

"Tell me again. You don't know anything else about this Albright guy? Where he works?"

"No, I really don't. Tom didn't tell me, anyway."

"What's his first name?"

"Red."

"Sounds more like a nickname."

"I know. Tom said his name was Red Albright, and he had four other guys, all experienced hunters, that they were heading for this lodge on Lake Peetwaniquot, and that they'd pick him up on the way."

"Where, at his house?"

"They met him at the duty-free shop by the bridge. They said they'd be driving a black Chevy Suburban. I drove him over there."

"But you didn't see them. I mean, you weren't there at the duty-free, hiding behind the cigarettes or anything."

"No, Alex. I was not hiding behind the cigarettes."

"You don't know anything else about these men, other than the fact that they were going to pay your brother three thousand dollars?"

"Every one of my cousins has asked me that," he said. "Every one of my uncles, two of my aunts, and, of course, my mother has asked me that maybe seven times on her own. The answer is no, I don't know anything else. And I'll give you the answer to your next question before you even ask it. Yes. Yes, I'm an idiot."

"That one I didn't need to ask," I said. "So try the lodge again. Maybe their phone works today."

"Maybe it does," he said, punching in the number. After a moment, he hit the End button. "It still doesn't go through."

We rode on another few minutes, through more trees, then over a small bridge. I could see a large bird, maybe a hawk, circling over the road ahead.

"So when do you call the police?" I said. "I mean, I'm just wondering."

He looked out the window. "I want to find him and bring him back home. Without getting him in big trouble."

"If you can."

"Yeah, if I can."

"And if you can't?"

"Then I call the police."

"Okay," I said.

"We take one shot at it," he said. "That's all I want to do."

"Fair enough."

We kept going. Four hours had passed. As we left the park, we saw signs for Wawa, the closest thing to a real town we'd see for the rest of the day, if you didn't mind the name.

"You getting hungry yet?" he said.

"You read my mind. We'll stop in Wawa, get some gas. See if they have a decent place to eat."

The first thing we saw was a goose. It was a good twenty feet tall, and it was standing on a pedestal that had to be another ten feet. A giant goose head thirty feet in the air, looking down at you—that's apparently how you know you're in Wawa. There was another goose, this one only five feet tall, in front of the first store we saw, then another goose about the same size in front of the motel.

"They seem to have a thing about geese in this town," I said.

"Where do you think the name comes from?"

I thought about it. "Wawa means goose?"

"In Ojibwa, yes."

"Now I know." I drove by a couple of fast-food places and pulled up in front of a place that didn't seem to have a name. "You don't mind stopping at a bar, do you?"

I knew Vinnie didn't drink, but I'd be damned if I came all this way up into Canada without having a Molson. We got out of the truck and stretched, looking and sounding like two men who'd been driving since well before the sun came up. There were only two other vehicles in the parking lot—one truck that looked about as old as mine, and an Impala that may have been white one day, a long, long time ago. Apparently, this place didn't draw much of a lunch crowd.

When we stepped inside, we saw a bar and six empty stools. The man behind the stick looked up at us and put down his magazine. Besides him, there were two men on the other side of the room, playing one of those barroom bowling games where you slide the metal puck down the wooden chute. There was a pool table in the middle of the room with two cues crossed in a large X on the green felt, and a jukebox that, thankfully, wasn't making a sound.

Everywhere else, there were photographs. On every wall, on

every available surface on which you could hang a picture, there was nothing but men standing next to dead animals, mostly deer, all of them strung up by the back legs and hanging upside down, tongues falling out of open mouths. Suddenly I didn't feel so hungry.

"Come on in, gentlemen," the man at the bar said. He was a big one. He had passed three hundred pounds a long time ago, and wasn't heading back anytime soon. "What can I get ya, eh?"

"You serve food in here?"

"Damn right we do. You in the mood for some nice venison stew?"

Vinnie and I both sneaked another look at the pictures on the wall. "You don't actually hunt deer around here, do you?" I said.

The man looked at us for a moment and then started laughing. "I thought you were serious."

"How about a couple of cheeseburgers," I said. "One Molson and one 7-Up."

The two men playing the little bowling game had stopped to watch us come in. "Where are you boys from?" one of them said, the one with the Maple Leafs jersey. His nose was taped up, and there were purple bruises running under both eyes. His friend was wearing his orange hunting jacket, with the license still pinned to the back.

"Michigan," I said.

"You up here hunting?"

"Nope, other business."

"Other business," the one with the taped-up face said to the one in the hunting jacket. "What the hell does that mean?"

The bartender brought our drinks over. We sat there and watched him grill up the cheeseburgers. The two men went back to their bowling game. The pins were attached to the machine from above, and you had to slide the puck over little sensors to make them flip up. They apparently thought you needed to slide the puck as hard as you possibly could, and that you needed to swear at it very loudly.

"You gotta excuse those boys," the bartender said. "They had a little run-in yesterday and they're still buzzing."

"I noticed the broken nose," I said.

"A couple strangers came in here. One of them had a real nose on him so these two clowns start making jokes. You know, like 'Tell us another lie, Pinocchio,' real intelligent stuff like that. These guys take it for about two minutes before the guy with the nose stands up and hits Stan right in the face. Says 'Here, let's see what your nose looks like tomorrow.' And the other guy, hell, he's about twice as big, so Brian wasn't gonna step in."

"Yeah, I'm so lucky having somebody to watch my back," the man with the broken nose said. "He's a real friend."

The other man just stood there with a bottle of beer in his hand. He still hadn't said a word.

"And this game is a piece of shit, too."

"Will you two knock it off?" the bartender said without turning around. "I swear, I'm gonna throw that machine out on the road."

"We need more sawdust," Broken Nose said. "This thing ain't sliding."

"Open up your brain and dump some out."

"Haw haw, that's funny."

"They got nothing better to do, eh?" the bartender said, apparently to us. "They gotta torment me every day of the week. Get in fights with the customers."

"We don't got 'other business' to do like these fellas," the man said. "We're not 'other business' kind of guys, you know what I mean?"

"What the hell are you talking about?" the bartender said, finally turning around.

"Ask the Lone Ranger and Tonto here," the man said.

37

I turned on my stool and looked at him. He and his buddy went back to their game. Vinnie sat next to me as cool as an ice sculpture. I knew he had a fuse about seven miles long, and that no matter what they said, it would get to me a hell of a lot sooner than it would get to him.

"Don't mind those morons," the bartender said as he served up the cheeseburgers. "They're the only two in town, believe me."

"Just our luck," I said. We ate our burgers. I drank my beer and had another one. Two cold Canadian beers were the easiest part of the day so far.

I could feel their eyes on our backs. When we were done, I turned around again and watched them slide their stupid little puck down the board. "Who's winning?" I said.

"Machine's broken," the man said. "It don't keep score anymore."

"Why don't you keep score yourself?"

They looked at me like I was from Mars.

"You know," I said, "when we came in, I was wondering why you guys weren't playing pool. Now I understand. Pool's too complicated."

"You wanna try me, old man?" he said. He looked like he meant it, even with an already broken nose. His partner was obviously not so sure.

Before I could say another word, I felt Vinnie's hand on my shoulder. "Come on," he said. "We're leaving."

"That's right," the man said. "Go do your 'other business' with your Indian boyfriend."

I would have taken him apart right there, but Vinnie had other ideas. "You wanna spend the rest of the day in the Wawa jail? Come on, it ain't worth it."

He steered me out of there and into the truck. "I didn't pay," I said.

"I left some money on the bar," he said. "Put the key in and drive away."

I did as he said, sending a spray of gravel behind us. We had to double back through town to get back to 17, so the giant goose was there once again to say goodbye to us.

"Vinnie," I said, a couple of miles later, "doesn't it even bother you when people say stuff like that?"

"Who says it doesn't? I just don't get in fights over it."

"I was sticking up for you, you know."

"How's that?"

"You're the one they were insulting. That Lone Ranger and Tonto business."

"That was for both of us," he said.

"No, the Lone Ranger was a hero."

"So was Tonto."

"He was the trusty sidekick," I said. "Believe me, this is one thing I know about. That was my favorite show when I was a kid."

"Of course," Vinnie said. "The Lone Ranger. That explains a lot."

An hour and a half after we left Wawa, we came to a little town called White River. The Canadian Pacific Railroad crossed the road here. We sat and watched the freight cars go by for ten minutes.

Route 17 turned west in this town, heading back to the upper shores of Lake Superior. We took a right turn on 631. We had to keep going north, as far as the roads would take us, deep into the heart of Ontario.

"I'm gonna try home again," Vinnie said. "See if he showed up."

"Wouldn't that be something," I said. "We're way the hell up here and he walks through the front door back on the rez."

"Right now I'll take it."

He punched the numbers and waited for the answer. "It's Vinnie," he said. "Just checking in."

He listened for a while. "Okay," he said. "We'll be there in a couple more hours. I'll call you back."

He hung up and sat there looking at the phone.

"No sign of him," I said.

He shook his head.

"Everybody okay back home?"

"They want to call the police."

I didn't say anything. I kept driving.

Another hour and a half passed. We went through more trees, and then the trees would open up to a wide meadow, or a marsh thick with tall grass and the cold remnants of cattails. We'd see another vehicle maybe once every thirty minutes. My eyes were getting tired.

Vinnie tried calling Albright's number again. No answer. He left a message this time, letting him know that we were in Canada. He left my cell phone number and told him to call the second he got in.

"I hope that went through," he said as he hung up. "The signal's getting pretty weak up here."

We finally came to a small town called Hornepayne, where another railroad crossed, this time the Canadian National. The train had just passed as we came to the crossing. As we bumped over the tracks, we could see the last car disappearing into the west.

"This line goes all the way to Vancouver, doesn't it?" I said.

"I believe it does."

"Hell of a long trip."

He let out a breath. "I'm sorry," he said.

"For what?"

"For dragging you all the way up here."

40

"You're not. I always wanted to visit Hornepayne, Ontario."

He laughed. "I think that was it already."

He was right. The road was empty again. It was another hour north, past a lonely lake called Nagagamisis, until we finally reached the end of the line, which in this case was the Trans-Canada Highway. We could turn left and head west to Longlac and then Geraldton, or we could turn right and head east to Hearst and then Kapuskasing. After eight hours of driving, we had gone as far north as we could go. From here it was nothing but wilderness, all the way up past the Albany River, then the Attawapiskat, then the Ekwan, through the Polar Bear Provincial Park, to the shores of Hudson Bay. There were small outposts here and there, but from this point on they were accessible only by plane.

"Which way?" I said.

"I think left."

"You think?"

"I know it's not too far," he said. "Either way. That much I remember. And I'm pretty sure Tom said west."

"So how were you supposed to find this place?" I said. "I mean, if you were with these guys—"

"If I was with them, they'd know exactly where to go. I'm sure Albright had the exact directions."

"Okay, okay," I said. "I get it. Let's give it a shot."

I took the left and drove west down the Trans-Canada. There were lots more trees. This was officially the most goddamned trees I'd ever seen in one day. About twenty minutes later, we saw a gravel road heading off to the right.

"Think that's it?" I said.

"There's no sign," he said. "Don't you think there'd be a sign?"

"I can keep going."

"Go a little while more. If we don't see something soon, we'll come back."

41

We drove ten more minutes. There was nothing but a sign telling us that Longlac was a hundred miles away. I stopped in the empty road, did a three-point turn, and headed back the other way.

"Let's try it this time," he said when we came back to the road. "If it's not this one, then it must have been east instead of west."

I took the gravel road, and held on tight as it twisted its way through the forest. It was one blind turn after another as I fish-tailed the truck on the loose gravel.

"Take it easy, Alex."

"Who are we gonna hit?" I said, turning the wheel hard.

"Look out!"

I slammed on the brakes, and felt the truck start to slide.

"Son of a bitch!"

We came to rest with all four wheels in half-frozen mud. The moose stood there in the middle of the road, all gangly legs and long nose, looking at us with mild interest.

"That would have been great," I said, as I put the truck in reverse. "We come all the way up here and get killed by a moose."

"Can you get out of this?"

I gave it some gas. The wheels spun. I tried putting it back in drive, to see if I could rock our way out. The wheels spun again. I turned the key, and we sat there for a while, listening to the engine cool off.

"Now what?" he finally said.

"Try the phone."

He turned it on. "It's not getting a signal now."

"I was afraid of that. We're too far north."

"We'll have to walk," he said. "Maybe the lodge is right up this road."

"I'm sure it is," I said as I opened my door. "The Lone Ranger never got lost when Tonto was around."

Chapter Four

As we got out of the truck, the moose stepped slowly off the road and into the woods.

"That's a big one," I said. "For a female."

"Yep. I'm glad you missed her."

"Which way you think? North to the lodge, or south back to the highway?"

"Let's try north first."

We started walking north. The air was a hell of a lot colder up here. I zipped up my coat.

"What's the Ojibwa word for moose?" I said.

"Moozo."

I nodded. "Wawa and moozo. So far, it's a pretty silly-sounding language, Vinnie."

"I just realized what your Ojibwa name should be," he said.

"What's that?"

"Madawayash."

"What's it mean?"

He smiled. "I'll tell you later."

We walked. The road twisted its way through more trees and more marshland with grass growing eight feet tall.

"Tire tracks," Vinnie said, kicking at the ground.

"Recent?"

"Looks like it."

"What kind of vehicle?"

He looked at me. "One with tires."

"Was the driver right-handed or left-handed?"

"You're funny."

"Come on, you're the Indian guide. Where are the tracking skills?"

We had walked maybe two more miles, and were about to give up and turn around. But then we went around a bend and the road ended. There were three vehicles parked among the trees— one jeep and two pickup trucks—and then through the trees we could see blue water.

"I'm guessing this is Lake Peetwaniquot," I said.

"I think we found it."

"They don't need a sign on the road. Either you know how to get here or you don't."

I looked at my watch. It was almost five o'clock. There was some daylight left, but the sun hung low enough in the west to cast long shadows. As soon as we had stopped moving, the air felt cold again.

"Let's go see who's here," Vinnie said.

"Lead the way."

We walked down the path, the trees opening up to a clearing and a large cabin overlooking the lake. As we got closer we could see a couple of smaller sheds set back in the woods, and a long dock. There was a floatplane tied up to it, and two aluminum boats with outboard motors.

"Hello!" Vinnie said. The sound died in the cold wind. Nobody answered.

"There's got to be somebody here," I said.

We walked down closer to the lake. The wind was just strong enough to kick up a light chop in the water. The floatplane bobbed up and down.

"Hello!" Vinnie said again.

Nothing.

We walked out onto the dock, passing a large weighmaster's scale and several propane tanks. There was no sound but our heavy footsteps on the wood, the wind blowing in off the lake, the hollow clunk when the boats came together, and the plane's left float working up and down against the rubber bumpers on the dock.

"It's a nice lake," I said. It was maybe a half mile across, with nothing but trees on the far shore.

Vinnie wasn't looking out at the water, but at the dark, seemingly empty window of the cabin "Let's see if anybody's in there," he said.

We were halfway there when the man stepped out from the shed.

Blood.

That's all I saw at first. The man was covered in blood.

"Whatcha boys need?" he said.

"You own this place?" Vinnie said.

That broke the spell. I saw the man clearly, with the full-length canvas apron, the gloves. He was a little guy, not more than five feet tall. And he must have been about my age, which made me wonder why he called us boys.

"Nah, you want Helen," he said. "I just work here."

"You're butchering something?" Vinnie said.

The man looked down at his gloves. "A moose," he said. "What a goddamned mess."

A woman peeked her head around the door behind him. She was the same size as the man, and you could tell in a second they'd been married forever. "Who is it, Ron?"

"Couple of men," he said. He didn't introduce us to her. Instead he just turned around and went back to her. They disappeared into the shed and closed the door.

"What's the matter with you?" Vinnie said. "You look like you've seen a ghost."

"It's nothing," I said. "I'm fine."

Just a little blood, I thought. No problem.

"I take it that woman in the shed wasn't Helen," he said. "You suppose she's in the main cabin?"

"Let's go see," I said. "I thought they'd never stop talking."

We went up the path to the front door of the cabin, climbing a set of wooden stairs that desperately needed a new coat of paint. The whole place had a run-down look about it, from the cracked foundation to the porch ceiling overrun with spider webs. We knocked on the front door. Nobody answered.

Vinnie looked at me, knocked on the door again, and then opened it. The room we stepped into was a lot nicer than what I expected, based on how the place looked from the outside. A big wooden table stood in the center of the room, with eight hand-carved chairs. There was a stone fireplace on the back wall that my old man would have approved of, and a great moose head looking down at us, its rack of antlers as wide as a piano.

"Hello!" Vinnie said. "Anybody here?"

"Back here!" a voice said. "Come on in!"

There was a door in the far wall of the room. As we stepped around the table, I looked up at the moose head. He seemed to stare right back at me.

Vinnie pushed the door open slowly and peeked inside. It was an office, with a rolltop desk and a big window overlooking the lake. The woman inside was fiddling around with the antenna on a small television. Where she expected to get a signal from, I couldn't even guess. Maybe a CBC station out of Timmins.

"We're sorry to bother you," Vinnie said.

The woman turned around and looked at us. "Oh!" she said. "I thought you were the men back from town."

"We're sorry to bother you, ma'am," I said.

"It's all right," she said. "You just surprised me." She had brown eyes, that was the first thing I noticed. She was about my age, maybe a couple years older, with brown hair just starting toward gray, and she was wearing a red flannel shirt a couple sizes too big. My overall impression was a nice lady who was a little tough, too. I suppose that's what it took way the hell up here.

"The couple outside told us to come see you," I said. "They said you owned the place. We tried calling you, but I think you have a problem with your phone."

"I'm Helen St. Jean," she said, standing up. She shook Vinnie's hand and then mine. "Yeah, that phone's been out for a week. If it wasn't so late in the season, I'd get it fixed so it could go out again."

Vinnie spoke up. "My name is Tom LeBlanc," he said. The old switcheroo was apparently alive and well. "This is my friend Alex McKnight."

"That was Ron and Millie you met outside," she said. "He was probably still working on that moose."

"He seemed to be up to his elbows in it," Vinnie said.

She frowned at that. "I don't know how many mooseburgers those men are gonna take home," she said. "They didn't seem too happy, is all I know. I don't imagine they'll be coming back next year. Not that we'll even be here next year."

"Who are we talking about?" Vinnie said. "You see, we're sort of trying to track down my brother. We know he came up here."

"I think I hear them now," she said. "Hank took them over to Calstock when they got back from the lake. You know how it is. Seven days in the woods and you need pizza."

Vinnie went to the window and craned his neck, trying to see who was outside. "I don't see him," he said. "Which party is this, ma'am?"

Before she could answer, a man came stomping into the office. "Son of a freaking—Helen, do you have the sheet for these clowns, eh? The sooner we can get rid of them—" He stopped when he saw us standing there. "Let me guess," he said. "The truck that some idiot ran off the road back there."

"That would be me," I said. "There was a moose."

"Uh-huh."

"I've got the bill all made up," Helen said, ruffling through the papers on the desk. "Let me just put one more thing on here. Gentlemen, this is Hank Gannon. He's usually in a better mood. Hank, this is Tom and Alex."

He stood there looking at us. He was a tall man, with a firm jawline and a commanding air. His name fit him perfectly. With the leather coat and wide-brimmed hat, he looked like the Canadian version of a Texas Ranger. "You boys need something here? Aside from a tow out of the mud?"

It was the second time in ten minutes we'd been called boys. It wasn't sounding any better.

"I'm looking for my brother," Vinnie said. "He was with the Albright party."

Helen stopped writing and looked up at us.

"Christ, Albright," Gannon said. "You guys are looking for him, too?"

"Was there somebody else looking for him?"

"Yeah, two other guys, just yesterday."

"Did they say who they were?"

"Nah, they just wanted to know where Albright was. I told them the same thing I'll tell you. The Albright party came and left. And good riddance."

"Albright and his men were here, then," I said. "Last week."

"That's right. I flew them back down on Saturday morning. They were gone by noon. Biggest bunch of jackasses I've ever had the misfortune of meeting. Even worse than these guys out here. I swear, Helen, it's just not worth it anymore."

She finished up her bill and gave it to him. "Here, send them on their way," she said. "So we can have some peace. Did you see Ron down there? He's probably done with the butchering."

"He's just wrapping it all up," Gannon said.

"These men who were here looking for Albright," I said, a sudden thought hitting me. "Did one of them have a big nose?" I was wondering if the two men who caused the trouble at the bar in Wawa were the same men who were here at the lodge.

"Yeah," Gannon said. "Matter of fact. He had a real smart mouth, too."

"Sir," Vinnie said. "Please. What can you tell me about Albright and the men he was with?"

"Ain't much more to tell," he said. "We flew them out to Lake Agawaatese and then we flew them out a week later."

"Right here," she said, pointing to a map on the wall above the desk. "See, we've got seven different lakes. Agawaatese is up here." She stretched to put her finger on the upper right corner. "Good lake for moose, although the cabin could use a little work."

"There were six men, right?" Vinnie said.

"No, five."

That stopped Vinnie for a second. "I thought there were six, but somebody might have canceled at the last minute."

"There were five of them," Gannon said. "Albright and his partners. What did he call them? His 'executive partners.' I was expecting a bunch of hotshots with cell phones and hundred-dollar loafers. But when they got here, eh? They were such thugs. My God, Helen puts up with a lot of shit from all the men who come up here, but these guys—"

"Needless to say," she said, "I passed on their offer to take me up to the lake with them."

"That just got them even more riled up, eh? They were ready to kill something. I couldn't get them out of here fast enough. And when I flew them back, hell, I made sure Helen wasn't even here at the lodge. She shouldn't have to put up with guys like that."

"Hank, I had to go into Timmins anyway," she said. "Don't make it sound like you were protecting me."

He waved that one off. "Bunch of clowns. President Albright and his executive partners, my ass."

"They weren't all partners," Vinnie said. "My brother was with them."

He shook his head. "The man said they were all partners."

"My brother was the guide."

He looked back and forth between us. "Let's get a couple of things straight here," he said. "Number one, if those men were gonna use a guide, they'd use *our* guide. We got an Indian fellow out there who knows these lakes inside and out. You don't need to be bringing in your own guide from America to hunt our moose, okay? If you're dumb enough to do without any guide at all, that's a different story. Number two, when this Albright called us, he made it crystal clear that he was bringing up four men who worked with him. And that they wouldn't be needing a guide. I tried to talk him out of it, but he dug in his heels. No guide necessary. He said they were all experienced hunters, and they didn't need our help. So I said, suit yourself, sir. If you don't want to actually find any moose, you go right ahead up there by your-selves. And that's what they did."

"Which kind of explains why they didn't bring any moose back with them," Helen said. "Not that they'd listen to that."

"You got that right," he said. "They came back dirty and tired, and pissed off at everything. And I told them, I said, you didn't even see the back end of a moose the whole time you were up there, eh?"

"No matter what they said," Vinnie said, "my brother did not work for Albright. I mean, just for the few days maybe. That's what he might have meant."

"I told you," he said. "We got this Indian fellow—"

"I know, you've got your own Indian. I'm telling you, Albright was just trying to get around your little rule, okay? He brought his own Indian with him. My brother."

The man looked at Vinnie, like he was really seeing him for the first time. It was something I'd witnessed before, many times. Some people look at Vinnie and see an Indian right away, like those idiots in the bar in Wawa. Others don't see the Indian in him until he points it out.

"He did look like you," Gannon said. "God damn."

"He never came back home," I said. "That's why we're here. He should have been home four days ago."

Gannon looked at Helen and then shook his head. "I'm sorry, I don't know anything about that. I flew them back out and they left. And fast. Lord knows they had nothing to load except the gear they were carrying. They were all driving this big SUV thing."

"A Chevy Suburban," Vinnie said.

"Yeah, a black one. Looked brand-new. They all piled in and left. Like I said, they were out of here by noon. Plenty of time to get back to Michigan the same day. If they didn't feel like driving all the way back to Detroit, I suppose they would have spent the night somewhere."

"My brother lives in the U.P. They would have dropped him off that night."

"Yeah, they would have. Like you say, that same night."

"He never came home," Vinnie said.

Gannon threw up his hands. "I don't know what to say. Although, come to think of it—"

"What?"

"Oh, I'm just trying to remember. On their way out, this Al-bright clown was saying something about how they didn't get their moose, and they were in no hurry to get back home. So maybe they'd have to go have some fun somewhere else."

"Like where?"

"He didn't say. I was just assuming he meant they'd hit some casinos or some clubs or something. I didn't think much of it at the time."

"Do you have a phone number for this Albright?" I said. "Or an address?"

"He paid with a Visa number," Helen said, "so I don't have a check. I'm not sure he ever gave me an address."

"You've got to have his address," I said. "That's just normal business practice, isn't it?"

She looked at me, and then at Gannon. "I'm not sure we even qualify as a business right now."

"I'm sorry," I said. "I didn't mean to criticize. We're just trying to find out what happened to Tom—" I caught myself. "Uh, Tom's brother." Real smooth, Alex.

She shook her head and looked through another pile of papers. Finally, she came up with a three-by-five card. "Here's his phone number." She read off the same cell phone number Vinnie already had.

"You don't have anything else?" I said. "Not even another number in case of emergency?"

"Just this one," she said.

Vinnie ran one hand through his hair. "What do we do now, Alex?"

"I don't know," I said. "Let me think."

Gannon stood there watching us. Helen was staring at the floor. It seemed ridiculous that we'd drive all the way up here and then leave so quickly.

"We'd appreciate any other help you can give us," I said to

them. "Do you have any idea where they might have gone, if not straight home?"

"Well," Gannon said. "I know what their first stop was gonna be. They ran out of beer their last night on the lake. Just one more thing they were complaining about."

"They were all drinking beer?" Vinnie said.

"Sure seemed to be. All five of them arrived pretty well lubricated, I remember that. Happens when you get Americans up here drinking Canadian beer the whole way."

"Are you positive they were all drinking?" Vinnie said. From the sound of his voice, he was already resigned to it.

"I know how many cases of beer we flew in with," he said, "and how many empties we brought back."

Vinnie seemed to lose his steam right about then. There didn't seem to be much left to say, so I thanked them for their time, and asked the man if he could help get my truck back on the road.

"You go on outside," he said. "I'll take care of these guys and then we'll go pull you out of the mud."

Vinnie didn't say a word as we went back down the rickety front steps and walked by the other hunting party. They were all standing around the butcher shed, these unshaven men with filthy sweatshirts and unwashed hair.

Four days ago, another group of men came back looking the same way and then disappeared off the face of the earth.

Or at least Tom did.

And two other men came up here looking for Albright. We were a day behind them.

As Vinnie and I walked up to the vehicles, I turned to look back at the lake. I saw a man standing on the dock, a man I hadn't seen when we first came down. He was young, and had the kind of dark features that left no doubt in your mind. He was an Indian.

"That must be the guide," I said to Vinnie.

He turned, and squinted in the last light of the day reflected off the water. "Where?"

"Right there," I said. But as I looked again, the dock was empty.

Chapter Five

The sun was going down when we left. It was a short ride in Gannon's jeep, not enough time to have a real conversation. But Gannon had something to say to us. "This is it, guys," he said. "We're done with the lodge business. It just doesn't make sense anymore. Less and less hunters, and the good hunters aren't passing it down to their sons anymore. It's just drunken jackasses now."

He let that one hang for a moment.

"Not to say that about your brother, you understand. The more I think about it, yeah, maybe he did stick out, eh? Maybe he wasn't a jackass like those other guys."

"Just tell me one more time," I said. "You brought them back Saturday, around noon, and then they drove away."

"Kicked up some mud on their way out," he said. "They were moving."

"And you have no idea where they might have gone, if not straight home."

"No sir, I really don't. I'm sorry."

That was about it. A few seconds later we got to my truck. Gannon backed up his jeep to it, looped a chain around my trailer hitch, and had me out with one pull. It was obviously something he'd done before.

I thanked him. He left. We got in the truck and got the hell out of there. Vinnie didn't say anything. He kept working his hands together into fists, then letting go.

"What do you want to do?" I said. I was heading back to 631. Unless he had some other idea, I assumed I'd just be pointing us south and heading home.

"I don't know," he said.

"Who do you think those other men were? The ones looking for Albright."

"No idea. Somebody else who was expecting them home a few days ago."

"That had to be them at the bar in Wawa," I said. "The guys who broke that joker's nose."

"We're on the same trail," Vinnie said. "And anybody coming up here pretty much has to stop in Wawa. It's not such a big coincidence."

"We'll keep trying Albright's number," I said. "When we get home, maybe we can find out his address."

He didn't say anything.

"Using his cell phone number, I mean. There's got to be a way. Hell, if you want, we can even go down there."

"All the way down to Detroit?"

"It's eight hours back to the Soo," I said. "What's another six hours?"

He shook his head. "I can't believe he was drinking."

"You don't know that for sure."

"Of course he was. Those men were in that cabin for what, seven days? With how many cases of beer?"

"If it was you," I said, "would you drink any of it?"

He looked at me.

"I'm serious," I said. "Would you?"

"I haven't touched alcohol in eight and a half years," Vinnie said. "You know that."

"How long has it been for Tom?"

He thought about it. "Maybe six months."

"But he was trying."

"I've been on hunts," Vinnie said. "Just like this one. I know how to deal with it."

"So maybe Tom did, too."

Vinnie shook his head again. "If he was drinking, all bets are off, Alex. There's no reason for us to even be up here looking for him."

"Come on, Vinnie."

"I'm serious."

"I never actually went to a meeting myself," I said. "But I know how it goes. You don't drink for the rest of the day. And then the next day, you do it all over again. If you fail, you just start over. You do the best you can."

"Yeah, that's how it works. You know the drill."

"Don't take it out on me, Vinnie. Okay? I'm just saying, maybe he's not as strong as you. Maybe he's gonna fall down a few times."

"I sent him into the woods for a week with a bunch of beer-drinking white men, and a stack of bottles about ten feet high. That's what I did for him."

I didn't say anything. The headlights hit the sign for 631. I took the right turn.

"I can't go home," he said.

"Why? You think your whole family is gonna hold you responsible for him?"

"Look at everything I did leading up to this," he said. "Letting him pretend to be me, violating his parole, sending him up here with strangers—"

"All right, it doesn't look good on paper," I said. "I'll grant you that."

"Don't mince words," he said. "Tell me straight. If it was your relative, and I did this to him, you'd be ready to shoot me."

"I would wonder what you were thinking."

"Yeah. You'd wonder."

I was tired. I didn't feel like arguing. "We should stop on the way back," I said. "Spend the night somewhere."

"I told you, I can't go back home."

"Vinnie—"

"I can't face them."

That was enough for me. I slammed on the brakes, just about sending him through the windshield. "Listen," I said, as he fell back into his seat. "I've had enough of this, all right? You want me to tell you it was a stupid thing to do? Okay, I'll say it. It was stupid. It was damned stupid. It was the stupidest thing I've ever seen you do. And yeah, everybody in your family is gonna be pissed off at you. And yeah, I would be, too. Okay? Have we settled that now?"

He rubbed the back of his neck. "Yes, we've settled that."

"Okay, then."

I put the truck back on the road and drove. Vinnie didn't say anything for another hour, until we hit Hornepayne. There was no train this time, so the whole town flashed right by us like an idle thought. There was nothing but open road again, and the headlights against the trees. Finally, he cleared his throat. "Don't you want to know why?"

"Why what?"

"Why I let Tom come up here?"

"You told me," I said. "You thought you were helping him. You thought he could use the money."

"No, that's not why."

"So tell me."

He settled back in his seat, looked out into the night. "About a month ago," he said, "I was coming home from the casino. It was like ten o'clock at night. I stopped by my mother's house, but it didn't look like anybody was home. I mean, the cars were all gone. The place was dark. So I figured, okay, they're all over at the healing center in Garden River or something. I'm about to back out of the driveway, and I notice that the porch light isn't on. Which is the first weird thing. The second weird thing is that there's a light on in the house. Believe me, when my mother leaves the house, she turns every light off, except the one on the porch. And God help you if you mess that up."

"I believe it."

"I went inside to see what was going on. At the very least, I figured maybe somebody else had left the house after she had. I was thinking I'd be saving somebody a lot of abuse if I turned that light off in the house and turned the porch light on. But when I got inside, I thought I heard something from one of the back rooms. I called out, you know, 'Hey, anybody home?' Nobody answered. But then another noise. It was dark, and hell, it had been a long day, so maybe my imagination got the best of me. I was thinking maybe it was a burglar back there, so I grabbed a fireplace poker, just like in the movies. I go down the hallway real slow, holding that poker, listening for somebody. And then I see there's a light on in the bathroom."

He stopped for a moment, took a deep breath.

"So I called out again," he went on. " 'Hey, who's there?' Nobody answered. So I went up to the door and I opened it."

He stopped again. There was nothing but the sound of the tires on the road, and the cold air whistling by.

"Who was it?" I said.

"It was Tom. He had stayed home, all by himself. You wanna know why?"

I didn't even try to answer.

"He stayed home so he could hang himself with an extension cord in the shower."

I kept driving. I waited for him to start talking again.

"His face was blue, Alex," he finally said. "It was actually blue. A minute later and he would have been dead. I grabbed him and tried to lift him in the air. And he started fighting me, kicking me all over. It was just ... I was so mad, Alex. It's almost funny looking back on it. I wasn't mad that he was trying to kill himself. I was mad that he was doing it in the bathroom. That was my first thought. This is the bathroom my uncles worked so hard on. Putting in all that new tile and the sink and the bathtub and the separate shower stall. And they're all gonna come home in a little while and find your dead stinking body hanging there."

He rubbed one hand over his face and through his hair.

"In the bathroom, Alex. God damn it. If you're gonna kill yourself, you go up to the old graveyard on Mission Hill. You know what I mean? You say hello to your ancestors and then you jump off the cliff. Just walk right out into the sky. That's how you kill yourself."

"So what happened?" I said.

"Well, at that point I'm fighting him, trying to get him down, and the stupid shower rod breaks. We both go falling in the shower and I just about crack my head open. The extension cord was coming loose and he's getting his breath back. He's trying to yell at me, and trying to punch me. I could have killed him right there. I could have strangled him with my bare hands. Which was kinda weird, I guess, after I stopped him from killing himself. But finally he gives up fighting me and he's just lying there, half in the shower and half out. He starts crying. I sat there with him for, what, maybe thirty minutes, just sitting there watching him cry. I finally asked him, 'Why, Tom? Why were you gonna do that?' And he says, 'This is the only way out. It's either go back to prison, or this.' "

"Okay," I said, after another long silence. "So how does that end up with you sending him up here?"

"You've got to understand, the only jobs he's ever had aside from leading hunts were either washing dishes or cleaning toilets. He can't even work at the casino, now that he has a record. It's just more of the same. Hell, I'd be going crazy, too."

"You wouldn't try to kill yourself."

"Who knows, Alex? Who really knows? If I had to stay in that house, with everybody looking at me all the time like I was a criminal."

"So what then?"

"I told him just to hold on, you know? Just give me some time to help him. And then when this thing came along. Three thousand dollars for a week of hunting. Only problem was, it was in Canada. There's no way they would have let him leave the country."

"Vinnie, I know it's good money, but—"

"It's more than that. Don't you get it? You know why he loves doing hunts so much? Same reason I do. It sounds kinda stupid, but going out on a hunt makes you remember who you are. I mean, most of the time, you're just hanging out with your own people, you know, doing regular stuff, sitting around or going to work, whatever. Then you go out in the woods with a bunch of white guys and all of a sudden they're treating you like you're fucking Geronimo. Like you're this amazing, wild Indian shaman who can hear messages in the wind and talk to the animals and learn their secrets. At first, you think, okay, these white guys are totally into some kind of cartoon character they saw on television. But then you realize, shit, they're right. I *am* different. My ancestors, they *did* know all this stuff. And I'm still a part of it. You know what I mean?"

"Yeah, I get it. So you decided—"

"He needed this, Alex. He really needed this. Otherwise—"

I shook my head.

"It was either that or let him kill himself," Vinnie said. "That was my choice. If I hadn't let him go, he'd be dead. No doubt about it."

I slowed down to let a string of deer run across the empty road. We watched five of them go by, white tails flashing in the headlights. I waited another few seconds. There's always one more.

Then it came. The sixth deer, smaller than the rest. It jumped into the brush, following the rest of its family.

"What would you have done?" he said.

"I'd have to think about it," I said.

"You of all people should understand."

"How do you mean?"

"You've been there."

I looked over at him. "Excuse me?"

"It's like my mother said, you carry around so much pain, and you won't let anybody else help you carry it. She says you have such a lonely heart, it's hard to even look at you."

"All right," I said, "can we leave me and my lonely heart out of this? I think I'm doing a lot better now, anyway."

"She says you need a woman."

"Your mother sees all this in me? How about Tom? How come she didn't see it in her own son?"

I regretted it as soon as I said it, but Vinnie just laughed. "Your own family," he said. "That's different."

We both seemed to want to leave it alone for a while, so another hour passed as we made our way down to White River.

"You know what we should be doing?" I finally said.

"What's that?"

"You said you were at the duty-free shop when Tom left with those guys. But you didn't see them."

"No. Just the van. Why, what are you thinking?"

"I'm just wondering," I said. "If they came this way on their way up, and then again on their way back down, somebody must have seen them."

"I suppose you're right," Vinnie said. "How many places could they stop?"

"We're about to hit one of them," I said. "Here comes White River."

The road ended at Highway 17. That plus the railroad going through was excuse enough to put a town there. White River had three different places where you could get something to eat and drink. "If you were a rich guy passing through," Vinnie said, "which one would you stop at?"

"They all look about the same to me," I said. I stopped at the first establishment, a little cinder block bar and restaurant called the T-Spot. It turned out to be a real mom-and-pop operation, with card tables spread out all over the place and a tiny bar that looked like it had once been in somebody's basement. We ordered a couple of cheeseburgers from a lady who looked like she owned the place. Hell, she looked like she had built it herself. When we asked her why she called it the T-Spot, she looked at us like we were idiots and asked if we had noticed the two highways forming a T in the middle of town.

"I've got another question for you," I said. "Eleven days ago, six men came through here on their way to a hunting trip."

"Five men," Vinnie said.

"Yeah, maybe five. They would have come back through again four days ago."

"Well, let's see. Men on their way to hunt. In October. Hey, Earl!" she called behind her. "Have we seen any men on hunting trips the past few days?"

"I haven't been counting them," he said, without even looking up. "I'd guess around a thousand."

"These guys were a little different," I said. "They were probably dressed a lot better than most of the hunters you get in here. And it sounds like they weren't exactly behaving themselves. At least, all but one of them."

"What did the other one look like?" she said.

"Like me," Vinnie said. "He's my brother."

The woman studied his face. "Five guys, you say? Rich white guys and one Indian?"

"Yes."

"I remember them. They stopped in for breakfast. Bunch of slick old boys. Four whites and one Indian."

"Breakfast?" I said. "That must have been on their way up, eleven days ago?"

"Yeah, that sounds about right. I remember they seemed like real pains in the ass, you know, sending the eggs back because they weren't done right. Making a racket. But then they left me a twenty dollar tip on a thirty dollar bill. In American dollars. A twenty dollar tip I'll remember."

"But you didn't see them again when they were on their way back?"

"Nope, just the one time."

"How about another two men?" I said. "One with a big nose. They might have come through here yesterday."

"We got a lot of big noses up here, hon."

"Okay, never mind." I thanked the woman, we had our dinner, and then we left.

"We're about three hours away from the lodge," I said. "So maybe they didn't need to stop yet."

"Or maybe they saw that little bar in there and decided to go somewhere else."

We checked the other two bars in town. We didn't get anything.

"Okay, so on the way back, they just kept driving. Maybe they stopped in Wawa."

64

"Let's see," he said.

So we did. Through the dark woods we drove another hour and a half. My eyes were getting tired. It was 10:30 when we hit Wawa again. The giant goose looked down at us once again, this time lit up by two spotlights.

"We know what our favorite bar in Wawa is," I said. "You figure these guys found the same place?"

"Might as well start there," he said. "Just promise me you won't get into trouble again."

"That wasn't trouble," I said. "That was just a misunderstanding with the locals."

The parking lot actually had a few vehicles in it this time, and when we stepped into the place, it almost looked busy. Every bar stool was taken, and a few more men were sitting at the round tables. There were two guys playing pool, the chalk dust hanging in the air below the single fluorescent light. Thankfully, our friends weren't trying to play the bowling game.

The same big man was behind the bar. He was working a lot harder now, trying to keep everyone happy, with apparently nobody to help him. He was sweating like he'd just buried a dead horse. He did a double take when he saw us leaning on one end of the bar. "You guys again," he said, his voice a hell of a lot less cordial than the first time we heard it. "Just what I need."

"We just want to ask you a couple of questions," I said.

"Can't you see I'm busy here? You want something to drink or not?"

"A Molson and a 7-Up," I said. "Our usual."

He didn't smile. He hit the draft handle, drew me a glass that was at least half foam, squirted some soda water out of his shooter into a glass and put it down next to the beer. "Five bucks," he said.

"Your prices went up," I said.

"It's a tough business."

"Whatever your problem is—"

"My problem is as soon as you guys left here today, Stan and Brian got in a big fight. Brian's in the hospital."

I almost laughed. "Stan's the guy who got his nose broken, right? And Brian's the guy who didn't stand up for him? What the hell does that have to do with us?"

Vinnie leaned in front of me. "We're just looking for somebody," he said, raising his voice over the noises around him. "Do you think you could help us out?"

"Who you looking for?"

"My brother."

"Go check the parking lot. That's about as far as an Indian gets before he passes out."

The look Vinnie gave him right about then should have scared him. But the bartender didn't know Vinnie like I did. He didn't know the kind of day we'd been having, or that Vinnie's seven-mile-long fuse was about to burn all the way down.

That's when our friend Stan showed up. There was fresh white tape on his face, and his two black eyes looked even worse. "Lookee here," he said. "It's the Lone Ranger and Tonto again."

He was still wearing his Maple Leafs jersey. It took Vinnie about two seconds to hit him twice in the face and then pull that jersey right over his head. Somebody else jumped in, and then me. Usually I'm smart enough to cover myself in a bar fight, especially when I'm fighting over something stupid in a roomful of strangers. But somehow it all boiled over at that exact moment, all the driving and the dead ends, and everything Vinnie had told me about Tom. Having your brother go to prison and then finding him in the shower, trying to hang himself. Somehow I was plugged into the same anger now, for Tom and for the men he had come up here with, and for everyone else in this goddamned backwoods bar. Fortunately, nobody else in the place seemed too interested in fighting. Most of them just watched us for a minute or two until they could step in and separate us.

"Easy now," a man said in my ear as he wrapped me from behind in a bear hug. "Just take it easy." I struggled to break free, but he was strong enough to wait me out.

Where all this anger had come from, I didn't know. I was thinking about it thirty minutes later, as two officers from the Ontario Provincial Police station down the street had us sitting at a table in the corner. They weren't happy about Vinnie not having a driver's license, but they ran mine and stood around for a while, figuring out what to do with us. It wasn't the first bar fight they'd seen that week—hell, maybe not even that night—so they let us go with the standard warning.

I was still thinking about it at midnight as we checked in at the local motel. I sure didn't feel like driving another four hours to make it home. Spending the night in Wawa wasn't my idea of a vacation, but at least it wasn't the local jail.

I got Vinnie some ice for the scrape over his left eye, used the toothbrush the man at the front desk had given me, washed it down with tap water that tasted like pure iron. When the lights were out and I was staring up at the ceiling, I tried to let go of the anger. I tried to let go of it the way you let sand run between your fingers. When it was gone, there was nothing left but a question. And then another.

"These guys didn't just vanish into thin air," I said. "Where in hell did they go?"

Vinnie lay on the bed across from me. "I wish I knew, Alex."

"And these other two guys, the ones who are looking for them. Who are they?"

He didn't answer. He stared up at the same ceiling. We both listened to the night, a long way from home, and waited for the morning.

Chapter Six

The chirping woke me up. Some kind of bird was making a racket, and it was doing it about three hours too early. I opened one eye and saw a dim ray of light coming through the window—whose window I could not say. I had no idea where the hell I was.

I sat up. There was a dull ache in my right hand. The bird started chirping again. What in goddamned hell, I thought. And then it came back to me.

I was in a motel room—in Wawa, Ontario, of all places. Vinnie was face down on the other bed, still wearing his clothes from the night before. The ache in my hand told me that I had gotten at least one good shot in before the fight was broken up. And that damned chirping had to be—

My cell phone rang again. Where the hell was it? I picked up my pants, then my coat, but I couldn't find it. Finally, I stood still and listened. The ring was muffled, and it seemed to come from

Vinnie himself, like maybe he had swallowed the damned thing. I rolled him over and picked it up off the bed.

"Hello," I said. I looked at the clock. It was 6:32.

"Mr. McKnight?" It was a woman's voice.

"Yes."

"This is Constable Natalie Reynaud of the Ontario Provincial Police."

I thought of two things at once. One was the sick feeling that the previous night was coming back to haunt us. Somebody must have filed charges—probably Stan, the guy Vinnie did a number on. The other thing going through my mind was just how little this woman sounded like a police officer. It was too early in the morning to be politically correct about it. Hell, most of the women officers I had known had voices like drill sergeants.

"Constable—" I said. That's all I got out.

"You left a message on Mr. Red Albright's cell phone," she said. "That's how we got this number."

I ran my hand through my hair. "Albright's phone? That was actually my friend calling."

"Mr. Albright's wife called the Michigan State Police yesterday. I assume they've been in contact with you already?"

"The police?" I needed to wake up, and fast.

"In Michigan, yes."

I stood up and gave Vinnie a nudge. "No," I said. "We haven't made it back to Michigan yet. We're in Wawa."

"You were up at the lodge yesterday," she said. "On Lake Peetwaniquot."

I nudged Vinnie again. He slapped me away. "Yes, we were," I said. "We were looking for Albright and the men who were with him."

"We just spoke to Mr. Gannon and Ms. St. Jean. They told us you were up there."

"Yes, we drove up to see if we could find out anything. The

men were due back a few days ago. Are you telling me that Albright never got home, either?"

"None of the men did. Mrs. Albright and the other wives apparently decided to give them one more night, and then call the police. It's been five days at this point. It doesn't take that long to get back down to Detroit."

"Even less to Sault Ste. Marie."

"Now, that's where we're getting a little mixed up. You see, I've got four names here, Mr. McKnight. These were the names called in from Detroit. I don't see anybody from Sault Ste. Marie."

"They picked up another man on the way," I said. "That's the man we were worried about."

"Okay, it's starting to make sense now. That's what Mrs. St. Jean seemed to be saying. There were five men on the hunt."

"Yes, exactly."

"Can I get this man's name, please?"

"LeBlanc."

"LeBlanc," she said. I could tell she was writing it down. "What's the first name?"

I looked over at Vinnie. He was out.

"Mr. McKnight? I need that first name."

"I know, I know." It was way too early to try to keep the story straight. And now that the police were officially involved, I figured it was time to end it. "You see," I said, "it's kind of a long story."

"If you're telling me I've got a fifth man missing who the families in Detroit didn't even know about, I'm going to need that name right now."

"Where are you calling from, Constable?"

"We're at the Hearst Detachment. It's about fifty miles east of the lodge."

"You think we could come back up there and talk to you in person?"

She hesitated. "Mr. McKnight, if you want to come up here, you can do that. But first I want that name."

71

"Thomas LeBlanc," I said.

"That was the fifth man on the hunting trip."

"Yes. I'm here with his brother, Vincent LeBlanc."

"Okay," she said. "See, that wasn't so hard."

I let that one go. As soon as she ran the name, she'd find out just how hard it really was.

"Listen," she said, "we're on our way over to the lodge right now. As long as you're still in Wawa, why don't you come back up and talk to us?"

"I think that would be a good idea."

"Okay, Mr. McKnight. We'll see you at the lodge. Drive carefully."

"You, too," I said. "Watch out for moose."

I switched the phone off. Vinnie slept in perfect peace, oblivious to what I'd just done. Like I had any choice.

"Wake up," I said.

He made a noise.

"That was the police."

He lifted his head. His left eye was still swollen. "What?"

"Albright never got home. His wife called the police down in Detroit."

He pulled himself up until he was sitting on the edge of the bed. "Man," he said. "My head hurts."

"That was the OPP," I said. "They're going to the lodge. I told them we'd meet them there."

"Okay."

"They wanted Tom's name. I figured it was time to come clean."

He looked at me. "You figured that, huh?"

"We're going up to see the police, Vinnie. These men are officially missing now."

He let out a long breath. Then he pushed himself up and for one second I thought he was going to jump on me. But instead he stumbled toward the bathroom. "I need to take a shower," he said. "I can't go see the police looking like a vagrant. It's gonna be bad enough."

An hour later we were both as cleaned up as we were going to get. We stopped in at a little coffee shop down the street, then at the gas station, and then we were on our way. The giant goose looked down on us one more time as we left town. It felt strange to be going north again.

The rest of the morning we spent retracing our route from the day before, through White River and Hornepayne, through miles and miles of lakes and trees. The air felt even colder. Vinnie sat on the passenger's side and looked out the window.

"I didn't have any choice," I finally said.

"I know."

"At this point, it's got to come out."

"You're right," he said without looking at me. "I'm not saying you did the wrong thing."

"Okay," I said, and then I settled in for two more hours on the road without one more word from him. I suppose if I had a brother and I knew he was probably on his way back to prison, I'd be just as talkative.

It was eleven o'clock when we hit the Trans-Canada Highway again. I knew to take the left, and to look for the unmarked road on the right. I kept the truck out of the mud this time. We didn't see our friend the moose.

When we came around the last bend in the road, we saw the police car parked behind the other vehicles. It was white and clean, with the blue OPP seal on the door. We stopped and got out of the truck.

"They must be inside," I said. The place looked just as deserted as the first time we had seen it. There was a wet wind coming in off the lake again. The air felt heavy.

We walked down to the main cabin. As we passed the butcher's shed, I expected to see the man come out with the blood all over his gloves again. I couldn't remember the man's name, although I knew Helen had told us.

"The plane's gone," Vinnie said. I looked out at the dock. There was just the two aluminum boats, bobbing up and down in the waves.

We went up the creaky old steps and into the main cabin. The big moose head looked down at us. "Hello!" I said.

Nothing.

"That's what I love about this place," I said. "They always know how to make you feel welcome."

We went back to the little office, but it was empty. A radio was on. A faraway station was barely audible through the thick buzz of static. It sounded like French.

"Where is everybody?" Vinnie said.

"Think they all went someplace in the plane?"

"They told us to meet them here, didn't they?"

"They did," I said.

We went back through the main room to the front door. It opened just as we got there. Helen St. Jean took one look at us and screamed.

"Oh, my goodness," she said when she could breathe again. "You scared the life out of me."

"I'm sorry," I said. "The police told us to meet them here."

"The police," she said. "Yes. Hank flew them out to the cabin."

"The cabin where the men were staying?"

"On Lake Agawaatese, yes. They wanted to see if the men left anything there."

"Like what?"

"I don't know," she said, looking out the window at the sky. "Some kind of clue. Something that might tell the police where they were going when they left here. I can't imagine what that would be."

"How long have they been out there?"

"They flew out around eight. I'm surprised they're not back already."

"Albright's wife called the police," I said. "And the other wives. Those men never did get back to Detroit."

"I know," she said. "That's what the constables said."

We all stood there for a moment. I wasn't sure what else to say. The door creaked open just then, and the man from the butcher's shed came in. He stopped when he saw us.

"They're still out there," Helen said.

The man nodded.

"Ronnie, this is Alex and Tom," she said. "They were here yesterday."

Vinnie looked down at the floor and shook his head.

"Yes, we met," I said. "You were butchering the moose."

He glanced upward, past my shoulder. I turned and looked up at the moose head with him.

"Sorry," I said. "Maybe we should change the subject."

The man didn't smile. He didn't say a word. He gave Helen a little nod and then he went back out the door.

"You'll have to excuse him," Helen said. "He doesn't say a lot, especially to strangers. Millie's kinda the same way."

"It's a good place to live then," I said. "How many strangers do you even see up here?"

She smiled. "Less and less every season. I don't imagine we'll be coming back next year."

"That's what Mr. Gannon told us yesterday. I got the impression it was a done deal."

"I suppose it is," she said. "It's hard to believe we'll be packing up for good this time."

"Where do you go when you're not up here?"

"We all live in Sudbury," she said. "For the last fifteen years, we've been coming up here for the summer and fall. Business was good the first few years, then it started to taper off. This year was the worst, and now, with this—" She looked out the window again.

"I'm sorry to hear that, ma'am," Vinnie said. "This isn't good for anybody."

She looked at him for a long moment. "You fellas want some coffee?"

"That would be nice," Vinnie said.

As she left the room, Vinnie went to the window and stared out. "I wish we were out there," he said.

"What do you think we'd find?" I said. "The men have been gone for five days now."

"People leave things behind," he said. "There's always something."

Helen came back out with a pot of coffee and three empty mugs. She poured it black and didn't ask if we wanted cream or sugar. Which was fine with me. We all stood there looking out the window for a few minutes, until finally we heard the distant whine of the motor.

"That'll be them," she said. "I'd know that sound anywhere."

We followed her outside. She went down to the dock and stood there watching the northern sky. A speck appeared above the trees. It got larger as the sound of the motor grew louder. The plane seemed to bob up and down in the wind as it cleared the tree line. Then it hit the water, touching down as smoothly as a loon returning to its nest. The plane cruised in across the length of the lake, slowing down as it approached the dock. I could see Hank Gannon's face through the windshield.

He cut the motor. The sound kept ringing in my ears. Helen stepped up and caught the plane with one hand, then looped two ropes around the cleats on the float, front and back. The door popped open, a small ladder came out, and Hank climbed down to the dock.

"Isn't this cozy?" he said, looking right at me. I was still holding my mug. "Did you bake them a cake, too?"

"The police told them to come back up," she said.

"Yeah, no kidding. It sounds like they've got some real good questions to ask them."

A woman stepped out next. This had to be Constable Natalie Reynaud, wearing the distinctive blue uniform of the Ontario Provincial Police. She had dark hair pinned up under her hat, and I would have put her age around thirty-five if I had to guess. She hopped off the last step of the ladder like it was nothing.

The man who followed her took a lot longer to get down that ladder, and he sure as hell didn't jump off the last step. He was wearing the same uniform, but aside from that he was everything his partner wasn't. He looked like he was in decent shape for a man in his sixties, but I knew that was old for a man on active duty.

"That was a bumpy ride," he said. "Feels good to be on the ground again."

"Did you find anything?" Helen said.

"Just a big mess," the old cop said. "Those boys don't know how to clean up after themselves."

"I tried to clean it up a little bit," Hank said. "Sorry we took so long." He looked at me again, and then at Vinnie. "We shouldn't have left you here, Helen."

"One of the windows was knocked in," the older constable said. "Looks like a black bear did it. Probably smelled the garbage."

Constable Reynaud came up to me and looked me in the eye. "You must be Mr. McKnight," she said. "And this must be Mr. LeBlanc." She had a nice face, and green eyes. But you could tell in a second she was all business. "This is my partner, Senior Constable Claude DeMers."

He shook out the kinks as he came over to us, and he shook my hand. "Thanks for coming up," he said. "I hope you don't mind if we ask you a few questions." All of a sudden, he didn't look so old anymore.

"Yeah," Gannon said from behind them, "start by asking them why they didn't give us their real names."

DeMers turned and gave him a look. "Hank, I told you. Let us handle this. I'm sure there's a good explanation."

Gannon just turned away and gave him a wave of his hand. He climbed back into his plane, grabbed a big trash bag from inside, and threw it down onto the dock. It landed with a heavy thud.

"Helen," the cop said, "is there someplace we can have a chat with these gentlemen?"

"Use the office," she said.

"You should send Hank back out to fix that window," he said. "You don't want any more bears in that cabin."

"Doesn't matter much now," she said. "They can move in for all I care."

DeMers shook his head at that. "Hell of a thing," he said. "I hope we find those boys soon so we can put an end to this."

"Where are you looking?" Vinnie said. "They've been missing for five days. Are you covering all the roads back to Detroit?"

DeMers looked at him. For one long moment the only sounds were the wind and the waves. "My partner tells me your name is Vinnie," he finally said.

"Yes."

"Not Tom."

"No, Tom is my brother."

"Well, Vinnie, like we said, we need to ask a few questions. What do you say we start with you? I mean, now that we've established your real name—"

"Vinnie," I said, "you don't have to say anything right now. I think maybe we should talk to a lawyer first."

"I'll tell them what they need to know," Vinnie said. "I'll tell them the truth."

The whole thing went downhill from there. They took Vinnie into Helen's office for questioning. I sat by myself in the main room, trying not to look up at the moose head.

An hour passed. It felt like a day. I got up and went to the window, watched Gannon cleaning out his plane. The other man appeared on the dock, the silent one. What was his name? Ron, that was it. He took the big bag of garbage away, then he came back with a broom and swept the dock. The man's wife appeared. Millie. She went to the end of the dock and looked out at the lake. Ron stopped sweeping and went out to stand next to her. He put his arm around her. She put her head on his shoulder.

I heard a noise behind me. The door to the office was closed. I heard the noise again—it sounded like . . . like a low wailing. Like somebody moaning. I stood still, holding my breath, listening.

There's nobody here, I told myself. Nobody but—

The moose, for God's sake. It sounds like it's coming from the moose. That would make this day complete. A haunted moose head.

I went over and stood below it. The sound came again, this time a lot louder. But not from above me. I bent down and looked in the fireplace. The moaning sound was the wind passing over the chimney. The updraft was so strong I could feel the air rushing past me.

Helen came in through the front door. "Are they still in there talking to your friend?"

"Yes," I said. "I'm next."

She stood by the door, looking uncertain. "I wanted to start packing up the office. I was hoping we could get out of here by tomorrow morning."

"This is quite a fireplace you've got here," I said.

"Oh, that. Yeah, we don't use it anymore. Hank says it doesn't draw well."

"Are you kidding? It's practically sucking me up the chimney."

"I think there was a nest up there," she said. "Raccoons or something. Maybe they're gone now. God, what a horrible thought. All those animals crawling around up there." She wrapped her arms around herself. "I'm sorry. Listen to me. Now that I know we're leaving for good, I just can't stand being here another minute. I hate it like a sickness. I think we all feel that way now, all four of us."

"You said you're all gonna move back to Sudbury?"

"Yes."

"Do you have family back there?"

"We have each other," she said. "We *are* a family."

"No children?"

"No," she said. "We sort of all have that in common."

I looked outside the window again. Ron was still standing at the end of the dock, his wife's head still on his shoulder. Her back was shaking now, like she was crying. Ron put his head on her head and pulled her closer.

Gannon had picked the broom up. He was holding it in both hands, his eyes closed. He kept tapping the dock with it, again and again.

A thought hit me. "The Indian you use as a guide," I said. "He was here yesterday, too. I saw him on the dock as we were leaving."

"Guy? No, I doubt it," she said. "I think he left as soon as he got back from the hunt."

"Those men who were hanging around, he was out on a moose hunt with them?"

"Yes, his last one of the year. The last one he'll ever do here, I guess. He left without even saying goodbye."

"I suppose if I was out in the woods for a week, I'd be anxious to get home, too."

"No, that was a four-day hunt, over on a different lake," she said. "Thank God. If it was a seven-day hunt, we'd still be stuck here waiting for them to get back."

"Well, either way, I'm sure I saw him."

"I don't know," she said, shrugging her shoulders. "Maybe he was still here. He's such an odd young man, I have to say. I never could figure out what made him tick."

The office door opened and DeMers stuck his head out. "What's going on out here?"

"We're just talking," I said. "If you're about done in there, Helen would like her office back."

"We're done with Mr. LeBlanc," he said. "Now it's your turn."

This will be loads of fun, I thought. I gave Helen a little smile and stepped up to the plate. As Vinnie came out of the office, he looked cool and unruffled, like he'd spent the last hour just having a nice chat. But that was something Vinnie had in his blood, going back a thousand years. I didn't have that. Not one drop.

"Right in here, Mr. McKnight," DeMers said. "Make yourself comfortable." As he closed the door I thought I heard the moose wailing again.

Chapter Seven

"Let's talk about you first," the senior constable said. He was sitting in Helen's office chair. Constable Reynaud was sitting next to him in another chair. A real chair. I got the rickety folding chair.

"Those men apparently told Gannon they were gonna have some fun before heading home," I said. "So they might not have gone straight home. Are you looking for them in Toronto? Windsor, maybe?"

"Constable Reynaud, did you say something?" he said. "I must be hearing things, because I know you and I are the only ones asking questions here."

"I didn't say a thing," she said.

"It's all part of getting old," he said. "Half of what you do hear is only in your head."

"Okay," I said. "I get the point."

"Alex McKnight of Paradise, Michigan," he said, smoothing out a wrinkle in his pants. I was starting to get a little better picture of the man. I was sure all of his socks were neatly folded and organized by color. "Constable Reynaud did some checking up on you. Turns out you were a police officer."

"Eight years in Detroit," she said, looking at her notepad. She was another type of cop entirely. The old line about a woman having to be twice as smart as a man to get half the credit was never more true than in a police station. I was sure her partner would do most of the talking, but she would be the one who really knew how to listen.

"More recently," she said, "you were granted a private investigator's license."

"I understand that's a pretty easy ticket in Michigan," DeMers said. "As long as you've got the years in law enforcement, it's pretty much automatic. Just fill in a form and you're in business, no matter what kind of person you are."

"I'm not practicing," I said. "That has nothing to do with why we're up here."

"In Ontario, it's a whole different ball game," he said. "You've got to be interviewed by the deputy registrar, provide a list of references. Then they do a thorough investigation, really turn you inside out. If anything looks fishy, you don't get that license."

"Yeah, good thing I didn't apply up here," I said. "I would have missed out on so much fun." I was trying very hard to keep cool. It was starting to make my stomach hurt. "Look, I'm not working as a private investigator. I came up here with Vinnie to help him out, because he's my friend."

And this is what I get for my trouble, I thought. I help out a friend and I end up getting grilled by another hard-ass cop. It was pretty much automatic. Come to think of it, maybe this senior constable was the only hard-ass cop left in the entire OPP. They wouldn't let him retire yet, just in case I ever decided to come to Ontario.

"Yes, about that friend," he said. "About Mr. LeBlanc. He told us quite a tale about his brother Tom, and why he felt it necessary to have him misrepresent his identity. Would you care to tell us your version?"

"He knows better than I do," I said. "I'm sure he gave you the whole story."

"Yes, but you know, it was such a compelling story, I think I need to hear it again."

"I know it looks bad," I said. "But this business with Tom is really a separate issue, okay?"

"Give me your version," he said. "And then we'll talk about how bad it looks, and how it may or may not be related to our situation."

Our situation, he calls it. I was about to say something cute, but restrained myself. No sense making it any worse. Instead I took a deep breath and gave them a quick rundown, beginning with Tom's release from prison, continuing through Vinnie's brilliant plan to let his wayward brother use his identification because it was just the thing to get his head on straight, and ending with our attempt to find out what the hell happened up here. Constable DeMers made an elaborate show of cleaning his glasses while I talked, while his partner hung on my every word and wrote notes on her pad. It may have been a new twist on the old good cop, bad cop thing. Or maybe he just liked clean glasses.

Either way, he put his glasses back on just as I finished. He took a moment to adjust them on his ears, gave his partner a quick glance, and then looked back at me. "Thank you," he said. "That was illuminating. Although I think you may have left out a couple of details."

"Such as?"

"Well, number one, where you fit into this whole thing. Surely you must have had some part in it from the beginning."

"I didn't," I said. "If I had any idea what they were trying to do, I would have stopped them."

"Being a former police officer and all."

"Former police officer or not, I would have known it was a bad idea."

"You didn't know anything about it until he went missing. At which point you dropped everything to come all the way up here to look for him."

"Vinnie's my friend," I said. "Tom's his brother."

DeMers sneaked another quick look at his partner. "The LeBlancs are very lucky," he said. "Most friends wouldn't go to such extremes."

"It was no big deal," I said. "We drove up, we asked some questions, we left."

"And the other two men? The ones who were up here the day before you?"

"We don't know anything about them. Gannon told us they were looking for Albright."

"Two men come all the way up here looking for Albright, and the very next day, two other men come looking for Tom LeBlanc."

"They were all due back," I said. "They didn't show. It's not so unusual people would come looking for them."

"And yet, according to Hank, you knew that one of them had a rather large nose."

"What?"

"You asked him that," he said. "You asked him if one of the men had a big nose."

"That's just because—" I stopped myself and counted to three. "Constable, what are you getting at? Is there some point to this?"

"You were a cop once," he said. "Put yourself in my place. Four men leave Detroit on a hunting trip. You want to tell me about those men, by the way?"

"I don't know anything about them."

"Nothing at all?"

"No. How could I?"

"You know where they live?"

"Detroit. You just said that."

"Their actual home addresses were all in Grosse Pointe. Does that tell you anything?"

"It tells me they had some money."

"Four seriously wealthy, well-connected men go on a hunting trip, and they never make it back home. The wives file missing-person reports. We get contacted to look into this end of things, because this lodge is the last place they were seen. We soon find out there was a fifth man on the team. Just enough for a hockey line."

"That would be six," his partner said.

He turned and looked at her. "Constable?"

"You need six men for hockey," she said. "You forgot the goalie."

"The goalie stays on the ice. That's why I said 'line.'"

"If you really meant a line," she said, "then that's only three. The defensemen come out separately."

He gave me a little smile and a shrug. "How about basketball, then. That's five."

"The fifth man was the guide," I said. "They picked him up in the Soo."

"So you say, and yet the good people here at the lodge know nothing about it. As far as they're concerned, he's just another one of this gentleman's business partners."

"I don't know for sure," I said, "but I don't imagine these people would have appreciated it if Albright had brought his own guide. They have their own man here."

"You mean to say it's either use their guide or none at all."

"He was taking a job away from a Canadian," I said. "I know you guys can get a little sensitive about that." It was my turn to give him a smile.

"Okay, well, assuming that was the case, don't you think it

87

looks kind of funny when this mysterious fifth man turns out to be a felon on parole who isn't even supposed to be in the country in the first place?"

"We're back to where we started," I said. "I already told you, I know it doesn't look good."

"So we agree," he said. He leaned forward in his chair. His face was two feet from mine. "Four rich American men, one American felon. All missing. Two mystery men drive all the way up here looking for them, without even giving their names. The next day, two more men drive all the way up here. One of them happens to be the man who loaned the felon his identification, and the other is a nonpracticing private investigator who's supposedly just along for the ride. And neither one of them can spend twenty-four hours in our country without getting into trouble."

"What are you talking about?" I said. I was afraid I already knew.

Constable Reynaud flipped through her pad. "Big Tony's Lounge in Wawa," she said. "Does that ring a bell?"

"That's the name of the place? Big Tony's Lounge?"

"Let me guess," she said. "The other guys started it."

"How did you know?"

DeMers stood up and opened the door. "What'll it take you, about nine hours to get home?"

"Eight if I break the speed limit." I stood up and stretched.

"That's not funny, Mr. McKnight. I hope you realize, we could have done this over at the detachment. Right now, I suggest you head directly home at a reasonable speed, and please make a point of not stopping at any bars, okay? We wouldn't want anyone else to drag you into a fight."

"We'll go right home," I said. "Believe me, it'll be my pleasure."

"As soon as you get there, you need to contact the Michigan

State Police in Sault Ste. Marie. They'll be waiting to hear from you."

"I got it."

He leaned forward again. I was waiting for another zinger. I didn't get it.

"McKnight," he said. From one second to the next, his voice had lost its edge. "Can I call you Alex?"

I hesitated. "Yes."

"Now that I've read you the riot act like I'm supposed to do, can I talk to you like a human being?"

"Yes," I said. I looked at Reynaud. She kept watching me.

"I understand why you came up here," he said. "I really do. Your friend did something really stupid, and you were just trying to help him out."

"That's right."

"But you know why we had to ask you these questions."

I looked at Reynaud again. Dark green eyes. "Yes."

"Okay, so now that it's out in the open, you've got to go back home and let us do our job. Right?"

I nodded.

"Okay then," he said. "Let's get you on your way."

He opened the door and led me back into the front room. Vinnie was standing alone at the front window, looking out at the dock, just as I had been. "That was quick," he said.

"Alex is an old cop himself," DeMers said. "He knows the drill."

I followed Vinnie onto the front porch. DeMers was right behind me, until Reynaud took him by the arm. They had their little conference while Vinnie and I went down the steps. Hank Gannon was waiting for us, his arms folded across his chest. When we were two steps from the bottom, he still hadn't moved.

"I'm surprised you're not wearing handcuffs," he said.

"Gannon, we've already had enough for one day," I said. "Step aside."

"Did you explain to the constables why you lied to us?"

"Yeah, we explained it. Now get out of the way."

"You feel like explaining it to me?"

"No," I said. "I don't."

He shifted his eyes to Vinnie. "How about you?"

"Where's Helen?" Vinnie said.

"She went for a walk. She couldn't stand to be around here anymore."

"I owe her an apology," Vinnie said. "I hope you'll give it to her for me."

He shook his head. "You just don't get it. She's been working so hard to keep this place going."

"That's got nothing to do with us," I said. I stepped down to put myself between them. "This place was in trouble long before those men went missing. You said so yourself."

"Yeah, no kidding," he said. "And this was just what we needed for a send-off—a bunch of drunken assholes from Detroit and a drunken Indian who didn't even know his own name."

The constables came out the door. A few seconds later and Vinnie might have found the end of his fuse again.

"Let them go, Hank," DeMers said. "They've got to get back home."

Gannon looked up at them, then at Vinnie, and then at me. After a long moment he stepped back. We walked up to the truck. Ron came out of his butcher's shed and stopped dead in his tracks. He watched us walk by. He didn't have to say anything to us. The look on his face was enough.

We got in the truck and I fired it up. Only then did Millie come out of the shed. She walked up toward us, moving quickly, like she wanted very much to tell us something. Ron caught her from behind and led her away, casting one last look over his shoulder at us, like even this sudden impulse on his wife's part was somehow our fault.

"Let's get away from this freak show," I said. "I hope I never see it again."

"They're packing up," he said. "Nobody will see it again."

I pointed the truck down the service road and punched it. "We'll go home," I said. "We'll get a good lawyer for your brother. Sooner or later, they're gonna turn up, and Tom's gonna be in big trouble."

Vinnie shook his head.

"As soon as he gets home and you know he's okay and you've got him hooked up with the lawyer, that's when you can kick his ass."

I got us down the twisty damned service road without incident. No moose, no running into the mud. When I hit the highway I took the left and headed back to 631. It appeared a few minutes later. I put on my right-turn signal.

I turned. Then I stopped.

"What's wrong?" Vinnie said.

"Is there a reservation around here?"

"I think so," he said. "They call them reserves up here."

"Okay, reserve. Where is it?"

"Let me think . . . There's one on Constance Lake. That's probably the closest."

"How far away?"

"Maybe twenty, thirty miles."

"Which direction?"

"East. It's just north of a little town called Calstock."

I swung the truck into a U-turn and went back to the highway.

"I take it we're going there?"

"You got it," I said.

"Aren't we supposed to be going straight home?"

"We're supposed to be, yes."

"So why are we going to the reserve instead?"

"There was a young Indian at the lodge," I said. "Yesterday. I saw him on the dock, just as we were leaving."

"You think he might know something?"

"Maybe he does. Maybe he knows something the other folks couldn't tell us."

"Couldn't or wouldn't?"

"Take your pick."

"I suppose we could try," he said. "We could ask around for the man who works at the lodge."

"Helen told me his name is Guy," I said. "That should help."

"Guy."

"She also told me he was out on a hunt with that other group of men we saw yesterday."

"So?"

"It was a four-day hunt," I said.

"Yeah?"

"That means he flew out on Saturday."

"The same day Albright's party flew back."

"Right. Their hunt was on a different lake, but they all take off from the same place. So he might have talked to them. Hell, maybe he did a little Indian bonding with your brother."

I headed due east on the empty highway. A sign told us that Calstock was fifteen miles ahead.

"He had long hair," Vinnie finally said. "He was maybe eighteen, nineteen years old. He was wearing jeans and a blue-and-white jacket. I think it had the Toronto Blue Jays emblem on it."

I looked over at him. "You saw him."

"Yes," he said. "I saw him."

Chapter Eight

We hit Calstock just after noon. There was a truck stop where the access road hit the highway. I pulled over and gassed up. The man behind the counter hesitated a moment over my American money, then said something in French.

"No parlez français," I said. "English?"

"Of course," the man said. "I was just asking you if you want your change in Canadian money."

"Whatever you got," I said. "How far up this road is Calstock?"

"About five miles. When you hit the sawmill, you're there."

We got back in the truck and continued north, bound on both sides by the thick walls of white pine trees. The sawmill came into view, just as advertised, along with a power plant that obviously burned all the bark and wood waste. The hot smell hung in the air.

Constance Lake appeared on our left just as we entered the reserve. There was a big wooden sign to let us know we were on Indian land.

"Are these Ojibwa up here?" I said.

"No, they're Cree."

"You guys get along?"

"Why wouldn't we?"

"Weren't they your mortal enemies?" I said. "No, wait, that was the Dakotas."

"The Cree and the Ojibwa are like family," he said. "It's been that way for hundreds of years. Now more than ever."

We passed a little shop that sold Indian crafts. Soon after that we were in the heart of the reserve. The houses weren't all brand-new like in Michigan. Most of the windows were taped up with plastic to keep out the coming winter winds. Thin spirals of smoke rose from the chimneys.

"How do we find Guy?" I said.

"There has to be a tribal center. Keep going."

We drove by more houses. Eventually we saw a school and beside that a big cement building that had to be something official. We pulled up next to a police car. There was a round seal on the car door that read NISHNAWBE-ASKI POLICE SERVICE.

"Maybe these police will be a little more accommodating," Vinnie said.

"Those two weren't so bad," I said.

Vinnie stopped and looked at me. "Just because one of them was attractive . . ."

"Has nothing to do with it," I said. "They could have been a lot worse, is all I'm saying."

He shook his head and smiled. "Come on." He got out of the truck and went in. I followed him. The door opened to a large meeting room, with a great round table in the middle. A young woman was vacuuming the floor. We stood there for a few seconds until she noticed us.

"Pardonnez-moi," she said. She had an unmistakably Indian face, with dark eyes and dark hair tied in a ponytail down her back. She wore thick boots under her long skirt. They clunked loudly on the floor as she came over to us.

"We're sorry to bother you," Vinnie said. "We're looking for a young man named Guy."

"Guy Berard?"

"I'm not sure what his last name is," Vinnie said. He looked at me and I shook my head. "We know he works over at the lodge on Lake Peetwaniquot."

"Yes, that's him. I haven't seen him around in a few days."

"Can you tell me where he lives?"

The woman looked at Vinnie, then at me, then back at Vinnie. "Who are you?"

"My name is Vinnie LeBlanc. I'm a Bay Mills Ojibwa, from Michigan. This is my friend Alex."

"Guy lives in his mother's house," she said. "Go south, take the first right. It's the last house on the left."

"Thank you," Vinnie said. "I appreciate it."

"Is Guy in trouble?"

"No," he said. "But my brother is. I'm hoping he can help me."

She nodded her head slowly. "Tell Mrs. Berard that Maureen sent you."

"Thank you, Maureen."

I added my own thanks, and we left. We went back down the road, past the school, and took the right turn. The road ended abruptly. Beyond the road there was a field of rocks and weeds, with a path leading down to Constance Lake. The water stretched out at least a mile, with low hills in the distance.

There were no other cars in front of the house. It was a small wooden affair the same size as its neighbors, and it had been bright yellow a few seasons ago. Now it needed paint.

Vinnie knocked on the door. We waited. A cold wind picked up and hit us like it was trying to blow us off the little porch. Vinnie knocked again. The door opened a couple of inches and stopped. The top of the door swung back and forth, until finally, with a horrible sound of wood scraping against wood, it flew open the rest of the way. The woman behind the door was practically knocked to the ground.

"Je regrette," she said, and then I caught something about "la porte," which I knew was the door. The rest I didn't get.

"We're sorry to bother you," Vinnie said. "Is Guy at home?"

She looked at Vinnie. Her hair was long and dark, like the woman at the tribal center, but it was untied and cascaded over her shoulders. She looked a little too young to be Guy's mother.

"He's not here," she said. "Who are you?"

"My name is Vinnie," he said. "I'm from the Bay Mills Reservation in Michigan. This is my friend Alex."

She looked over at me without smiling.

"Maureen sent us," I said.

"Bay Mills?" she said, looking back at Vinnie.

"Yes, ma'am."

"Please come in," she said. She stepped back to let us into the house. There was a small living room, with barely enough room for a couch and a chair. The carpeting needed replacing even more than the outside needed the paint. The curtains were closed, and a television cast a pale blue glow over the room.

"Can I get you something?" she said.

"No, thank you," Vinnie said.

"Then please sit down."

She turned off the television and sat down on the chair. Vinnie and I sat on the couch.

"Your son," Vinnie said. He apparently had no trouble believing this was his mother. "He works at the lodge on Lake Peetwaniquot."

"Sometimes," she said. "When they need a guide."

"Do you know when he's going to be home?"

"No," she said.

"Excuse me for asking," I said. "How old is Guy?"

She looked me in the eye for an instant, and then looked down. I remembered something Vinnie had told me, about how some Indians consider looking you right in the eye to be rude.

"He's nineteen," she said.

"Do you happen to know if he was out at the lodge yesterday?" I said.

"He was gone yesterday," she said. "But I really don't know."

That was something else Vinnie had told me—this business of not interfering in other people's lives, even your own son's. It always seemed a little contradictory to me, how the Indian culture was so centered on family, and yet they believed that you chose your own path in this life, and that nobody should try to change it.

Don't try to understand it, Vinnie had said. That's just the way it is.

"Can we leave a message for him?" Vinnie said. "A number he can call when he comes home?"

"You can do that," she said.

I had a pen in my coat pocket. I took it out and gave it to him, along with the receipt from the gas station. He wrote my cell phone number on the back.

"My brother is missing," Vinnie said as he gave it to her. "He was last seen at the lodge. I was hoping maybe your son might have some kind of information to help us find him. That's all."

There was a noise in the room behind us. It sounded like something bumping into the wall.

"That's Guy's grandfather," she said. "I thought he was asleep."

"I hope we didn't come at a bad time," Vinnie said.

"No, not at all," she said. She stood up. It was our cue to do the same.

"Please have Guy give us a call," I said. "We'd really appreciate it."

"Of course," she said. She didn't look me in the eye at all this time. Not for a second.

As she showed us out, I couldn't help noticing the coats hung on hooks beside the door. One of them was blue and white, with the Toronto Blue Jays emblem. I didn't say anything. I left with Vinnie and thanked her again. We watched her struggle with her sticky door. Then we left.

"Did you notice the coat?" I said when we were back in the truck.

"Yes."

"Did that whole conversation strike you as a little strange?"

"I'm not sure it even qualified as a conversation," he said. "But yeah, you're right."

"What do you think? Was she lying?"

"Indians make terrible liars," he said.

I drove south, away from the heart of the reserve, back toward Calstock. I was going very fast, because I wasn't sure if I really wanted to leave.

"What do we do now?" I said.

"I don't know," he said. "I'd like to find out what's going on with Guy."

"Maybe he just didn't want to talk to a white man."

Vinnie looked over at me.

"Maybe he saw me through the window," I said.

"Yeah, you are pretty scary-looking."

"I'm just saying, this might not mean anything at all."

"I suppose."

"We can look up the number for the tribal center," I said. "If we don't hear from Guy in a couple of days, we can give Maureen a call and see if she can help us."

"Yeah."

"Indians make terrible liars, huh? If I said something like that, you'd hit me in the mouth."

"It's true," he said. "As a general rule."

"Whatever you say."

"What? You don't agree?"

"I'm hungry, all right? Let's stop somewhere. I thought I saw a place in Calstock."

"Okay."

We drove by the last of the houses. The sign told us we were leaving the reserve. "They could use a casino," I said. I shouldn't have said it.

"Why's that?"

"This place looks like Bay Mills before the casino," I said. "That's all."

"They've got tiny little houses. So what?" he said.

"So maybe they wouldn't mind having bigger houses. And a new school, and a health center. What's the matter? I'm just saying—"

"Never mind," he said.

We were back in the trees again. The sunshine was obliterated. It was so dark it felt like the end of the day.

"I know, Indians don't care about money like white men do. Just like they can't lie."

"You're saying that, not me."

"Yeah, just like the tribe in Saginaw. They're putting on quite a show." The *Detroit News* had done a whole series on them, and the fights they'd been having over the casino money. One word against the tribal leadership and you were out of the tribe forever. With no way to appeal.

"Money makes an Indian act like a white man," he said. He looked out the window. "I'm not denying that."

"You mean money makes everyone act the same," I said. "It proves we're all exactly alike."

"Alex, wait . . ."

"Look, we don't have to—"

"Alex, *stop!*"

I slammed on the brakes. "What is it?"

"Back up," he said.

"Why?"

"Just do it."

I put it in reverse and turned around to see where I was going. It was a good thing we were on one of the loneliest roads in the world. I backed it up about fifty yards before he told me to stop. The wheels were still rolling as he threw his door open and jumped out, the door catching him in the arm as he headed for the woods.

I pulled the truck off the road and killed the engine. I stepped out into the cold air. There was a silence in the trees. All the birds had already left for the winter.

"What's going on, Vinnie?"

"Come down here," he said.

I took a few steps over the gravel shoulder and stepped down into the drainage ditch. Vinnie had already pushed his way through the brush. There was a gap maybe ten feet wide in the line of trees.

"What is it?" I said. "What do you see?"

As I got closer, I saw for myself. There was a vehicle back in the thick undergrowth. To the right of it a small pine tree was leaning over at an angle.

It was a black Chevy Suburban.

Vinnie had already fought his way through and was standing on the driver's side with his face pressed against the glass. I caught up to him and looked inside. In the dim light I could make out sleeping bags and boxes and long, leather cases that must have contained rifles. Vinnie was breathing hard next to me, making fog on the glass.

"Do you think this is it?" I said.

He didn't answer.

I pushed past him and tried the driver's side doors. They were locked. Inside, I could see the keys hanging from the ignition. I moved around the front of the vehicle, feeling the sudden sting of thorns on my face. I ducked under the branch and got around to the other side. These doors were locked, too. I could see an empty beer bottle lying on the front passenger's seat.

I started to feel a dull sense of dread. This looked bad, and it didn't even make sense. Why would the vehicle be here, miles off the main road? Unless—

Before I could finish the thought, I heard the sound of breaking glass. As I looked through I could see Vinnie raising the rock in his hand again, and smashing it into the driver's side window.

"Vinnie! What the hell!"

By the time I got back over to the driver's side, the door was open and he had climbed inside.

"Vinnie, you've got to get out of there!" I was already thinking ahead to the phone call we'd have to make, and what the police would think of this when they got here.

Vinnie climbed over to the second row of seats. There was a pile of wallets on the floor. He started picking them up one by one. His hand was bleeding.

I looked at the broken glass that had sprayed all over the front seat. I looked back at the road. It was still empty, still silent. When I looked back at Vinnie, he had stopped going through the wallets. He was frozen still, one wallet held tight in both hands. A drop of blood fell from his finger.

"Whose is that?" I said.

He didn't say anything. He just opened it up and showed me the picture of himself.

Chapter Nine

A couple of constables showed up within three minutes of my call. They weren't Reynaud and DeMers, that was for sure. They were both in their thirties, both rock hard if a few pounds overweight, the way cops get from sitting around too much. One had scar tissue laced through both eyebrows. An old boxer, I would have bet money on it. Probably a middleweight. The other guy had never been hit in the face, and he had a deep suntan, even by American standards. I was guessing a lot of time on a fishing boat.

They pulled up behind my truck, radioed in the basics—exact location, license plate of the vehicle, our names—and then stood there for a moment, looking at us. The cop with the suntan took out a first-aid box and wrapped up Vinnie's right hand, while Boxer Face took a few steps down into the ditch. He came back up and stopped right in front of me.

"Did you break the window, sir?"

"That was me," Vinnie said. The man turned and looked at him, then addressed me again.

"As of this morning, we've been trying to locate five men who didn't make it back to America after a hunting trip."

"I know," I said. "We spoke to two other constables this morning."

"So how did you end up finding this vehicle?"

"We got lucky. We were driving by and we saw it."

"And the reason you broke into it?"

"I told you," Vinnie said. "I did that."

"I heard you the first time," the cop said. "Maybe you guys shouldn't say anything else for the moment, eh? I think we need to take you back to the detachment."

"Are we under arrest?"

"Not at the moment," he said.

"This man had nothing to do with this," Vinnie said. "It was all me."

"Vinnie, shut up," I said. "Just cool it."

We all stood there while my man went to the car and talked on the radio. They'd need some more men down here, to set up a crime scene and to take over while they transported us to the detachment.

Twenty minutes later, constables DeMers and Reynaud arrived. DeMers was driving. I saw his grim face through the windshield as he slammed on the brakes. He got out of the car and came over to us, probably moving faster than he had in twenty years. He looked at us without saying a word, then took a flashlight off his belt and climbed down the drainage ditch to the Suburban. After fighting his way through the brush, he shined the flashlight into the interior. He stopped short when he got to the shattered window. Constable Reynaud stayed up on the road. She looked at me and shook her head slowly.

And this time around she looked even better. It was a hell of a thing to notice under the circumstances, but damn.

As DeMers was fighting his way back, he tripped over something and ended up flat on his face. When he stood up again, both knees were soaking wet. "Son of a bitch," he said. When he was finally back on the road, he tried brushing himself off. It didn't do much good.

He came and stood in front of me. "The window," he said.

"That was me," Vinnie said. I wanted very badly to smack him in the face.

"Yeah, I sorta figured that," he said, eyeing Vinnie. "The bandage on your hand was my first clue. You wanna tell me why you broke in?"

"I wanted to see if Tom's stuff was in there."

"And was it?"

"Yes."

"I saw some wallets on the backseat. Did one of those belong to your brother?"

"Yes. I mean, it was actually my wallet."

"Your wallet was in the vehicle."

"The wallet I let Tom use."

"Naturally," DeMers said. "Because he was supposed to be you."

"Yes."

"I trust you left the wallet in there. You didn't remove it, did you?"

"No."

DeMers nodded his head, then came back to me. "How about you, Alex? Did you compromise the crime scene, as well?"

"No," I said.

"I suppose you know better, being an ex-cop and all."

"That plus the fact it wasn't my brother's stuff in there."

He narrowed his eyes. He was about to say something but stopped. "I'll take these men," he finally said to the other cops. "You guys stay here."

DeMers opened up the back of his car and motioned us inside.

He didn't look me in the eye as I walked by him. He looked down at the ground and it sounded like he was trying very hard to measure his breathing.

As soon as we were set, he flipped the car into gear and turned it around. He drove through Calstock, back to the main highway, and took a left, pushing eighty-five as he hit the highway. Reynaud was frowning as she watched him drive. She looked back at us, catching Vinnie's eye for a quick second before settling on me. "Claude, please take it easy," she said, turning away from me. "You wanna get in a wreck three months away from retirement?"

"These guys," he said. "God damn it all."

"I know," she said. "I know. Just take it easy."

About a half hour later, we hit a small town. He pulled into a parking lot, next to a long single-story building. The sign read ONTARIO PROVINCIAL POLICE, HEARST DETACHMENT.

DeMers opened the car door and let us out. "This way," he said. He led us through the front door, past the reception area, down a hallway, into an interview room. It looked like most every other interview room I had ever seen. A table and four chairs, gray walls, a big mirror on one of them. Before he could close the door, another officer stuck his head in and gave us all a quick once-over. He had white hair and the kind of face I'd often seen on desk cops—the kind that could register ten levels of irritation, and today it looked like he had turned it up to seven or eight. The man called DeMers out into the hallway, while Reynaud stayed with us. She sat down on the opposite side of the table.

"Is that his superior?" I said.

"The detachment commander, yes. Staff Sergeant Moreland."

"He doesn't look happy."

"I don't think he is."

"You said DeMers is three months away from retirement?"

"Yes."

The fluorescent lights buzzed overhead.

"How long have you been a constable?" I said. I couldn't help thinking, if I were twenty years younger, or even ten years, and I was still on the force, and this woman was my partner—how would I handle it? In eight years as a cop in Detroit, I never had a female partner.

"Five years," she said. "Do we really need to talk about this?"

"Okay," I said. "I just have one more question for you."

"What's that?"

"I know how tough it can be for women cops. I don't imagine it's changed much."

"And your question is?"

"Getting stuck way up here, miles from anywhere, is it a test or a punishment?"

She looked at me. If she was going to answer, she didn't get the chance. The door swung open and DeMers came back into the room. His knees were still wet.

"All right," he said as he sat down. "All right." He took off his glasses and went into his whole cleaning routine again. If he were my partner, he'd get to do that about three or four times before I grabbed the damned glasses and broke them in two. "Here's where we are. We were already searching for some trace of those missing men. The Mounties were helping us out. Now that we have the vehicle, we'll take it over to the main detachment in Timmins, see what they can come up with. Of course, we already know a couple of things they're gonna find, don't we?"

He paused and looked at both of us.

"They'll find a lot of shattered glass," he said. "Some blood. They'll find the wallets, which might be the most important piece of evidence. But, of course, they'll all be moved and they'll have a new set of fingerprints on them. That's gonna make their job a hell of a lot harder."

He stopped again. The lights buzzed above our heads. I wondered if anyone was watching us through the two-way mirror.

"Here's the thing," he said. "I asked you to go back to Michigan. Instead of doing that, you guys headed right over to the Constance Lake Reserve. You wanna start by explaining that one?"

"I thought I saw a young Indian at the lodge," I said. "I thought he might know something that could help us. Constance Lake is the nearest reserve, so I figured that's where we'd find him."

"Did you?"

"No, he wasn't there."

"Have you ever been on the reserve before today?"

"No, of course not."

"You have no connection to anyone there."

"No," I said. "How could I?"

"And you, Mr. LeBlanc? You haven't said anything yet. Do you have any connection to anyone on the Constance Lake Reserve?"

"No," Vinnie said. He sat there with arms folded across his chest.

"You live on a reservation in Michigan, don't you?"

"No."

DeMers looked a little surprised. "Even so, you felt comfortable trying to contact this young Indian Mr. McKnight said he saw at the lodge."

"I saw him, too."

"So you went to find him, but he wasn't there. Then you left."

"Yes."

"Who spotted the vehicle?"

"I did," Vinnie said.

"That's pretty amazing. The vehicle was deep in the woods."

"Maybe thirty or forty feet," Vinnie said. "I happened to be looking out the window."

DeMers turned to his partner. "I still think it's amazing," he said. "Don't you?"

She thought about it for a moment, or at least pretended to. "I think it's safe to say it was amazing, yes."

"I know I wouldn't have spotted that vehicle," DeMers said. "Not in a million years. Now, if I knew to look for it, that would be a different story."

"We didn't know it was there," I said. "You don't even have to take our word for it. Just think about it."

"The fact that you broke into the vehicle makes me wonder," he said. "Maybe you were trying to retrieve something important."

"And then we called you," I said. "Instead of just leaving."

"You knew it would be found eventually. Why not just call it in and get it over with?"

"What are you suggesting?"

"That you either had a very good reason to find that vehicle and break into it. Or else you were so lucky you just happened to stumble over it, and so stupid that you'd intentionally compromise a crime scene. Which is it?"

"I don't know about lucky," I said, "but we'll cop a plea on stupid."

Vinnie gave me a quick look. He kept his arms folded.

"Those men left the lodge five days ago," DeMers said. "Instead of going home, they did God knows what, and their empty van ends up ditched in the woods, just outside the reserve. Which, as you know, is most definitely *not* on the way to anywhere. Certainly not on the way home. So you tell me. What do you think happened?"

"One of those men is my brother," Vinnie said.

I recognized the tone of voice. Please no, I thought. This would be a bad time to run out of fuse again.

"You got the Mounties helping you now?" Vinnie went on.

"It's about time. Why don't you get out there, too? Instead of asking us all these stupid questions."

"Vinnie, knock it off."

"Why don't you go change your pants," he said. "And then get out there and look for them."

That was enough for DeMers. He stood up and told us to do the same. Then he led us out of the conference room and deep into the back of the building. There were three holding cells there, all of them empty. The doors were open. He showed us into the first of the cells and slammed the door shut behind us.

"Are we officially charged?" I said.

"How does obstruction of justice sound?" he said.

"You didn't Mirandize us yet. You should have done that before asking us all those questions."

He came back to the bars and put his face six inches from mine. I could see my reflection in his glasses. I could smell his aftershave. "First of all," he said, "we're in Canada. They call it the Charter of Rights and Freedoms. Second of all—"

"What is it?"

He put his hands on the bars. Once again, just when I expected him to explode, he surprised me. "You guys are making this really hard," he said. "Don't you see that?"

I didn't say anything.

"We're trying to find these guys, eh? We're trying to do our jobs. Why can't you just let us do that?"

I was about to answer him, but he cut me off.

"You think that helps us? Breaking into the van and messing everything up? For God's sake, guys. Didn't I tell you to go home?"

"Constable—"

"You can call me Claude, all right? Will you do that?"

I hesitated. "Claude—"

"We're on the same side, eh? All of us, including my partner. We're just trying to find those men."

"Okay."

"Okay, nothing. Why don't you try cooperating for a change, eh? Do you have any idea how much trouble you're causing?"

I wasn't sure what to say.

"Just sit tight here for a minute," he said. "I'll be right back." He walked away, shaking his head.

Vinnie was already sitting down on one of the two beds in the cell. There was a small sink between them, and a metal toilet. I sat down on the other bed. It was softer than I thought it would be. As holding cells went, these were deluxe accommodations.

"What the hell is going on?" Vinnie said. "It's like he's Jekyll and Hyde or something."

"Son of a bitch," I said.

"What?"

"I know what he's doing."

"He's trying to trick us? Set us up for something?"

"No," I said. "Not at all. That little show in the room, that was for his boss, the staff sergeant. The guy must have been behind the glass."

"What are you talking about?"

"DeMers is springing us," I said. "Don't you see? He ran us through the wringer because he had to, just on the face of it. But now he's going out of his way to get us out of it."

"Why would he do that?"

"Because we're such nice guys."

"Seriously, Alex."

"I don't know, Vinnie. He's been a cop a long time. He must know we're being straight with him. So he blows off a little steam and then he does the right thing. He's gonna kick us out of here."

"Whatever you say."

"Remember the last time you were in jail?" I said.

"What about it?"

"It was a crappy cell, you had three strangers in there with you, and your face was a mess."

"I remember."

"You're moving up in the world."

"Is that supposed to be funny?"

I sat back on the bed and leaned my head against the hard wall.

"Let me ask you something else," I said. "Why would that van be ditched in the woods like that?"

"DeMers was right about that road," Vinnie said. "It's not on the way to anywhere, except the reserve."

"When you were looking through those wallets, did you happen to notice if the cash was missing?"

He looked up at me. "There was no cash."

"How about credit cards?"

"Those were gone, too."

"You think it's a coincidence Guy's mother was acting so strange?"

"That doesn't make any sense," he said. "If he was involved in this, he wouldn't dump that vehicle a mile from the reserve."

"No, not if he had a choice. Hell, I don't know."

Vinnie stared at the floor. "How long do you think we're gonna be here?"

"I'll bet you he comes back in five minutes," I said.

He was back in four. Reynaud was with him.

"Ready to go?" he said as he opened the cell door.

"You guys don't know how to play this game," I said. "This cell feels like a three-star hotel."

"You should see the food," he said. "Same stuff we eat in the cafeteria."

112

"Canadians," I said. "You probably give them beer, too."

DeMers slammed the door shut and led us down the hall. "What are you guys gonna do as soon as you get outside?" he said.

"Is my truck here?"

"We towed it over, yes."

"Then I'm gonna get in and drive home."

"Good man," he said. "If you don't, God help me, I'll find you and kick your ass all the way home myself."

I smiled at that one. Reynaud smiled, too. Just a little bit.

"That's not meant to be funny," DeMers said. "I'm doing you a favor here. Don't make me regret it."

"We're going," I said. "And I suppose we owe you some thanks."

He shook it off. "Thank me by never letting me see your face again."

When we hit the front door, we could see that the world had changed in the past hour. It was late in the afternoon, and there was snow in the air. The wind was swirling it around in every direction. It hit us when we opened the door. As we walked to the truck I took one last look behind me. They were both standing there watching us through the glass. I gave them a little wave, but they didn't wave back.

I fired up the truck and got us the hell out of there. The town was right on the highway, so it was just a matter of pointing us west, back to 631. We'd take that south and if we made good time, we'd be home by midnight.

"It's too bad you won't see her again," Vinnie said.

"What do you mean?"

"Constable Reynaud. She's strong and quiet, like a wolf."

"You're so full of it."

"Myeengun. That's the Ojibwa word for wolf."

"Thank you."

"Shit, I should call home," he said, picking up the cell phone and turning it on. "We actually might have a signal here."

"There must be a cell tower in Hearst. Better call now before we get too far away."

"It says you missed seven calls."

"Are there any messages?"

"No, the little envelope thing would appear, right?"

"Right."

"No, no messages. They must have called and hung up."

"It's probably your family," I said.

"Yeah, probably." He dialed the number and waited. A few seconds later, he had his mother on the phone. He described what we had found, and how he didn't know what it meant yet, and how everyone was looking for them and she shouldn't let herself imagine the worst. I could tell by the look on his face that she was already doing just that.

At that point, Vinnie listened to something his mother was saying, and didn't seem to like it. "They did what?" he said. "How could you let them do that? You didn't have to let them, even though they asked." He rubbed his forehead while he listened some more. "No," he said. "No, no, no, no. Oh, God." It went on that way for another minute or two, until he finally told her we were on our way home and that she should just sit tight until we got there. Then he hung up.

"What's going on?" I said.

"The Michigan State Police came to the house already."

"That was fast."

"They told her about the vehicle, and they asked her a bunch of questions about Tom. Then they asked if they could search his room."

"And she said yes."

"Of course she said yes. It wouldn't have occurred to her to say anything else. And none of my uncles were around."

"Did they find anything?"

"A bag of marijuana."

"How big?"

"Not big at all. But under the circumstances—"

"I thought he was clean now."

"Yeah, well, I guess he was still smoking a little weed now and then. Just to mellow out. That's exactly what he would have told me. Just to mellow out."

"How's your mother doing now?"

"We've got to get home, Alex. She doesn't know what to do with herself."

"We're going," I said. I pushed the pedal down. The snow was still swirling around in the air, making crazy designs all over the road, but it wasn't sticking yet.

"By the way, those calls on your cell phone, they weren't her."

"No?"

"No. You want me to check? You've got call history, right?"

"Yeah, but you've got to go into the menu and turn that little wheel. Here, let me have it."

He handed me the phone. Before I could do anything, it rang in my hand. I looked at the display. The call was coming from a 313 number. That meant Detroit, although if it was a cell phone, the caller could have been anywhere at that moment. I hit the button and said hello.

"Who is this?" It was a man's voice.

"This is McKnight," I said. "Who is this?"

"Somebody left a message on Red's machine," the man said. "They left this number."

"That was my friend," I said. "We were trying to find out if he'd gotten back home yet. Who am I speaking to?"

The signal wavered. For a few seconds all I heard was static, until finally the voice broke through again. "The police said they found Red's van in the woods up there. You wanna tell me what's going on?"

"That's what we're trying to find out," I said. "Are you gonna tell me who you are or not?"

"Red is my brother, all right? Now just tell me what the fuck is going on up there."

"You gotta talk to me first," I said. "You're one of the men who came up here, aren't you? Are you the guy with the big nose?"

"Friend, you are really pushing your luck. You know that?"

"You were up here, looking for Albright," I said. "Where are you now?"

The line was silent for a few seconds. I wasn't sure if I was still connected. Finally, the voice came back on. He spoke slowly, as if he could barely control himself. "I will find out who you are. And I will break every bone in your body. You got that? Every fucking bone in your body. And when I'm done, I'll go back and break every bone again. Okay? Are you hearing me?"

He said a few more words, but I didn't catch them. Then the signal went out for good. I threw the phone on the seat.

"What was that about?" Vinnie said.

"One of those other men who were up here," I said. "He said he was Red's brother. He must have gotten into Albright's phone messages."

"What did he say?"

"He just wanted to know what's going on up here. You should've heard this guy, Vinnie. I gotta tell ya, this is getting worse by the minute."

"His brother's missing. I can relate to that. Of course he's gonna be mad."

"No, it's more than that. He sounded like the kind of guy who gets mad for a living."

"Meaning what? You think Tom got hooked up in something?"

"It doesn't look real good right now. You've got to admit it."

He didn't say anything.

There was no need to push it any further, so I settled in for the long drive. The snow started to let up. I drove for a while, never thinking about looking in the rearview mirror. Up here, you don't even need one.

I heard the buzzing noise, then finally looked up and saw the motorcycle closing on us from the rear. My first thought was the police—this was DeMers coming to hunt me down like he said he would. But no, he'd be the last man on earth to get on a motorcycle.

My second thought was the phone call. Red's brother had connections in Canada, and this was his way of letting us know he didn't appreciate my attitude.

The motorcycle moved over to the other lane and drew even with me. The rider gestured for me to pull over. He had a black helmet on, so I couldn't see his face. But I recognized the blue-and-white coat. I pulled over.

The motorcycle fishtailed as it came to a stop in front of us. The rider got off and walked over to us. He shook his hands. With no gloves, they must have been colder than hell. When he got to the truck, I rolled down my window. He took his helmet off.

"You always drive that fast?" he said. He had long dark hair, dark eyes, and the wide cheekbones of a full-blooded Indian. He looked in past me at Vinnie.

"You must be Guy Berard," I said.

If he was surprised, it didn't show. "You're McKnight and LeBlanc. I've been trying to catch up to you ever since you left the police station."

"How'd you know we were there?"

"I saw you guys on the road," he said. "Where that van was. I saw the police take you away."

"Yeah? And how did you know who we were?"

He gave me a slight smile. "My mother told me all about you."

"You were at home, weren't you," I said. "How come you were hiding from us?"

"Can we go talk about this somewhere? I'm freezing my ass off."

"What do you know about the men on the hunting trip?" Vinnie said.

Guy looked past me again. The two of them stared at each other for a long moment. "You're the brother."

"Yes," Vinnie said.

"We need to talk," he said. "Follow me."

"Why should we?" Vinnie said. I was surprised at the hard edge in his voice. "If you know something about my brother, just tell me now."

The wind came up again. It kicked up a riot of snowflakes. Guy buried his hands in his armpits.

"I'll tell you one thing," he said. "And then you can decide if you want to hear the rest. I was there at the lodge on Saturday."

"We already figured that out," Vinnie said. "That's the day Tom's group flew back from the lake."

"Did you talk to them?" I said.

"No, not that day," Guy said. "They were already gone."

"Okay, so what's the big deal?" Vinnie said.

"I don't think they came back that day at all," he said.

"What are you saying?" I could feel Vinnie sliding over on the seat.

"I'm saying I think they either came back on a different day," he said. "Or else they never flew out to that lake in the first place."

Chapter Ten

We followed Guy back to the reserve. I got a little anxious driving by the crime scene again. There were five OPP cars parked up and down the road, along with three cars from the Royal Canadian Mounted Police. A thin yellow tape was stretched from tree to tree, forming a loose circle around Albright's Suburban. Some of the officers on the scene looked up at us as we passed, but nobody stopped us.

Just for the hell of it, I turned my cell phone back on. Our new friend from Detroit had called three more times just in the past few minutes, and left one message. I tried calling in to hear it, but the signal faded out almost immediately. I left the phone on the seat and got out of the truck.

"Same guy?" Vinnie said.

"Apparently."

"Shouldn't we call him back? He might know something."

"It sounds more like he wants us to tell him what's going on.

But yeah, I suppose we should. As soon as we head south a little bit, we'll pick up a signal again."

Guy parked his motorcycle behind his house and came back around to lead us through the front door. His mother nearly jumped out of her skin when she saw us.

"It's okay," Guy said. "I stopped them on the road. I decided I needed to talk to them."

She nodded her head, but kept staring at us with wide eyes. Guy sat down next to her on the couch and slid over to give Vinnie room. I sat on the chair next to the television. The air in the room was hot and stale.

"So why are you talking to us now?" I said. "Earlier today, you were hiding from us."

"A lot's happened since then," he said. "They found that Suburban in the woods, for one thing. Then the police came by looking for me. Just to ask me some questions, they said." His mother closed her eyes as he said that. "They must have got my name from the lodge. And with me living here on the reserve, I mean, you can imagine what they were thinking. I know they'll ask me if I had ever met Tom before, or if I had talked to him at the lodge."

"Did you?" Vinnie said. "You said they were already gone when you got there on Saturday."

"It was the Saturday before, when they first got there. I had just come back with a group that day, and I was still hanging around when they pulled up. Mr. Gannon had told me they didn't want a guide. So when I saw Tom, I said to myself, no wonder, these jokers brought their own guide. I was a little upset. Then I heard these guys carrying on, and I wasn't upset anymore."

"What do you mean?"

"They were just a bad bunch, you know? The white guys, I mean." He slipped me a quick look. "Not Tom. He was cool about it. These guys were all hitting on Mrs. St. Jean and making all

120

these jokes about shooting anything that moved. I mean, you hear that kind of stuff a lot, but these guys— There was something about them, like they weren't just kidding around. I was pretty sure Tom was at least part Indian, so I went up to him and asked him what the deal was on these guys. He said they were all a little drunk already. I guess it was quite a trip getting up there. I asked him if he was up for spending a whole week with these guys, and he said he'd deal with it."

"Had Tom been drinking?"

"I don't think so."

"Are you sure?"

"Pretty sure, yeah."

"Okay. So what happened then? They loaded up the plane and flew out?"

"I don't know. I left. I had just been out in the woods for a week. So I wanted to get home and take a shower."

"So you never actually saw them fly out in the plane."

"No," he said. "I just assumed they did. The next time I was at the lodge was this past Saturday, the day they were supposed to come back. By the time I got there, they were already gone. The plane was back on the dock, and their Suburban wasn't there anymore."

"So what makes you think they never flew out there?"

"It's just a bunch of things, you know? I never really put it together in my head until today, when they were asking me all those questions. When I got to the lodge on Saturday, it was like nobody had been there at all. The butcher shed was clean, the dock was clean. It was just . . . weird."

"Gannon said they didn't get a moose," Vinnie said. "So of course the shed's gonna be clean."

"Yeah, well, I asked him about that. And that's what he told me. He flew them back that morning. No moose. No nothing. They got in their van and left. But it was just— I don't know, the way he said it. It just gave me a funny feeling. And then when the other group got there, I was busy helping them get their stuff together, while Mr. Gannon fired up the Otter. That's his plane— it's an old DHC-3 Otter. Sometimes it takes a while to get warmed up, you know. Anyway, I'm helping out these guys and I can't help noticing, he's cranking and cranking that thing until it finally starts. If he had just been out that morning, the engine would have still been warm."

"Are you gonna tell the police this?" I said.

He raised his hands. "I'm gonna tell them I've got this funny feeling Mr. Gannon never actually flew out on Saturday to pick them up? And that everybody at the lodge is lying to them? How do you think that's gonna go over? They're already asking questions about me, like they're thinking maybe me and Tom had something to do with this."

His mother closed her eyes again. She put her hand to her face and took a deep breath. "Guy, mon coeur," she said.

"Don't worry, Mom. It's gonna be okay."

"It's not good," she said. "For any of us. It's the last thing this place needs right now."

"I don't know," I said. "Just from my old days as a cop, I gotta tell ya. The odds of getting four people to all tell you the same lie . . ."

"Did you talk to all four of them?"

"Well, actually no. Just Helen and Gannon."

"And let me ask you this," he said. "How was Mr. Gannon acting?"

I thought about it. "Like he was unhappy we were there," I said. "Like he couldn't wait to get rid of us."

"Okay, then."

"What do you think, Vinnie?" I said.

"We can't just go back to the lodge and ask them. Is there some other way we can tell if they went out there?"

122

"Yes," Guy said. "As a matter of fact, there is."

"How?"

"I was out at that cabin three weeks ago. I remember how we left it. If we go there now, I'm sure I'll be able to tell if someone else has been there."

"Gannon took those two constables out there yesterday," I said. "They looked all around the place. It sounded like it was a real mess."

"Maybe it was," Guy said. "But who knows if those men really made that mess?"

"What, you mean somebody else did?"

"If they can lie about them going out to that cabin, they can certainly take a few minutes to make it look like they were there."

"So how will you be able to tell?"

"I'll know," he said. "If somebody's really spent some time up there in the last three weeks, I'll know."

"Okay, so how do we get out there? Gannon certainly isn't gonna fly us."

"He doesn't have to."

"Who else has a plane?"

Guy smiled. "I'll show you."

Guy led us back outside and down the street to the house next door. If Guy's house needed a little work, this house needed to be run over by a bulldozer. If you believed what was left of the paint, it looked like one side had been green and the other side red. A thin stream of smoke rose from a metal chimney pipe, set at a crazy angle in the middle of the roof. Someone had put down the black tar paper on that roof, but had never bothered with the shingles.

Guy pushed open the front door. "Grandpère?"

We followed him into the room. The television was on, and a fire glowed red through the glass door of the wood stove.

"Grandpère!" Guy said, a little louder.

A man came in through the back door. He was carrying enough firewood in his arms to keep the house warm all night. He dropped it all in a heap next to the stove and clapped the wood chips off his bare hands.

"You're back," he said to Guy. "What's happening?"

"I want you to meet Alex and Vinnie," he said. "Vinnie's brother was one of the men in the hunting party."

He looked at us carefully. His face was wrinkled, but he had the barrel chest of a circus strongman. His black hair was streaked with gray, and even longer than his grandson's. A great red flannel shirt hung untucked over his waist.

"Some people call me Maskwa," he said.

"The bear," Vinnie said.

"Yes, very good." He shook my hand. His skin felt as tough as an old catcher's mitt.

"Pleased to meet you, sir," I said.

"And you," he said, shaking Vinnie's hand. "You're not Cree, are you?"

"No, I come from the Bay Mills Reservation," he said. "In Michigan."

Maskwa nodded at that. "Casinos."

"Among other things."

"Casinos and a golf course."

Vinnie just smiled.

"Grandpère," Guy said, "Alex and Vinnie were at the police station."

I wasn't sure if this was the best way to make an impression, but Maskwa seemed pleased by it. "They have a good jail there," he said. "It's all brand-new."

"We were the lucky guys who found the vehicle in the woods," I said.

"And this was your reward," Maskwa said. "A fine thing."

"Grandpère, these men came all the way up here to find out what happened to Vinnie's brother. We've got to help them."

"Excuse me for saying so," he said. "Why do we need to do this?"

"Because something's not right," Guy said. "And it might end up hurting all of us."

"That sounds like something your father would have said. Or even me, about forty years ago."

"We need to fly out to Lake Agawaatese," Guy said.

Maskwa looked at us all, one by one. "Fly to Lake Agawaatese? Are you making a joke?"

Guy ran down the quick version of what he had told us, and his suspicions that everyone at the lodge had been lying to us. "We have to find out if they were really there," he said.

Maskwa listened carefully, and when it was over he stood there with a troubled look on his face. He stepped in front of Vinnie and grabbed him by the shoulders. "What's your real name, young man?"

"Misquogeezhig."

"That means . . . red sky, right?"

"Yes, sir."

"What's your brother's name?"

"Minoonigeezhig."

Maskwa hesitated. "Pleasing sky? Where the sun sets?"

"Yes."

"Those are very old names. You don't hear them anymore."

"I know."

"Where do you think your brother is right now?"

"I don't know, sir."

"Do you think he's in trouble?"

"I think so, yes."

"Does your heart tell you he's in trouble?"

"Yes."

Maskwa nodded his head. "Okay. So we'll go to the lake. We'll see if that tells us anything."

"Do you have a plane?" I said.

He said a couple of words I couldn't understand. Guy laughed, and Vinnie apparently understood enough to laugh, too.

"It's too late to fly now," Maskwa said, smacking me on the shoulder. "We'd never make it back before dark. So first thing tomorrow morning."

I looked at Vinnie. I didn't have to say anything. He knew what this meant.

"You should go home," he said. "I'll stay and go out there."

"I'm not leaving you here," I said.

"DeMers will kill us if he finds out."

"He can try," I said. "I think he's too old to catch us."

Vinnie smiled. Without another word, we were both in all the way.

"You'll stay here," Maskwa said. "Have you eaten yet? Come, sit down."

We had dinner with them, all five of us crowded around Maskwa's little table in the kitchen. Guy's mother kept sneaking sly looks at Vinnie and me, and then looked quickly away. After dinner Maskwa fixed us up with sleeping bags on the floor of his living room. He went off to his little bedroom behind the kitchen, leaving us alone. We watched the fire through the glass doors of his stove as the wind blew outside.

"Where do you think they really are?" Vinnie finally said. It was another night, just twenty-four hours later, and we were asking ourselves the same questions as we tried to go to sleep. Tonight it all looked a lot worse.

"The police have everybody looking for them," I said. "They'll find them."

"What if Guy's right? What if they never flew out to that lake?"

"We'll find them, Vinnie."

"Do you think they're alive?"

I didn't have an answer for that one. I didn't even try.

Chapter Eleven

Maskwa woke us up with the sun. Guy was already in the kitchen, filling up a big Styrofoam cooler with ice.

"If we're gonna fly all the way out there," Maskwa said, "we'll need some food. Do you want me to throw some beer in there, too?"

"I won't stop you," I said. "As long as you're not drinking it while you fly."

He laughed. Then he slung a big bag over his shoulder and told us to follow him. "It's time to show you my plane," he said.

He led us out the back door and down the path to the lake, the same path I had noticed the day before, leading past Guy's house into a rough field of rocks and weeds. "I do hunts myself," he said as we picked our way down the trail. "I take them even farther north."

"Do you have much business?" Vinnie said.

"Less and less. I used to do them with my son, Guy's father. We were a good team."

"Your son's not around anymore? I'm sorry, is he—"

Maskwa waved his hand at that. "I did a couple with Guy, but he can make a lot more money over at the lodge. I don't blame him." He sneaked a look back at his grandson, who was bringing up the rear. I tried to take the heavy cooler from him, but he shook me off.

"I do some guide work myself," Vinnie said. "When I'm not working at the casino."

"What's your job there?"

"I deal blackjack."

Maskwa laughed. "Blackjack," he said. "All day long, right? Taking the white people's money?"

"Something like that."

"And then you take them into the woods so they can feel connected to nature."

"Just like you," Vinnie said.

Maskwa laughed again. "Yes! Of course I do. Why shouldn't I?"

The weeds got taller as we got to the lake. We finally came to an old building that looked like a boathouse. It might have been a boathouse at one time, but when Maskwa opened the door we saw an airplane inside. He told us it was a DHC-2 Beaver, not quite as big as Gannon's Otter, but more than enough plane to get the job done. "Her name's Mikiskon," he said. "That was my wife's name."

He started pulling on a chain to raise the big lakeside door. When it was open he hopped up on one of the floats and climbed the ladder into the cockpit. He gave the engine a few cranks until it finally caught. The noise was downright painful. He came to the door and took the cooler from Guy, and then waved Vinnie and me up the ladder. As soon as we were on board, sitting on seat cushions that looked like something out of an old boat, Guy pushed the plane out onto the lake, jumped onto the float, and climbed the ladder to join us. He closed the door and sat down beside his grandfather.

"Everybody ready?" he said.

I wasn't sure, but I wasn't going to say anything. We had come this far.

Maskwa grabbed a handle mounted on the floor and pumped it up and down a few times. Then he let the throttle out and pointed the plane toward the far end of the lake. The plane gained speed, the floats riding rough over the waves.

"Next stop, Lake Agawaatese!" Maskwa said. He had to yell over the din of the motor. "Vinnie, did you tell Alex what the name means?"

"It's kind of a complex word," Vinnie said. "It literally means 'He casts a shadow while flying.' "

"You mean like a bird?" I said.

"Bird, cloud, whatever."

"How about an airplane?" I said. But I don't think anyone heard me. We were getting closer and closer to the far shoreline. Maskwa pulled the yoke back, and the plane fought its way off the water and into the air. It didn't look like we'd have enough room to clear the trees, but I figured the man knew what he was doing. I sat back in my seat and tried to relax. It almost worked.

We cleared the trees with three inches to spare. Hell, maybe it was four inches. The plane kept climbing into the sky, higher and higher, until the whole forest was laid out below us from one horizon to the other. Many miles to the north, Lake Agawaatese, with its flying shadows, was waiting for us.

We flew for the better part of an hour, passing over a thick pine forest broken only by lakes and streams and wet marshlands. I looked down and saw a moose cow standing up to her knees in water. She didn't seem to notice us.

The morning clouds had moved off to the east, but the wind was still blowing. A gust would catch the plane now and then, dropping the bottom out of my stomach. At one point, the plane took a sudden dip and half the dashboard came loose and landed in Maskwa's lap. Guy reached over and calmly pushed it back in place.

I felt Vinnie tapping me on the shoulder. I looked over and saw an eagle soaring in the sky. "Migizi," he said. "Maybe that's good luck."

Maskwa banked the plane and started his descent. Through the windshield I could see the lake coming up fast. He brought the plane in just over the trees, with what looked to be about three inches to spare again, and then touched down. We skipped a couple of times until the water finally grabbed us for good.

"A little rough, Grandpère," Guy said.

"Let's see you do it," Maskwa said.

"I've watched you enough times, I bet I could."

Maskwa cut the throttle back and drove the plane through the water. There was a light chop, just enough to make the plane rattle like it would fall apart any second. I didn't see the cabin at first, but then we rounded a slight bend and there it was on the far shore, a small white building with an L-shaped dock, an aluminum motorboat tied up to it. As we got closer, I saw another smaller building by the water, and a third back in the woods.

"There's a boat here," Vinnie said.

"Yeah, we keep the motor in the shed," Guy said. "Along with the gasoline. I helped Mr. Gannon bring that boat out in his plane last year. There's no way he'll ever bring it back."

Maskwa cut the motor just before we got to the dock. We drifted the rest of the way. Guy climbed out his door and jumped onto the dock. When the plane was tied down, we followed him. I could still feel the vibration of the plane's engine in my legs as I walked up the dock. The buzzing still rang in my ears.

"All right, let's take a look around," Guy said. He led us into the cabin. There was a small wooden porch and a screen door in front, with two screened windows. One of them was pushed in. "Goddamned bears," he said. "If they smell garbage—"

When I stepped into the cabin myself, garbage was exactly what I saw. There was one picnic table in the center of the room, with enough spilled breakfast cereal and ketchup and fish batter and God knows what else to draw a dozen bears. The stale smell of beer hung in the air, and the wooden floor was sticky to walk on. There were unwashed plates stacked up on the counter, and three pots on the propane stove. When Guy opened the propane refrigerator, there was a carton of eggs on the bottom shelf and nothing else.

While the other men stood there looking at the mess, I went into the other room. There were three separate bunks—just bare wood to put your sleeping bags on—and a wood stove. I opened the little door and looked inside. I couldn't tell how old the ashes were.

"My God, what an unholy pigsty," Maskwa said. He picked a skin magazine off the floor and threw it in the empty trash can.

"It obviously wasn't like this the last time I saw it," Guy said. "But you could fake this, you know what I mean? If you wanted to make it look like somebody was here, you just come in and trash the place."

"They could fool the police that way," Maskwa said. "But not you."

Guy nodded his head. "First, the propane," he said. He went outside to the big tank on the side of the cabin. "When I left here last time, it was three-quarters full. Now it's . . . Let's see . . ." He checked the gauge. "About one quarter."

"Is that how much gas you'd use if you were here a week?" I said.

"Yeah, pretty much. You got the oven and the refrigerator, plus the two overhead lights."

"So maybe they were here," Maskwa said.

"Unless somebody switched the tanks. Hold on." He went

133

down to the little shed by the dock and looked inside. He took out two red gasoline cans and shook them one by one. "Damn, these are empty," he said. "How much could they use?"

"They must have gone out in the boat a lot," Maskwa said.

"Two cans worth?"

"You think they switched the cans, too?"

Guy shook his head and looked around the place. "I don't know."

"If there's no way to know for sure—"

"Hold on," Guy said. "The outhouse. When I left here, I made sure there was toilet paper in there. I know for a fact that there were exactly four rolls in there, with half a roll on the wall. I'm positive."

I stayed on the dock while they went to check. This was one mission I didn't need to be a part of. I stood there watching the lake, as the colors changed with each passing cloud. We were so far away from anywhere else right now. We had taken the last road, and now an hour's worth of flying had put us here on the shores of this lake. I zipped up my coat.

"Okay," Guy said as he joined me on the dock. "They were here."

"You have to admit," I said, "it was pretty unlikely from the beginning. I mean, I suppose it was good to come out here in any case. This is the last place they spent any time. But right now I don't see how it can help us."

"Something's still wrong," Vinnie said. He had been quiet since we had landed here. "Something is very wrong."

"How do you mean?"

"Let me ask you something," he said to Guy. "If you were leading a hunt here, would you leave this place looking like this?"

"No, of course not."

"Even if you couldn't stand the men you were with. And it was them that made the mess?"

134

"I'd still clean up before we left," Guy said. "And they'd hear about it, believe me."

"Exactly. That's the same thing Tom would have done."

"So what are you saying?" I said.

"They didn't leave here under normal circumstances," Vinnie said. "Something happened. Maybe they had to leave in a hurry."

"Or maybe," Maskwa spoke up behind us, "they never left at all."

Vinnie turned around and looked at him.

"Maybe they got lost hunting," Maskwa said. "The people at the lodge, they didn't want to deal with it. So they lied."

"Tom wouldn't get lost," Vinnie said.

"Your brother is a long way from home. These are not his woods."

"If that's what happened," Vinnie said, looking beyond the cabin at the thick wall of trees, "then he's still out there. Tom knows how to survive. He knows how to find plants he can eat, how to make shelter, how to make a fire."

"But what about their wallets?" I said. "Why would they be in the Suburban?"

"They may have left them here at the cabin," Vinnie said. "When Gannon came out here, he found them. Maybe Maskwa is right, Alex. Something may have happened. The people at the lodge are just covering it up."

Maskwa stepped up to Vinnie and grabbed him by the shoulders. "We will look," he said. "I promise you. We can't panic, Vinnie. We can't run around here like chickens."

"I know."

"Let's eat first, okay? Then we'll look."

Maskwa sent Guy back to the plane for the big bag and the cooler. Then he sat down on the dock and took out two long salamis and a loaf of bread.

"Grandpère," Guy said. "How much food did you bring?"

135

"I had an intuition," he said. "Something told me we'd be here all day."

We all sat down on the dock with him and ate. Maskwa passed me one of the cold Molsons from the cooler. The sun came out and shone on the surface of the lake, making it feel a lot warmer than it really was. Under different circumstances, it would have been a hell of a nice day.

I couldn't stop thinking about that Suburban ditched in the woods. It seemed too far-fetched, that they'd dump it there just to cover themselves. The whole thing was starting to feel wrong, from top to bottom. The real answer was probably something simple. It almost always is.

"You and Vinnie can go out together," Maskwa said as we finished up. "Alex will come with me." He looked at his watch. "We should meet back here at 3:00. The days are getting shorter— any later and we won't have enough daylight to fly back."

Vinnie and Guy picked the trail that went north from the cabin site. The other trail curled around the rim of the lake before heading west. The pine trees were thick enough to obliterate the sunlight. Maskwa led the way.

"If they're lost," I said, "then they could be miles away from here. How are we gonna find them?"

"We won't," he said. "But we may find which way they went. A man can't walk in the woods without leaving some trace behind."

I followed him deeper and deeper into the woods. The trail seemed to disappear every now and then, but Maskwa didn't hesitate. He kept moving forward, and inevitably the trail would appear again. "You see all these tracks," he said.

"What are they?"

"Look at them. You tell me."

The tracks were about four inches wide, with five distinct toe-prints and little gouges in the dirt where the nails must have dug in. They kept appearing in pairs, with one print right in front of the other.

"Bears?"

"Yes, black bears," he said. "You see how they walk? Each back foot almost steps into the front track."

"There's a lot of tracks here."

"You can tell how fast they're going from the spacing. You can even tell if the animal was limping."

"Are you seeing any human tracks around here?"

"Of course, aren't you?"

"I'm sorry," I said. "I'm not good at this."

"You just have to look," he said. "I mean really look. Come here." He went to the edge of the trail and crouched down close to the ground. I leaned in close to him.

"Come all the way down here," he said. It was a position I knew well, of course. Most catchers crouch down behind the plate a few hundred times a day until they're done playing ball. And then they never crouch again if they can help it.

"See right here?" he said. He brushed away some pine needles. "Here's a boot print. What does it tell you?"

"Looks like about a size twelve," I said.

"What else?"

"I'd guess it's not very recent."

"Why would you say that?"

"Well, number one, the fact that we don't see any tracks in the middle of the trail. It's all bear tracks. That means the bears have been here more recently."

"Okay, what else?"

"The pine needles," I said. "It would take some time for the needles to fall and cover the tracks."

"Couldn't this man have stepped on top of the pine needles?"

I looked more closely. "If he did, then the pine needles would be pushed into the mud. And some would be bent."

"Very good," he said. "It's all common sense, isn't it?"

"Yes. So what now?"

"So we go back. It doesn't look like this trail has been walked on in the last couple of weeks. The men went a different way."

We retraced our steps to the cabin site. It was just after two o'clock when we got there. Maskwa and I sat on the dock again, and I had another beer.

"This is a beautiful lake," I said. "It's too bad we had to see it this way."

"You must be a good friend," he said. "You came all the way up here."

"Vinnie would do the same for me."

"Do you have a brother, Alex?"

"No, Maskwa, I don't."

He nodded and looked out at the lake. "I had two. They're both gone."

"What about your son? Guy's father."

He threw a small rock into the water.

"Never mind," I said. "It's none of my business."

"He's gone, too. He killed himself."

"I'm sorry."

He shook his head, threw another rock in the water. "He has peace now."

We kept sitting there on the dock. The sun shifted west, making the shadows longer. Three o'clock came and went. It was almost three-thirty when Vinnie and Guy finally came back.

"What did you find?" Maskwa said.

"Lots of bear tracks," Guy said.

"A real bear highway," Vinnie said. Even in the cold air, he was sweating.

"There were boot prints, too," Guy said. "As far as we could tell, they looked pretty recent. The trail split off, though. And then again. There might be four or five different spurs."

"And in that one spot—" Vinnie said.

"Yes, a lot of boot prints together. It was hard to say what was going on there."

"Just a bunch of men standing around?" Maskwa said. "Maybe they were waiting for somebody."

"I don't know," Guy said. "Some of the prints were uneven." He leaned his leg so that most of his weight was on the inside of his foot. "Like this."

"We don't have much light left," Maskwa said. "I think we should go back. Tomorrow we can bring radios with us, and more food. We'll search again. We can even fly over the area if we want."

"I can't leave," Vinnie said. "I'd like to spend the night here."

"There's no need to do that," Maskwa said. "We'll come back tomorrow."

"You brought plenty of food," Vinnie said. "If you'd be good enough to leave some with me, I'll sleep here in the cabin."

"Vinnie," I said. "I don't think that's a good idea."

"I need to do this, Alex. Tom was here. He slept here. I can feel it. Being here might help me find him."

"If you're gonna spend the night here," I said, "then I'm staying, too."

"Me, too," Guy said.

"You're not staying here," Maskwa told him. "You'll come home with me, and help me get ready for tomorrow. Go get two of those sleeping bags from the plane. And two flashlights."

Guy put up a small fight about it, but eventually gave in and climbed up into the plane to get our supplies. Vinnie thanked Maskwa a couple of times for everything he had done.

"We will find your brother," Maskwa said just before he left. "I promise you."

We stood there and watched the plane take off. As it cleared the trees, it banked and circled us once and then headed south.

We could still hear the sound of the plane, long after it disappeared.

Vinnie started walking around the clearing, collecting sticks. The trees were close on all sides, with the edge of the water just a few yards away. It was so small, this cabin site, a tiny speck in a huge wilderness.

"What are you doing?" I said.

"Making a fire."

I helped him build a teepee-shaped pile of wood. He put some birch bark in the middle and lit it with a match. The bark burst into flame.

"Best fire starter there is," he said. "It'll even burn when it's wet."

"I'll remember that."

An hour later, the sun was going down and painting the sky in deep shades of red and orange. Vinnie and I sat by the fire, eating more salami sandwiches and finishing off the Coke and beer.

"It's a nice sky," Vinnie said. "Tom probably sat right here and watched it."

"What you said about feeling him here, do you really mean that?"

"Yes," he said. "Don't you believe me?"

"I'm not saying I don't."

"Tom and I used to fight a lot when we were kids. My grandmother told us we shouldn't fight because we had the same blood in our veins. We were part of each other. I didn't really listen to her back then. I wish I could talk to her now. She'd know what to do."

"You're doing everything you can."

He put some more wood on the fire. A dry pine log crackled and sent sparks into the air. The sky got darker.

"It's getting cold," I said. "We should get some sleep."

"You go ahead. I'll put out the fire."

I went in and got one of the pots off the stove, cleaned it out as well as I could and then went down to the lake to fill it with water. I heated the water on the propane stove and washed my face. Then I unrolled a sleeping bag on one of the bottom bunks and climbed in, with my coat balled up as a pillow. I lay there awhile, listening to the night, wondering when Vinnie would come inside.

I must have dozed off. I woke up some time later in total darkness. I grabbed the flashlight off the floor and shined it around the room. Vinnie wasn't there. There was a scraping sound somewhere close to me. I couldn't tell where it was coming from. It sounded like—

The wall right next to my bed. Something was scratching the wall, but it wasn't big. It was the slightest sound, like a whisper. Here, then here, then here—all over the wall.

No. It was inside the wall. I put my ear against it and listened. I heard the scraping noise like it was being done a thousand different ways, and then I heard a thousand little squeaks.

I got up out of the sleeping bag. The wooden floor was cold beneath my feet.

"Vinnie?"

There was no answer.

I went through the main room, out the front door. Vinnie was sitting there on the porch, facing the lake.

"I'm right here," he said in a quiet voice.

"What are you doing out here?"

"I'm listening."

There was a quarter moon in the night sky. Silver clouds raced in front of it. And then a darker cloud, rising from behind the cabin, that broke up into a thousand dark pieces.

"Oh shit, those are bats," I said. "My God. They must live inside the back wall. You should hear them in there."

He put his finger to his lips and shushed me. I listened to the wings fluttering and the high squeaks.

"I'm sure they were hibernating," he said. "We must have disturbed them."

"Doing what? We haven't made any noise."

"*Something* woke them up."

"Yeah, well, I'm gonna hibernate a little bit myself," I said. "You should, too."

"I'll be in," he said. "Go to bed."

I went back in and climbed into the sleeping bag. The bats kept moving around inside the wall. I tried not to picture them, crawling all over each other and flying out into the night. A thin layer of plywood was the only thing separating them from me.

I heard Vinnie come in and take the bunk next to me.

"You didn't have to stay here," he said.

"I'm in this far, Vinnie. I'm gonna help you see it through."

"I don't understand you," he said. "Why are you doing this?"

"I made a promise to your mother."

"You know that's not the only reason."

"Don't worry about it. Just get some sleep."

"I know you don't like to talk about it," he said, "but there's something inside you that makes you do things like this."

"Yeah, it's something."

"I'm serious, Alex. You can be a real pain in the ass, but underneath it all you're the most loyal person I've ever known."

"Vinnie, I don't have that many friends, okay? It makes me want to hold on to the ones I've got."

"Okay," he said. "Okay. That sounds good to me."

"Okay then."

"I'm glad I'm one of them."

"Me, too," I said. "Now shut up and go to sleep."

He settled in and said good night. I listened to the bats in the wall for a while, and I thought about what he had said.

He's right, I thought. Vinnie can see right through me.

I finally slept for an hour, maybe two. Then suddenly I was awake again. There was another noise in the room, this one a lot louder than the bats.

"Vinnie, what is that?"

I heard him sit up. His flashlight came on, blinding me.

"It's in the other room," he said.

We both got up at the same time. When he shined the light at the front wall, we saw an enormous face looking at us through the window.

"Go on! Get out of here!" Vinnie yelled. He went into the front room and banged two of the pots together.

"That was one big bear," he said. "Did you see him?"

"Yeah, Vinnie, I saw him."

Vinnie pushed the front door open and went out onto the porch. I followed him. We could hear the bear crashing through the brush.

"Alex," Vinnie said, his head back. "Look."

I looked up at the sky. The quarter moon had gone down behind the trees. The clouds had disappeared. It was so dark up here, so far away from any other kind of light. It was just the stars, every star in the heavens, the great expanse of the Milky Way spread out above us.

I stood there with my friend, watching the sky.

Until the sound came. A lonely, inhuman sound, far off in the distance. It was joined by another. And then another. The sound rose and fell, stopped and started again.

"What the hell is that, Vinnie?"

"I think those are more bears, Alex. Black bears."

"Black bears? From what planet?"

"Shh, listen," he said.

We stood there under the stars and listened to the wailing of the bears. If I lived a million years, that sound was something I'd never forget.

Chapter Twelve

There's nothing like waking up in a cold, filthy cabin, a hundred miles from anywhere, with no running water and nothing to eat but salami and bread.

When I looked over, Vinnie's sleeping bag was empty. I pushed myself up to a sitting position, feeling the stiffness in my neck, and my shoulder, and my back. After that, I stopped counting.

I stood up and put my shoes on. There was a pot of water on the propane stove. It was just starting to boil. One of the front windows was on the floor. The big bear had pushed it right in.

When I went outside, I saw Vinnie on the dock. He was on his knees, washing his face with lake water. He had his shirt off, which wouldn't have bothered me if it wasn't about thirty degrees. "Morning," I said. "Mind if I use the sink?"

"It's a bit cold," he said.

"I think maybe I'll keep my clothes on. That should help."

"Suit yourself."

"Your water's boiling in there," I said. I knelt down and just about pitched myself into the lake.

"I'll let it boil for a while," he said. "It's lake water. I found some instant coffee."

"That actually sounds pretty good right now." I splashed the water on my face. In ten seconds, my hands went from painful to numb.

We sat on the front porch, having our breakfast of salami sandwiches and hot instant coffee. We watched the morning fog drifting across the lake.

"I saw Tom last night," Vinnie said. "In my dream. He was trying to tell me something, but I couldn't make out what he was saying."

"Did it seem like he was in trouble?"

"No, not at all. He was happier than I've seen him in a long time. He was laughing."

"When do you suppose Guy and Maskwa will get here?"

"I imagine they've already left," he said. "How long did it take us to fly here yesterday? About an hour?"

"I think so, yeah."

"So they should be here soon."

"They're really going out of their way to help us," I said.

"It's not so surprising," he said. "It comes naturally to them."

"Being Indians and all."

He looked at me. "No, just being good people."

"Okay," I said. "No argument there."

We waited around for another hour. The sun came up and burned off the rest of the fog on the lake, but it didn't do much else. "I can't just sit here," I said. "I'm gonna be so stiff, I won't be able to move."

"I hear you," he said. "They might be having some trouble getting that old plane started. I'd hate to sit here and waste half the day. Why don't we go up this trail a little bit, start looking around."

"We could leave them a note."

"Yeah, and we'll hear the plane coming."

"Okay, let's do it," I said. "Anything to get moving."

I found an old notepad in the cabin and a two-inch stub of a pencil, wrote them out a quick note, and put it on the front porch. I put a rock on it so it wouldn't blow away. "Okay, show me this trail," I said.

We set off north, picking up a wide trail that led deep into the woods. If I'd forgotten just how far away from civilization we were, it took about ten minutes of walking through the trees to remember. There were no signs of human life whatsoever—none of the little things you find on just about any trail in America if you look close enough, like cigarette butts or gum wrappers. There were no wooden signposts, no little trail marker tags nailed to the trees. The trail belonged only to the animals. For all we knew, it hadn't changed in a thousand years.

Vinnie was walking slowly, looking at the ground in front of him. His footsteps didn't make a sound. "There are so many bear tracks here," he said.

"Can I ask a dumb question?" I said.

"Go ahead."

"How many moose tracks have you seen?"

"Not one," he said.

"So how good could the moose hunting be on this lake?"

"Sort of explains why they didn't bring one back," he said.

"Those other guys we saw," I said, "the first day we got here. They got a moose, but they were out on a different lake, remember?"

"I remember. So you're wondering why Albright and his guys came to this lake instead."

"There being no actual moose here, yeah."

"It's a good question."

Something moved ahead of us. We couldn't see what it was, but we heard the brush moving. Then we heard the sound, the same sound we had heard the night before as we stood on the porch of the cabin. It was like a low growl, but with an eerie, glottal pulsing to it. It was almost what a giant dog would sound like if it could purr like a cat.

"Vinnie, you're telling me a bear's making that noise?"

"Yes, Alex."

"How come I've never heard that before?"

"People don't realize how vocal bears can be," he said, "or how strange they can sound. Did you know when they do bear scenes in movies, they usually dub in some other animal's growl? Like a wolf?"

"That so?"

"And this time of year, hell, some of these bears are still desperate for food. They've got to put their fat on before the winter comes."

"That bear we saw last night, it was hard to tell in the dark, but it looked like it had brown fur."

"I'm sure it wasn't a true brown bear. Even black bears can have brown fur."

"How do you tell the difference?"

"The face and shoulders," he said. "And the size. Browns are bigger."

"Whatever you say, Vinnie. All I know is, I've never heard a sound like that."

We were maybe three miles up the trail when we came to a stand of white birch trees. The leaves were long gone. The cold sunlight lit the ground through the bare branches.

"This is where we stopped yesterday," Vinnie said. "Can you see all the marks on the ground?"

I bent down and looked. "All I see are bear tracks," I said.

"Yeah, but besides that. Over here toward the sides." He pointed a few feet off the trail, by the base of the biggest birch tree. "Careful where you walk."

"You make it sound like a crime scene," I said. Then it occurred to me. A crime scene might be exactly what this was.

"You see the boot prints?"

"Yeah, I think so."

"There are several together, right here." He stepped carefully and leaned against the tree. "I think there's at least three different boats here."

"So they were all walking in a line."

"But why so close to the tree? The trail's wide-open. There's no reason to walk all the way over here. And this is what we were talking about yesterday—you see here how this boot print is deep on the inside edge? And this one here, too. You wouldn't see that if somebody was just walking normally."

"So what do you think happened here?"

"I don't know," he said. "We need to keep looking."

"How far up this trail do you wanna go?"

Vinnie didn't answer me. He stood there looking up into the sky. "Do you hear that?"

"What?"

"Listen."

It took a few seconds to pick up the sound. It was a faint buzzing, in the far distance. "The plane," I said.

"They're coming. It's about time."

"So let's go back."

He looked back down at the ground. "You think you can find your way back to the cabin?"

"I suppose so, why?"

"We're just gonna go meet up with them, and then come right back up here. I'd rather just stay here and look around some more."

"Well, don't go wandering off too far. We don't want to lose you, too."

He looked at me.

"Sorry," I said.

"Are you sure you can find your way back?"

"Vinnie, I'm not that hopeless. I can follow the trail back to the cabin."

"Bring me some food when you come back," he said. "And some water."

"Will do," I said. "I'll be back soon."

I turned around and took two steps, then stopped. "Are you sure this is a good idea?" I said.

"Alex, I'm just gonna look around. Go get the guys."

"All right," I said. I shook off the little chill that had run up my spine and started down the trail. You're starting to imagine things, I thought. Damned bears and those noises.

I retraced our steps, leaving the white birches behind and heading into the deep shade of the pine trees. The pine needles were a soft blanket beneath my feet. The only sound was the steady buzz of the plane, getting louder and louder with each passing minute.

I came back to the small stream we had crossed, jumping over the water and landing hard on the rocks. Then it was back into the pine trees, more darkness, more pine needles. I saw bear tracks all over the place.

And no boot prints.

Shit, I thought. Leave it to me to get lost walking back three miles to the goddamned cabin.

"All right, stay calm," I said out loud. I didn't sound very reassuring. I wasn't fooling anybody. "Just retrace your steps a bit." When I turned around there was nothing to see but trees. A million trees and no recognizable trail.

The plane got louder. It seemed to be circling overhead now, but I couldn't see it through the branches. Maskwa must have flown right over the lake. He was probably scouting out the terrain up here along the north trail.

I took a few steps back the way I had come, following my boot prints, all the way back to the stream. The plane was north of me now, assuming I had any idea where north was anymore. I tried to locate the sun. "Okay, if the sun's there," I said. "It's late in the morning, which means that south would be——"

Thataway, you stupid useless white man. I found our boot prints, right down the original trail. How I'd missed them coming over the stream, I had no idea. I kept walking, making a promise to myself that I wouldn't tell anyone about my little detour. The plane was passing overhead once more. Again, I couldn't see it through the trees, although this time I did see the plane's shadow darken the sky for just a moment. The sound receded for a few minutes, and then stopped. They're at the lake, I thought. They're getting out, wondering where the hell we are.

I kept walking. They're reading the note, maybe shaking their heads at our impatience. They're settling down to wait for us. Or more likely they're coming up this trail to find us. With lots of cold water, I hoped. All this walking through the woods, not to mention getting lost, was making me pretty damned thirsty.

I was about a mile away from the cabin at that point. As I came around each bend in the trail, I kept expecting to see them. But I didn't. They must be unloading stuff from the plane, I thought. Or maybe they saw something else and went down a different trail. Which would mean I'd get there and find the place deserted, and wonder what the hell to do next.

I walked the last mile. The trail opened up to the cabin site. There was nobody there.

"Ah, horseshit," I said. "I knew it. They went off somewhere else. Now what the——"

I stopped. There was no plane at the dock.

I stood there for a full minute, trying to make sense of it. I had heard the plane in the air, had heard it land. I went over to the cabin and looked on the porch. The note was just where I had left it. I went to the dock and looked out at the lake. It was calm and empty. There was no sound at all. No wind. Nothing.

"What the hell?" The lake bent around to the right—maybe they had seen something on the far shore, and had landed the plane over there. I remembered the trail that Maskwa and I had explored the day before and how it had followed the curve of the shoreline.

I found that trail again and began walking. I moved fast. I wanted to find that damned plane so I could stop wondering, so I could get rid of this prickly little ball that was forming in my stomach. I flashed back on the way Maskwa had to muscle that flimsy old plane into the sky, how he just barely cleared the trees, how half the instrument panel fell right into his lap.

I moved faster. I was running now, trying to see through the trees. "Be there, God damn it. I want to see that plane."

How old was Maskwa, anyway? He was Guy's grandfather, so he had to be what? Sixty years old at least? Closer to seventy? And that plane, hell, for all I knew, it was just as old.

The trees opened up. I went up over a rock and landed in the shallow water. I didn't even think about how cold it was on my feet. Where was that plane?

Guy got his Grandpère to fly us all the way up here in his tiny little airplane. They were the only people on this earth who even knew we were up here. And today . . .

I waded out into the lake, until I was standing up to my knees in the freezing water.

Lake Agawaatese was empty.

Chapter Thirteen

The water was so cold, my feet were already getting numb. I came back to the shore, climbed over the rock and landed on the trail. I had two wet boots now to go along with all the rest of my problems.

My problems, hell. If Maskwa and Guy went down in the woods—

I tried to replay it in my head. I had heard the plane above me. It seemed to circle and head back south, which meant it would have approached the lake from that direction. Which was more or less the exact direction I was walking. I hadn't seen anything. I sure as hell hadn't heard anything. Wouldn't a crash make some sort of noise? Or would the trees just reach up and . . . God, catch them?

I headed back to the cabin site, squishing my way down the trail in my soaking boots. At some point, I'd have to make a fire and dry them out. Right after I found Maskwa and Guy sitting there on the porch of the cabin, having a good laugh. They had hidden their plane, just to play a joke on me.

Yeah, where'd they hide it, Alex?

"Holy fuck," I said. "Holy fuck holy fuck holy fuck holy fuck." I started to run again. That little ball of dread in my stomach, it felt like it was spreading through my entire body. I could feel it burning in my intestines, squeezing my lungs, and tightening all the muscles in my back.

When I got back to the cabin, I was fighting for breath. "Get a hold of yourself, Alex. You've got to think."

Water, that was the first thing I needed. Get some water in your body, and then you can think straight. I went into the cabin. It was exactly as we had left it. The big pot was still on the propane stove. We had boiled our water there in the morning and covered it with a lid when we left. I picked the lid up, dipped a coffee mug in, and drank. I took a deep breath and then drained another cupful.

Okay, I thought. That's good. That's just what you needed. Now what?

Now you go out and start looking for that plane. It can't be too far away. They may both be alive. They may both need your help, very badly.

Vinnie. I'll go back up the trail. I'll get Vinnie, we'll come back down here, and we'll find them.

Vinnie will need water, too, I thought. I looked around for something to carry it in. A canteen, a water bottle. Anything.

There was nothing like that. Just a few pots and pans, and a lot of garbage.

Plastic Coke bottles. That's what I needed. I went back outside and grabbed two empty liter-size bottles from the cooler. I came back in and filled them. Okay, I thought. I'm ready. Let's go.

When I was outside, I couldn't help looking at the lake one last time before I started back up the trail. I stopped. As if I didn't have enough to think about, another horrible thought came to me.

Could that plane have sunk?

No. No, it can't sink. It has floats. That's why they call it a floatplane, you idiot. It can't sink.

I carried the two bottles of water, one in each hand. Find Vinnie, I told myself. Look all around while you're walking. And find Vinnie.

I hurried up the trail, looking into the shadows on either side of me. I kept expecting to see the plane. I imagined seeing it leaning nose down against a big pine tree, one of its wings sheared off and lying on the ground next to it. I imagined it so hard I made myself see it, again and again.

Easy, Alex. I made myself slow down a notch. Blind panic wouldn't help anyone at this point. I kept walking, a mile into the woods, over the stream, then another mile. For a moment I thought I caught the far-off sound of a bear again. It didn't chill me to the bone this time. I had bigger problems now.

I opened one of the water bottles, took a quick drink and recapped it. I wiped away the thin line of sweat that was running down the side of my face, even in this cold air. My feet were still wet. I kept walking.

I finally got to the stand of birch trees. Vinnie wasn't there.

"Vinnie!" I yelled. "Vinnie! Where the hell are you!"

Nothing.

"Vinnie!"

A bear. In the distance. Nothing else.

"Where the fuck are you, Vinnie?" I went up the trail, trying to pick up his boot prints on the ground. I had already proven to myself just how bad I was at tracking, but I didn't know what else to do. It turned out to be easy, because he had just been walking here within the last couple of hours, and a dozen god-damned bears hadn't messed up the trail yet.

The trail split off into a couple different directions. I followed his tracks left. It split again. The tracks went left again. I picked up the sound of running water. And something else I couldn't quite make out. Probably more bears.

"Vinnie!"

Did I hear something then? It was hard to tell. I kept walking. The water sounds grew louder. Finally, I came to a waterfall. The water was coming down, maybe eight feet from top to bottom, and splashing on the rocks.

I looked again and saw that there was a great beaver's dam in the stream, raising the height of the falls. From where I was standing, the whole thing rose above my head. On another day, I would have stood there and admired it.

Then I saw the bootprints. Vinnie had gone up the side of this stream, up this jumbled mass of rocks and dirt, all the way to the top. I followed them. There were big depressions in the ground, where he had no doubt buried his boots halfway to his knees in the mud. Mine were already a soaking mess, so I had nothing to lose. I fought my way up the incline, grabbing on to rocks and roots and God knows what else.

I heard them. Before I got to the top, I heard the throaty roaring of the bears.

As I stumbled onto the top, I saw it all at once. I saw the bears, two of them, one black, one cinnamon brown, all fur and teeth and nails, one of them on its hind legs for a moment, suspended in the air. Vinnie swinging a long stick in slow motion, making a wide arc that would have been graceful in any other place than this sudden hell. The ground all churned up, like a battlefield. Freshly dug dirt, all along the bed of this creek. A clearing, the sun shining down. The sleeve of Vinnie's coat in tatters, blood on his arm.

I saw it all for a moment that lasted forever, feeling like I was seeing it from far away, out of my own body, until finally it all snapped into place and I heard the noises again and I knew what was happening.

The bears were attacking Vinnie. He was screaming and trying to beat them off with a stick.

I yelled something and ran forward, sliding through the muck and landing hard on my back. I clawed my way back to my feet and ran to him along the edge of the stream. The bears were on either side of him now, the ground itself a morass of black soil and stones and dead grass, torn up in strips.

And something long and white.

Bones. God help me, bones.

As I came to him, I saw the bones in the dirt. A hand. Black fingers locked in a twisted claw. White fingernails. A leg. The ribs of a man, half buried in the dirt.

This is what happened. They are dead. All the men are dead. The bears killed them and now they will kill us, too.

"Get away!" Vinnie's raw voice. "Get out of here!"

I screamed at the bears. I waved my arms. "Go! Get away! Go! Go!"

The smell. It washed over me. The stench of it, God, the dead rotting bodies.

And something else.

Vinnie swung his stick. A sudden pain in my arm as the end of the stick hit me and broke off.

I knew that smell.

"Get away!" he yelled. "Get away! Get away!"

One bear turned away, the one with the brown fur.

"Get away! Get away, God damn you!"

I couldn't even tell which of us was yelling anymore. That smell.

The black bear made his horrible inhuman noise and turned around. He looked back at us with yellow eyes and went away, toward the woods.

Vinnie kept screaming.

A long time ago. How many years? The same smell. The bodies in bags, zipped up tight. And yet the smell still hit me right in the face. I'm there in that same place now, as if it just happened, the way only a smell can take you back.

That house in Detroit. That burning house.

The fire.

I looked down at it. I had to look down. The white bones, the flesh ... Black. Blacker than the bear. Blacker than the dirt. Blacker than evil.

They were burned. The bodies were burned. The bears didn't do this. The bears didn't kill these men.

And the bears weren't attacking Vinnie. It was Vinnie who was attacking the bears. He saw what they were doing, saw the bears digging here in the ground, desecrating this shallow grave of dead burned men. He had tried to drive them away.

Vinnie was bent over now, with his face in his hands. There was blood all over his arm. He dropped to his knees. "Oh my God, Tom, oh my God."

"Vinnie," I said. "Vinnie." I grabbed his shoulders from behind.

He sat back on his heels and cried. The stream went by, the bears moved through the woods. The sun went behind a cloud and it got colder. The bodies of five men were spread all around us, some piece of each man above the ground, another piece below, and some inside the bears.

I dug into the dirt, took it in both hands, and threw it over what was once a man's head. I did it again and again, digging with my bare hands and covering the bodies. Vinnie stayed still. I worked all around him, spreading the dirt over everything I could see. My hands were hurting, scraped raw by the rough earth. But I kept at it. It was a primitive need to bury something dead and that was all I was capable of doing.

When I had done as much as I could do, I went to Vinnie and pulled him up by the armpits. I turned him around and held his head on my shoulder. He didn't fight me.

I looked at his left arm. A bear had raked a claw down his forearm, right through his coat, leaving three deep cuts. I needed to clean his arm off and wrap it up. That was the next thing I had to do. "Come on," I said. "We have to go."

I grabbed his other arm. He was holding something tight in his hand. "What is it, Vinnie?" I said. I lifted his hand and looked. It was a watch, caked with dirt, the crystal shattered.

"Come on," I said. "Come on." I led him back down the stream. He walked slowly, staring at the ground, his eyes half closed, as if he could barely stay awake. I took him back to where the trail led down over the ledge, next to the waterfall. I tried to help him climb down, but he was moving automatically, with no thought. We both ended up sliding down in the muck until we landed hard at the bottom. I found one of the water bottles there, opened it, and poured the water into his mouth. He swallowed it. I took a drink and then put it in my coat pocket. "We've got to move," I said. "We've got to take care of you. Okay?"

I picked him up, helped him out of the mud and onto the trail. He finally started to resist me. "No," he said. "No, no."

"Come on, Vinnie."

He looked behind us. "No."

I pushed him. "Let's go."

"No," he said. But he was too weak to fight me. He had nothing left. I turned him like a robot and pointed him south.

"Let's go, Vinnie."

We walked all the way back, three miles down the trail. I kept Vinnie's body moving forward, but I had no idea where his mind was. I couldn't even imagine. A good hour later, I had him back in the cabin, sitting at the kitchen table. I filled the big pot with water and put it on the stove to boil. I didn't see a first-aid kit anywhere, so I stripped down and took off my undershirt, and tore it into strips. I threw the strips in water, and added the dish towel that had been hanging on a nail in the wall. Vinnie sat there the whole time, looking at nothing.

I looked around the place while the water was heating up, on the off chance there might be a first-aid kit lying around. There wasn't. I left him there at the table for a minute while I went outside to check the little shed by the dock. When I opened the door, I saw an outboard motor leaning against the back wall, and several life preservers hanging on hooks. Two five-gallon gas cans sat on the floor. That was it.

I was about to close the door when a horrible thought came to me. I picked up both gas cans, shook them, and remembered that Guy had done the same thing yesterday. At the time, he had been surprised that so much gasoline was gone.

Ten gallons of gasoline.

I dropped the cans and slammed the door shut. Vinnie was still sitting at the table when I went back into the cabin. He hadn't moved, not an inch.

"Vinnie," I said.

He just sat there, staring straight ahead.

"My God," I said. "Vinnie." It all washed over me in one moment, how tired I was, how hungry, how much my back hurt for some reason, how miserable my feet felt in the wet boots. I couldn't solve anything else, so I focused on the small stuff. Get Vinnie cleaned up, and then get these boots off.

The water was finally boiling. I stirred it all up with a big spoon, and then I fished out the dish towel. I grabbed the little bottle of dishwashing soap, went over and sat down next to Vinnie, and went to work on him.

"This is gonna hurt," I said as I put his left arm on the table, pushing the sleeve of his coat up. As soon as I touched his arm with the hot towel, he stood up and pushed me away.

"Tom," he said. "I've got to help Tom."

"Vinnie, get back here."

He went out the door and jumped down off the front porch. "I've got to help him," he said. "The bears."

I chased him down, grabbed him around the waist.

"The bears," he said. "The bears."

"They're gone," I said. "Come on, Vinnie. Sit down. The bears are gone."

I pulled him back to the porch and sat him down on it. We were back outside in the cold air now. I took a deep breath and tried to clear my head. Then I squeezed out the soap onto the hot towel and pressed it onto his arm. He closed his eyes.

I washed him off as well as I could, starting with the cuts in his arm, then his face. The blood turned the towel pink. "Stay here," I said. I went into the cabin and took the pot off the stove, brought it outside and put it down next to him. I took out a strip of fabric and pressed it against his arm.

"These cuts aren't as bad as I thought," I said to him. "It's a good thing you had this coat on."

He looked at me. For the first time since I found him up there, he looked right at me. His eyes were red.

"We've got another problem," I said. I took another strip out of the pot and wrapped it around his arm. "The plane came back a while ago. It circled around a couple of times and then it landed. Or at least I thought it did. But when I got back, the plane wasn't here."

With the fabric wrapped around his arm, I took two more thin strips out of the pot and tied them around the edges, tight enough to keep the bandage in place.

"The plane didn't land on the lake, Vinnie. It must have gone down in the woods."

Vinnie kept looking at me, until it finally sank in. He turned his head and looked out at the lake.

"You can't land anywhere else," I said.

As soon as I said it, I knew it wasn't true. You can land somewhere else. There were other lakes. If you flew over this lake and kept going north, and you saw that the bears were uncovering your secret, the secret you had buried in the loose ground on the side of the stream, you would know that Vinnie and Alex were about to become your biggest problem. And so you would circle back and land your plane, but not on this lake. You would land on a different lake.

I thought back to our trip up here, flying over the trees. The other lakes, all strung out like pearls on the ground, connected by the thin streams. There was one lake, to the south of this one. I tried to remember how far away it was.

You land on the nearest lake. You get out of your plane. You know these woods. You know there's a trail to Lake Agawaatese.

You come quietly.

"Vinnie," I said. "We've got to get out of here." I stood up and looked around, leaving Vinnie on the porch. I followed the line of trees with my eyes, all the way around the lake.

That's when I heard the first gunshot.

Chapter Fourteen

Vinnie was down. That was the first thing that came to me. I ran over to the front porch and said his name, saw blood on the side of his face. I heard another shot. Wood chips flew from the side of the cabin.

I grabbed him by the coat and pulled him to his feet. There was another gunshot, and then another. Everything after that was a mad rush of fear and adrenaline. We ran like animals, tripping over rocks and roots, pine boughs lashing our faces. There was nothing left but running. No thought. No sanity. No reason. Just running through the trees with our hearts pumping in our throats.

Vinnie tripped and went down hard. I picked him up, just as we heard a branch snapping somewhere behind us. We kept running. He went one way around a great rock, I went another. I thought I'd pick him up on the other side, but he wasn't there.

There was a stream here, maybe the same stream we had seen before, maybe not. I had no idea where the hell I was. I almost called his name out loud, then realized how suicidal that would be. I stopped and listened. I could hear nothing but my own breathing and the soft sound of the water on the rocks.

Something moved in my peripheral vision. I ducked instinctively, waiting for the rifle blast. Vinnie's face appeared around the trunk of a tree. He was holding his right ear, the whole side of his face painted in blood. He was leaning against the tree like it was the only thing holding him upright.

I went to him, pushed his hand away, and looked at his face. He brushed me away and pointed at the ground. I looked down and saw my own footprints. We were making it pretty damn easy for them to find us.

"Come on, this way," I said. I was about to take him up the stream but thought better of it. That's exactly where they'd expect us to go. Instead, I led Vinnie downstream for a good hundred yards, cutting back against our original direction. The water was cold and it soaked my boots again, but what the hell.

We jumped out of the stream and hit the woods again. We couldn't run anymore. But we kept moving. There was no trail here. We didn't want a trail. We squeezed our way between trees and climbed over rocks. I don't know how long we kept going. I don't know how far away we got from them, or how hard we made it for them to find us. When Vinnie started to slow down and stumble, I figured we had gone about as far away as we were going to get.

We came to a large ridge of exposed rock. I peered down over it and saw that there was an overhang. "Vinnie, down here," I said.

I helped him crawl down over the ledge. He collapsed right there, his back against the wall of rock. I grabbed the trunk of a big pine tree that had fallen down and muscled it over, leaning it against the overhang. When I ducked inside, I saw that I had showered Vinnie with brown pine needles.

I brushed him off and finally got a good look at his face. There was a long furrow in his cheek, where the bullet had grazed him. His right earlobe was gone.

"Ah, fuck, Vinnie," I said. "God damn it all."

He was breathing hard, a long line of mucus hanging from his nose.

"Give me your arm," I said. He was losing blood a hell of a lot faster from his face, so I rolled up his sleeve and untied his bandage. I took it off and pressed it against his cheek and his ear. He struggled, but I held on tight. Finally, he gave up and went limp against me. I leaned back against the rock. He slid down with his head in my lap. I kept the cloth pressed against his face, closed my eyes, and listened.

Every sound in the forest, every mouse running over a leaf, every breath of the wind—it all made me wonder if they had found us yet. They could be standing on top of the ridge right now, looking down at us, waiting for us to move so they could shoot us.

It's just a matter of time, I thought. I couldn't stop thinking about it, just how fucking hopeless it was. You've got no food, no water, no weapons, no way out. You're gonna die here, just like Tom and those other men.

Those other men. They have to be the reason for all this. Somehow, they got hooked up with something bad, and Tom went down with them. And now us.

Fuck that, I thought. We're not dead yet.

We are not dead yet. Five words. Keep saying them to yourself, over and over.

We are not dead yet.

Vinnie shivered. He tried to say something, but I couldn't make any sense of it.

"You've got to hang on," I said. "For God's sake, just hang on, okay?" I tried to huddle up closer to him, to keep him warm.

"Don't give up," I said. "Please, Vinnie. We'll get through this."

I hung my head down. I was so exhausted, I felt myself sliding into a half-awake dream. I felt pine branches hitting me in the face, felt my legs running, my lungs aching for air.

I saw dead bodies in the ground. I smelled the burned flesh.

Minutes passed.

Hours.

The shadows grew longer all around us. I kept slipping in and out of the dream.

Running. Running away from the men in the ground.

The hand reaching out like a claw.

The smell. God save me, the smell.

Something woke me up with a start. A sudden noise above us. I held my breath and listened.

Nothing.

I looked down at Vinnie. His eyes were open. "Alex," he said.

"What is it?"

"Is this really happening?"

"Yes," I said. I was still holding the cloth against the side of his head. The whole thing was stained red. "We've got to figure out what to do."

He took the cloth from me and pushed himself up. Blood dripped down his neck.

"Keep holding that," I said. "You've got to keep the pressure on."

He winced as he put the cloth back to his face. "I think we're having ourselves a bad day," he said.

How he could make a joke like that, I couldn't even imagine. But it made me feel better. Somehow, the Vinnie I knew was back. It made me feel like we still had a fighting chance.

"This might be a dumb question," I said, "but why would they leave us out here overnight and then come back the next day? Why didn't they just kill us yesterday?"

"Alex, that wasn't Guy and Maskwa shooting at us."

"They're the only people who knew we were up here."

"It couldn't have been them."

"Why not?"

"They would have found us by now, for one thing. And they wouldn't have shot at us from so far away."

"Why is that?"

"Guy and Maskwa knew we weren't armed."

"They knew we'd run away as soon as we saw them."

"They could have still gotten a lot closer. Anybody else would have had to be a lot more careful."

I thought about it. "Okay, so who is it?"

He took the cloth off his face, turned it over, then put it back. "God only knows, Alex. Whoever did that . . ." He pointed in the general direction behind us. I didn't have to wonder what he was talking about. "Whoever that was, I think that's who we're talking about here."

"If it's not Guy and Maskwa," I said, "then where are they? They were supposed to be here today."

"Maybe they already got to them," he said. His voice was drained of all emotion. "First them and now us."

"If that happened, then there's nothing we can do about it. We've got to think about getting ourselves out of this."

"Time's not on our side," he said. "I'll probably stop bleeding, but we've got to find some food. I saw juniper by the stream. And some dandelions, but that's not gonna do much for us. We've got to get to them soon, while we still have some strength left."

"Do you think they're at the cabin?"

"Probably. Our only chance is to try to sneak up on them. We should wait until nightfall."

"What, try to go back there in the dark? They'll have lights."

"Exactly," he said. "That'll be our only advantage. If it's like last night, there'll be enough moonlight for us to see everything we need to. If they have flashlights, their eyes will never get adjusted to the dark."

"Okay," I said. "We take our shot at 'em. We do it tonight."

"Look at that sky," he said. Through the branches we could see another blazing sunset. It looked just like the sky from the night before, but of course everything was different now. The whole world had tipped upside down.

"Last night," he said, "I was thinking to myself, that's Tom's sky, the 'Pleasing Sky,' the sun going down in the west. I thought it was a good omen."

He closed his eyes and kept them closed for a long time. His breathing grew ragged.

"Vinnie, are you all right?"

"Our grandmother used to tell us these stories," he said. "These stories about our ancestors, all the things they did, the ceremonies, the medicines. Here's Tom and me, growing up in this house on the reservation, going to the public school. We didn't know anything about this stuff. But our grandmother, she made sure we learned our real history. She made us promise we'd remember it and tell it to our own children."

He stopped for a moment to wipe his eyes with one hand. He kept the other hand held tight against his face. The blood was drying on his fingers.

"You don't go to war for land, or for power. You go to war to avenge your brother's death. You gather your warriors, you gather your medicines. You make a war pole, you do your war dance. You sing the war song. I don't remember how the song goes, but there's one part that always stuck with me. Something about looking up at the sky and seeing the red, and knowing that someone would die. 'Blood is the sky.' That's the line I remember. 'Blood is the sky.'"

He dipped one finger into the dirt and rubbed a streak across each cheek. "You paint your face with black," he said. He dipped his finger in the dirt again, leaned over close and put a streak on each of my cheeks, as well.

He took some of his own blood and rubbed another streak on each cheek, above the black. "And red," he said. He took more blood and rubbed it on my face.

"Then you're ready," he said. "You're ready to go to war."

Chapter Fifteen

We waited for the sun to go down. The darkness seemed to creep in all around us until we were totally swallowed by it. Under our little overhang with the dead tree covering us, the darkness made me realize how alone we were, how far away we were from anyone who could help us.

We kept close together, trying to stay warm. As I shivered I could feel the last gallon in my tank burning away to nothing. Without food or shelter, I didn't see how I could live to see another night.

"How are your eyes?" Vinnie finally said.

"What do you mean?"

"Look out at the trees. Can you see them?"

"Not very well."

"Use the sides of your eyes," he said. "You have better night vision if you don't look at things directly. Try it."

I picked a tree, tried to look away and still be aware of it. "All right, I think I see what you mean."

"Okay, good. Are you ready to go?"

"Of course." I said it like I actually believed it.

Standing up was an ordeal. We had just spent the last few hours sitting on the cold ground, leaning against the rocks. It took me a full minute to straighten out my back. Vinnie had to keep his head down even longer than that to keep from passing out. When we were both finally on our feet, there was enough moonlight for us to see each other's faces. The war stripes on our cheeks were like a cruel joke.

"Do you remember the way back to the cabin?" I said.

"I think so. Back to the stream, and then we can work our way back to the trail."

"What if they're out looking for us?"

"They won't be, not unless they have flashlights. And then we'll see them long before they see us."

"Okay," I said. "Let's do it."

We climbed back over the little ridge and started picking our way through the trees. My feet were numb from the cold and from the moisture still in my boots. I didn't want to even think about what they'd look like if we ever got through this. My stomach was growling so loud, I was sure they'd be able to hear me from a mile away.

A branch caught me full in the face. I shook it off, kept walking, and took it right in the face again.

"Alex, don't look right at where you're walking," he said in a low voice.

It took a few minutes until I got the hang of it. Once we got out from under the trees, the moonlight made everything come alive with an eerie glow. Every star was burning in the cold distant space, just like the night before. I stopped to catch my breath.

"Alex, are you thirsty?"

"God, yes."

"The stream's just up ahead."

"Can we drink from it?"

"There might be a few little things swimming around in it," he said. "Right now I wouldn't worry about that."

We heard the stream long before we got to it, the sound of the water carrying far in the night air. The trees opened up and there was moonlight shining bright on the rocks. Vinnie held me back for a moment. He stood there and listened for a long time, and then we both went to the stream, got down on our knees, and drank the cold water.

I drank as much as I could, and splashed the water on my face. It made me feel a hell of a lot better, and even made my stomach stop hurting for a while. Beside me I could hear Vinnie gritting his teeth as he splashed the water on what was left of his ear.

"I'm gonna tear up my shirt," I said. "You need something else to stop the bleeding."

"Hold on," he said. "Let's see what happens at the cabin first. If they're not there, we can use the other stuff you boiled."

"How far away are we?" I said. "It felt like we were running forever."

"Probably not as far as you think. That trail has to be down here pretty soon."

We followed the stream maybe a half mile until we found the trail. Vinnie bent down to look closely at the ground. He stood up and looked all around us. "They were here," he said. His voice was a hoarse whisper.

"Can you tell how many?

"No, not in this light. I can make out some tracks, though. Somebody was here."

We headed south down the trail, making as little noise as possible. When I stepped on a twig, the sudden snap was like a gunshot.

"Fucking shit," I said. "Sorry about that."

Vinnie let out his breath and kept walking. He seemed to know just how to pick up and plant his feet without making the slightest sound. I tried to follow in his exact footsteps. A few minutes later, he stopped.

"What is it?" I whispered.

He didn't say anything. Then I noticed where we were. It was the stand of birch trees, looking ghostly white in the moonlight. This is where he had found all the bootprints, and now it all made a horrible sense. There was some sort of struggle here. The bodies were only a half mile away.

I heard the sounds again. I knew Vinnie could hear them, too. I put my hand on his back and led him away. "Come on, let's keep going."

I couldn't take seeing that scene again. Not in this moonlight.

He didn't resist me this time. Instead, the sounds seemed to give him new life. He took off down the trail, walking quickly. He wasn't quiet anymore. He was kicking up dead branches and leaves, and if anybody was waiting to ambush us, Vinnie was suddenly making it very easy.

I caught up to him and slowed him down. I could see new blood on his face, running all the way down his neck.

"Find something you can swing," he said. "A good solid stick." He picked up a long stick from the side of the trail, dropped it, looked for another.

"Vinnie, you've got to get a hold of yourself. They're gonna hear us."

He picked up another stick and swung it. "I want to kill some-body, Alex. For the first time in my life I really want to kill somebody."

"I'm with you," I said. "Let's do this right. We'll only get one chance."

He tapped the end of the stick in his free hand, testing its weight. "This one will do."

I looked around for my own club. As I picked up a branch, I flashed back on my playing days. How long ago now? It was forever. Back when I'd pick a good bat out of the bin, swing it a few times, and tap my spikes with it. That's what I needed right now, a good 34-ounce Louisville Slugger.

I finally settled on a straight piece of pine I picked up off the forest floor. It was light enough to swing, and hard enough to really hurt somebody. If I got the chance to use it.

A single cloud moved across the sky and hid the moon. It was too dark to see anymore. We waited for the cloud to pass and then finished our journey to the cabin, slowing to a crawl as we got closer. Finally, we left the trail altogether and made our way through the dense trees. I held my breath with every step.

At last, we were close enough to see the cabin through the trees. It was completely dark. We each got down on one knee and stayed there, perfectly still, watching the cabin and everything around it. Nothing moved.

"What do you think?" I whispered.

"I don't think they're in there."

"How can we tell for sure?"

He shook his head. "We can't just walk in. We've got to fake them out somehow."

"The only windows are in front," I said. "We should go one on each side, until we get to the door. We'll throw something, see what happens."

"If they shoot?"

"Then we've got to go for it. Hit them as they come out the door."

"All right," he said. "I'll take the left side, you take the right."

"If nothing happens, I'm gonna go in," I said. "You should move back into the woods."

"No," he said. "I'll try to cover you. If they're out there and they start shooting, just get down. You'll be pretty safe inside if they're outside. I'll try to pick up on where they're shooting from."

I took a deep breath and let it out. "Okay," I said. "Here goes nothing."

"Wait," he said, looking up into the sky. "Another cloud's gonna pass over the moon."

We waited another few minutes. The cloud came in front of the moon and cast a shadow over the whole scene. We picked our way through the brush and into the clearing. I expected the gun-shots at any second. The only question was which one of us would be hit first.

We crept closer to the cabin. A slight wind picked up. It carried the trace of a noise from far away. The bears again. I swallowed hard and kept moving.

Then another sound. A sudden rush of air. I grabbed on to the club, got ready to swing.

Bats. The goddamned bats woken-up from the back wall of the cabin. A couple dozen of them flew out from the bottom of the wall and into the night. I took a breath and kept going.

When we got to the cabin, I went around the right side. It was unnerving, not being able to see what Vinnie was doing. I found the plastic lid from a garbage can. That would be my decoy. When I got to the front of the cabin, I peeked around the corner and caught Vinnie's eye.

He gave me a little nod of the head.

I threw the lid at the front door. It hit the frame and then the ground. Clunk, clunk.

Nothing happened.

I waited another minute. Then I turned the corner and made my way to the door, keeping low to the ground. I looked in through the screen window, couldn't see a damned thing. The door creaked when I eased it open. Fucking door, I thought. Fuck-ing son of a whore door.

When the door was open just enough, I slipped inside. After

all the moonlight outside, in here I was totally blind.

I sat there for a while, giving my eyes a chance to adjust. Outside, the cloud moved past the moon. A thin stream of light came in through the front window, and shapes started to appear in the room. I saw the table, the stove, the refrigerator. The door to the back room.

They had trashed the place. It was already a mess before—now it was completely destroyed. There were pieces of Styrofoam all over the floor, and what looked like the stuffing from our sleeping bags. When I moved back and took a look in the back room, I saw the wood stove pushed completely over, the exhaust pipe pulled right out of the ceiling. I came back out into the kitchen, checked the refrigerator and the cupboards. Every bit of food was gone. The pots and pans were gone, even the utensils. Old Mother Hubbard, I thought, and what a fucking strange thing to think of at a time like this. They had probably taken everything that could have been of any use to us and thrown it right in the lake. For the hell of it, I tried turning on the stove. There was no propane.

I got down on my hands and knees and checked the floor. Maybe they had missed something. There was an empty plastic bottle under the table. Good for holding water. I put that in my coat. And what was this? It was something silver. I reached under the table and grabbed it. A half roll of duct tape. I put that in my coat, too. You never know.

A sound. Outside. Something close.

Where's that club? Where did I put that fucking club?

Over there by the door. I grabbed it and crouched down next to the door, waiting for it to open. The sounds got closer. My heart was pounding in my chest. This is it. This is the showdown.

It was joined by another sound. Some kind of hissing. It sounded like—

Fuck, it was Vinnie. What was he doing?

I looked out the window. A big black bear was coming toward the cabin. His fur glistened in the moonlight. Vinnie was hissing at him, trying to keep him away.

I slipped out the door and waved at him. We met up on the back side of the cabin, moving quickly, back into the cover of the trees. "I didn't know what to do," he said. "I didn't want that bear to come right through that window again."

"He can have the place now," I said. "They totally destroyed everything inside."

"That figures. If they're not gonna be there themselves to-night—"

"Maybe they'll come back here. Should we stick around?"

He leaned over with his hands on his knees. "I don't know, Alex. I don't know what the fuck to do now."

"Let's move back in the woods," I said. "If they come back, we should be able to hear them."

We made our way through the trees until we were about a hundred yards from the cabin. We found a thick mass of hemlock, perfect for hiding behind. If they came this way tonight, we'd hear them long before they got to us.

I took the roll of duct tape out of my coat pocket, made Vinnie roll his sleeve up, and taped up his arm. "It ain't perfect," I said. "But it'll do for now."

His face was a different story. I knew I had to do something with it, but the slightest touch made him flinch. "Here," I said, grabbing a stick. "Bite this. And hold your hair up."

He did as he was told. I stretched a piece of tape from his jaw, down his cheek, over his ruined ear, and around to the other side of his face. He closed his eyes and bit right through the stick. I put another piece of tape over the first, and then another. It looked like hell, but it seemed to stop the bleeding.

He sat down in the dirt and leaned back against a tree trunk. I sat down next to him. I listened closely to the night, but didn't hear a thing. The crickets were all asleep, buried under the ground. The birds had all flown south. The bears were out there somewhere, but at that moment I couldn't hear them.

"We need another plan," I said.

Vinnie didn't answer me. His head bobbed down, snapped back up, then bobbed down again.

"You should rest awhile," I said. I pulled him closer, so he could lean his head against my shoulder, with the bad side of his face in the air.

"No," he said. But he put his head on my shoulder and kept it there.

I spent the next couple of hours just sitting there, careful not to move. No matter how much I thought about it, I couldn't make things look any better. We were lost.

As I drifted off, I wondered if the next time I closed my eyes would be my last.

Chapter Sixteen

I opened my eyes. There was a dim light, and a wet fog hung heavy in the air. I could feel the cold dew on my face. When I tried to straighten out my neck, the pain ran right down my back. Holy God, I thought. This cannot be happening.

My heart stopped when I realized Vinnie wasn't sitting next to me anymore. For one horrible moment, I wondered if they had gotten to him somehow. They had killed him like the others and now they were on their way back for me. Then I heard him behind me.

"Good morning," he said. He was working on a long stick, carving the end into a sharp point. The duct tape was still wrapped all around his head. The black and red stripes had run into two great smudges on his face.

"Is that a knife?"

"Just a little jackknife. Too small to hurt anybody." He put the stick down and started on another. "Now if you had brought your gun—"

I thought about it. "My gun's on the bottom of Lake Superior right now."

"Too bad," he said. "Want some breakfast?"

"What do you mean?"

"Here," he said. He threw me the plastic bottle I had taken from the cabin. He must have gone to the stream to fill it with water. "I found some dandelions. It's just something to put in your stomach, if you want." He dropped a couple of plants in my lap.

I took a long drink of water and tried taking a bite of one of the leaves. It tasted like bitter lettuce.

"I can't find any insects," he said. "It's too late in the year."

Insects, I thought. If he had found any, I'd be eating them. The way my stomach is feeling right now, I'd do it.

"Today's the day, Alex. Are you ready?"

I looked at him. I couldn't understand why he suddenly had so much more energy than I did. "Vinnie, are you all right?"

"For now, I am. Tonight will be a different story."

"What are you talking about?"

"By the end of the day we'll be really hurting. There's hardly anything edible up here. We can't signal for help, not that anybody else is even gonna fly over here. We can't build a fire. They'd find us in a minute. We can't get back on our own. It's too far. We've only got one hope."

"What's that?"

"Their plane."

"What are we gonna do? Steal their plane and fly it?"

"Not unless you know how. I was thinking about their radio."

"How do we get to it?"

"Think about it, Alex. We know the plane's still here, right? We would have heard them if they had left. We know they're somewhere south of here. We have to find the plane."

"Okay, that makes sense."

"You know what else? If we find their plane, we'll find them.

Or at least one of them. That plane is their only way out, too."

"The plane is their only vulnerable spot," I said. "They have to protect it."

"Exactly. We have to hit them there. We don't have any other choice."

"Except sitting around and waiting for them to make a mistake."

"Which we can't do," he said. "Not for much longer."

I grabbed the tree and pulled myself up. I had never felt more drained in my entire life. Vinnie handed me one of his sharpened spears. "One way or another," he said. "We have to end this today."

We went back through the trees, toward the cabin. When we got to the edge, we both stopped in our tracks.

"If there's more than one of them," I said, "there might be somebody watching the cabin now."

"Could be. In the daylight, we'd be easy targets."

So we made our way around the lake to the western trail, keeping ourselves hidden in the woods. When we got to the trail, Vinnie checked the ground. "Somebody came this way," he said. "Heading away from the cabin."

"We've got to be careful. They could be anywhere right now."

He nodded as he looked all around us. "They know we're coming."

"What, to their plane?"

"Yeah, think about it. They know the same thing we know. Getting to that plane is our only hope."

"They'll ambush us on this trail," I said.

"We've got to go around the trail, get to the plane some other way."

It's not what I wanted to hear, but I knew he was right. We left the trail, climbing rocks to the higher ground that seemed to run parallel, using our spears for leverage. The loose pine needles on the rocks made the going tough. More than once we both slipped and just about killed ourselves.

When we got to the top, we saw that what we thought was higher ground was just an illusion. The land gave way again and then rose to yet another hill, and then probably another. We had to climb back down and then fight our way through thick brush, and then climb again. The sun came up, but it wasn't enough to burn off the morning fog. After an hour of picking our way over the rocks and through the brush, we were both soaking wet. It might as well have been raining.

We stopped to rest. We emptied the bottle of water. "We should come to another stream," he said. He was breathing hard, and his breath made little clouds in the cold morning air. "All these lakes are connected."

"Are your feet killing you, too?" Beyond the cold and the wet, I could feel the blisters growing with each step.

"I'm trying not to think about it," he said. He rubbed at the duct tape on his face.

We kept going. As long as the rising sun stayed on our left, we knew we were moving in the right direction. But God damn it all, it was too slow. We went for another hour. Then another. The sun rose higher in the sky.

Strange thoughts came to me—memories of things that had happened years ago. Things I had forgotten. A day walking in the woods when I was a kid. The sudden fear that I was lost.

Vinnie tried to step over a great fallen tree. He misjudged the height and ended up tumbling right over it. He lay on the ground with his head on the rotting wood, his eyes closed. His spear lay across his chest.

"Vinnie, are you all right?"

"I'm sorry."

"Come on, get up." I grabbed his hand.

"I'm sorry, Alex. I'm sorry. It's all my fault."

I sat down on the log. "Just rest a minute," I said.

"I'm trying to get us out of here."

I looked down at him. All that energy he seemed to have when he woke up, that was all just a show. It was for me. Now he was paying for it.

"The lake's gotta be close now," I said. "We're almost there."

He didn't move. "Guy and Maskwa," he said. "A kid and his grandfather. They're dead, Alex. And we're next."

"Get up, Vinnie." I reached down and hooked my hands under his arms. When I pulled him up, everything went black for a moment. I fought off the dizziness and pushed him forward.

We walked for another hour. There were no words spoken between us. We just kept moving. We met up with the trail again, and saw a perfectly preserved bootprint right in the middle of it. When we crossed over to the other side of the trail, we heard a stream. When we got to it, we both dropped our spears, fell down on the ground, and drank the cold water. If someone had seen us at that moment, he could have walked right up and shot us in the head.

I sat up and splashed the water on my face. It was so cold it hurt. The sun was above us, shining down on us with no warmth at all. It felt like even the sun had abandoned us, another strange thought. I shivered.

"This stream must lead to the lake," I said.

Vinnie didn't answer me. He was on his hands and knees, the water dripping from his face.

"Vinnie."

"Do you hear it?" he said.

"Hear what?"

"The music."

"Vinnie, there's no music."

"The water," he said. "It's making music."

"Don't leave me, Vinnie. Don't give up."

"The water flows from the four hills to the Path of Souls."

I crawled over to him, grabbed his collar and pulled his shoulders up so he was facing me. The tape was coming off his face. New blood ran down his neck.

"Vinnie, I'm gonna tape you up again. And then we're gonna go get the guys who killed your brother. Okay? We're gonna go fuck them up right now."

His eyes came into focus. "The Path of Souls, Alex. Tom's already there."

"Yes," I said. "He's there. But it's not your time yet. Or mine."

He looked into my eyes for a long time. Then he nodded. He pulled the bloody tape off his face without flinching. I dried everything off as well as I could with my shirttail, and then I put new tape on his face while he held his hair back. When I was done, he stood up and gave me his hand to help me up.

Vinnie reached into his pocket and pulled out Tom's wristwatch. I had forgotten all about it. He wiped some of the mud off the band, touched the hands through the broken crystal. "Let's go find them," he said.

I picked up my spear. It was a good heavy stick, with a sharp point on one end. This is what we had. This and the element of surprise.

We followed the stream for the next half hour. The sound of the water running over the rocks was hypnotic. It made me drift off into more memories. The flashing lights on a patrol car, the patterns the lights would make on a wall. Riding on a bus, working a baseball in my hands.

Then, a sudden noise. We both froze. It sounded like something moving in water. A boat, maybe?

We walked slowly, careful not to make any noise, holding our spears with both hands like a pair of primitive hunters. I could see the water now through the trees. The stream ran down a little wash and into the lake, maybe fifty yards away.

We made our way down to the shoreline, hiding behind the thick wall of trees. Finally, we saw what was making the noise.

It was a moose, calmly chewing on a great green mass of water plants. On another day it would have been funny, finally seeing a moose up here.

I let my breath out.

And then I saw the plane in the distance.

"That plane—" Vinnie said. He stood behind the tree next to mine, looking out at the water.

"It's Gannon's."

"That's what I thought."

It was a small lake, maybe a quarter mile across. The plane was right in the middle, spinning slowly in the wind. It had to be anchored there. The nose of the plane drifted around toward us.

Somebody was sitting on one of the floats.

"Alex, who is that?"

The bottoms of his boots were just skimming the water. He was wearing a green poncho.

And that hat. I recognized it.

Gannon was right there in front of us, sitting outside his plane. The way his hat was tipped forward, it looked like he was asleep.

"Am I seeing things?" Vinnie said.

"If you are, then I am, too."

"Is he really just sitting out there taking a nap?"

"If he is, we've got to get to him before he wakes up. Think we can swim out there without making too much noise?"

"We don't have to," Vinnie said. "Look."

He pointed to a spot along the shoreline, maybe a third of the way around from where we were standing. A yellow rubber raft was drifting lazily, just a few feet from shore.

"You figure that boat was tied up to the plane?" I said. "And somehow got loose?"

"It looks that way."

"I don't like this, Vinnie. It's too easy."

"How many men flew in, do you think?"

"Well, if Gannon is involved in all this, then everyone else at the lodge has to be, too, right?"

"You would think," he said. "Unless—"

"Unless he did this all on his own," I said. "Or with somebody else we don't even know."

"Didn't Helen say she wasn't even there at the lodge when they came back?"

"Yeah, you're right," I said. "And Ron and Millie. Hell, we didn't talk to them at all. For all we know, Gannon was the only person around that morning."

"The morning they supposedly left the lodge."

"Maybe they just assumed he flew them back and saw them off."

"Gannon brought their stuff back in the plane," Vinnie said. "He put it all in the Suburban, and then ditched it in the woods by the reserve."

"There's gotta be somebody else involved."

"Yeah, and they're somewhere around here, waiting to shoot us as soon as we get in that boat."

"Or else they're back on the trail," I said. "Waiting for us there."

"Or else they're buried in the ground with my brother."

"Yeah," I said. "Yeah, could be."

"So if he's really here alone, maybe he was up all night, waiting for us. Maybe he really is asleep now."

"In which case we'd better do something before he wakes up."

"So which is it?" he said. "Is this a trap? Or is this our only chance?"

Chapter Seventeen

"Vinnie," I said. "What does your gut tell you right now?"

"It tells me this is all a setup. How about you?"

I looked out at the lake—the plane slowly turning, Gannon on the float, his hat turned down, the rubber raft drifting along the shoreline.

"Look at Gannon on the plane," I said.

"What about him?"

"Something's just not right. The plane too slumped over to be comfortable. You know what? I don't think that's a person at all."

"You mean it's a dummy? Like a pair of pants stuffed with something, and some old boots?"

"Can you even see his arms?"

Vinnie shielded his eyes and took a long look. "I don't see his arms, no."

"Of course not. That big poncho covering everything? And the big hat covering his face? There's no way, Vinnie. We're not falling for it."

He took a breath. "Okay," he said. "So they're on the perimeter somewhere. We've got to sneak up on them. They won't be expecting us to come at them through the woods. That'll be our only advantage."

"I don't know, Vinnie. I don't think that's enough. They'll pick us off in two seconds."

"If we try to come at them from behind—"

"I guess so," I said. "What other choice do we have? Unless we can make them tip their hand somehow."

As soon as I said it, I knew the answer.

"Alex, are you thinking—"

"Yes," I said. "Just like we were thinking back at the cabin. If I can draw their fire, we'll know where they are. And they'll be distracted, too."

"How are you gonna do that?"

"I'll take the boat out. If they start shooting, I'll try to get back to shore. Or something."

"Alex, look how small this lake is. If they've got a good rifle with a hunting scope, you'll be dead on the first shot."

"Vinnie, I can't sneak up on them like you can. I've got to go out there and give you a chance to get to them. Okay? I don't know what else we can do at this point."

He looked at me, then out at the lake. "If they see just you, they'll know something is up."

"They shot you, remember? As far as they know, you bled to death."

He shook his head. "God damn it."

"If you were them, where would you be?" I said. "I mean, where on the lake would you wait to get a good shot."

"The trail's over there," he said, pointing to our right, past where the boat was floating. "If I had a good scope, I'd want to be somewhere over this way." He pointed back to our left. "So I'd have a clear line of sight."

"Give me a few minutes to get over to the boat," I said. "Then move down that way. If you watch carefully, you should see some movement when they start shooting."

"What if there are two of them? On opposite sides of the lake?"

I squeezed his shoulders. "Then we go down together," I said. "We go down fighting."

He gave me a little smile and nodded his head.

"Here, take this," I said. I gave him my spear.

"Get under the boat."

"What do you mean?"

"Don't get in the boat. Get under it."

"That'll be pretty damned cold."

"Water slows down bullets," he said. "You want cold or you want dead?"

"Good point."

"I'll buy you a beer when we get out of here."

"I'll remember that."

"One more thing," he said. He closed his eyes and winced as he pulled the tape away from the side of his face.

"What are you doing?"

He put his hand under the tape, brought the blood out on two fingers and painted my face again, right below my eyes. He did the same to himself, and then he bent down to the ground and took the dirt onto the same two fingers. He drew the second stripe on my face, and then on his.

"Just touching you up," he said. "Now you're ready."

"Thanks," I said. And that's how I left him.

I started walking, making my way around the lake. I couldn't help wondering if I was going to run into them here in the trees, before I got to the raft. That would pretty much end things right now, before we got to try out our brilliant plan.

I almost laughed out loud. I don't know why I was feeling so calm. I should have been scared out of my mind. Hell, maybe I was. Maybe this is what scared feels like when you haven't eaten in two days, and you've walked for hours in the cold, with wet, hurting feet. Maybe this was finally the end, and I was already walking down that Path of Souls that Vinnie was talking about.

Get a grip, Alex. Get a fucking grip.

I stumbled over something, landing face first in the dirt and pine needles. I got up, caught my breath, kept walking. God, I hurt. Every part of me. Through the trees, I could see the yellow raft bobbing in the water. Once I leave the trees, I'm gonna have to do this fast. Get in the water, get under the raft, and start moving.

I worked my way down to the water. I was twenty yards away now, hiding behind the last tree. Okay, so I am scared. This is okay. What the hell.

Take a few deep breaths, Alex. You're gonna need them. Once you hit that water, it's gonna get serious.

I looked down the shore. I couldn't see Vinnie, but I knew he was there.

Breathe. In, out. Lots of air.

I kept my eyes moving, scanning the shore, all the way around. Nothing but trees.

My hands were shaking. Easy, man.

The plane was maybe two hundred yards away. It kept turning slowly. The dummy Gannon with his hat down, slumped against one of the float supports—how stupid did they think we were?

This is insane. Here we go. Wherever you're hiding, boys, wake up. It's showtime.

I took my coat off. In the water, it would be dead weight, and if I happened to live through this, I'd need it when I got back out. I didn't want to give them a free shot at me on the shore, so I tried to get in the water and get under the raft all in one quick motion.

It didn't work out that way.

Instead, I took one step into the water and sank all the way up to my knees in cold muck. I spent what felt like minutes trying to get myself unstuck. Surely the men with the rifles already had me sighted in. They were probably just amusing themselves for a moment, watching me struggle in the mud, before putting their bullets right through my head.

With a desperate lunge I fell forward and caught the raft with one hand. The strain on my ankles, the sudden sharp pain in my shoulder as I reached out, were obliterated by the icy shock of the water, my entire body suddenly overwhelmed by the cold. Everything I had been through came rushing out in one primal scream as I pulled the boat over my head and the first bullet came ripping through all in the same moment. The crack of the gun sounded far away, quickly lost in the hissing of the punctured raft and my own voice in my ears, the cold gripping me and turning into blood fear and back to cold.

I kicked at the bottom of the lake, untangling myself from more muck and weeds and trying to push myself out into the lake, trying to move, God damn it, as another bullet punched through the rubber and made a splash right next to my ear. I dropped my head under the water, more icy shock and the whole world gone silent except the ringing in my ears. The water was dark with the stirred-up muck and I was going numb. Only seconds gone by and no hope for Vinnie to do anything at all.

I am losing it, I thought, in a little voice that seemed to be watching the whole struggle from outside my body. I am fighting the water and the weeds and the cold itself and I'm a goner.

I went up and took a breath, went back down, tried to kick my way into the lake, get the raft moving for God's sake, back up for a breath and back down. A mouthful of dirty water and I'm coughing it up now, my face above the water and the raft folding in on itself.

Another shot and I pushed the raft away from me, the little

voice telling me in its obscene calm that the raft was the target and I needed to get away from it. I'm pushing it with both hands but it's like a wet parachute draped all over me until I go back down and claw at it until it's moving over me and away at last.

I am upside down now in the water, looking up at the surface without seeing it, my eyes stinging in the filth and weeds and I must be still. God damn it, be still and don't kick or thrash your arms or your life will end right here in this water.

I am seizing up now with the cold, but the voice says to stay flat and to grab on to the weeds with my hands and keep everything under water, everything but the very tip of my nose, which I must finally slowly slowly move up out of the water, yes, that's it, just enough to finish breathing out and to draw another breath and pull myself down again, just like that, the voice says, just like that and hold it as long as you can. Vinnie is running in the woods, I can see it in my mind's eye, running as silently as the wind, as hatred, as vengeance, God damn it, I am so cold I cannot stay like this anymore. I cannot, I cannot.

Another breath, hold it, Alex, hold it, your whole body, just like that, just like that. I am so close to the surface now I can see the sky, see the trees, a cloud, the sun, the sun, the sun, God damn it, I'm gonna have to get out of this water. I'll run for it and he can shoot me in the back if he wants, I don't care, I can't do this for one more second. This is it.

I got up on my hands and knees, fighting my way through the green tentacles and the goddamned muck and tearing up both ankles and both knees getting onto the shore and up the slope into the trees. I knew the shots would come at any second and cut me down, but somehow it didn't happen. I was up the bank and into the woods, scrambling on ruined legs, finally falling to the ground, sitting up, dripping cold water and covered with dirt and leaves and pine needles. Somehow, I was holding my coat. I didn't remember grabbing it, but there it was. I wrapped it around myself and looked out at the lake. The raft was mostly submerged, a faint yellow secret in the dark water.

I listened hard. There was nothing to hear but my own breathing.

Vinnie, where are you?

I kept listening. Nothing.

I got to my feet, limped back down toward the water. I stood by a tree, my cheek against the rough bark, and looked out across the water and all along the shore.

Nothing.

The hell with it. I gathered my breath. "Vinnie!"

The sound echoed across the lake and back, then died. There was no answer.

"Vinnie!"

The wind picked up. I was shivering so hard now.

"Alex!"

Dear God. "Vinnie! Where are you?"

"I'm here," he said.

I looked in every direction. I couldn't see him.

"To your right," he said. "About two hundred yards."

He was in the opposite direction from where we had started, which meant he had to run all that way around the lake. How did he do it?

I made my way over to him, holding the coat tight around me, stumbling my way through the trees. When I finally got there, he was standing still, his back to me.

"Vinnie."

He didn't say anything. He didn't move. When I came up to him, I saw what he was looking at.

Hank Gannon was on the ground, lying on his side. The spear had run clean through his back, out through his chest. There was blood on his shirt, the blood that pumps bright red out of a chest wound and nowhere else. He was shaking and spitting up more blood, and clenching his hands at the spear without touching it. He looked up at us.

"I've been asking him why," Vinnie said.

Gannon moved his lips. He couldn't speak. He bled and bled and looked at us. A bolt action .306 rifle was lying on the ground behind him. I reached over him and picked it up. I saw a boater's key chain sticking out of his hip pocket, the kind with the float attached to it. I took the key chain and put it in my own pocket.

"He won't tell me," Vinnie said. "He won't tell me why he killed my brother. He won't tell me why he—" Vinnie leaned down to him, "burned him."

He was about to do something—take Gannon by the throat, kick him, take the spear out and run it through him again. I didn't want to see it.

"Vinnie," I said, grabbing his arm. "We need to get out of here. If there's anybody else up here, they heard the shots. You know they'll be here soon."

He wouldn't move. He kept watching Gannon bleed.

"Come on, I'm going out to the plane." I didn't want to leave him there. If someone else was on their way, I didn't want him to be an easy target.

I pulled him away. When I looked back at Gannon, he was still bleeding, still shaking. He was not dead yet. I knew it would happen soon, but, God help me, when I walked away from him, he was still very much alive.

The last thing I wanted to do was get in that water again, but the raft was long gone, and we needed to get to that plane. "Take your coat off," I said. "Hold it over your head."

He took his coat off. He had that same blank expression on his face, the way he looked when I found him fighting off the bears. "We've come this far, Vinnie. You've got to hold it together just a little bit longer."

"I'm together, damn it. Let's go."

I took my coat off and wrapped it around the rifle. When I waded out into the water, it didn't even feel cold. I was past feeling it. But I had second thoughts about getting Vinnie out here. I was about to send him back to the shore, but he was already in the water up to his chest. He was gritting his teeth.

I had to fight my way through the muck again, working hard to keep my coat dry, along with Gannon's rifle. When we were both deep enough, we swam sidestroke, moving slowly through the water.

"Vinnie, you all right?"

He didn't answer, but he was still swimming. So I kept my eyes on the plane and made myself do it.

Kick, God damn it. Kick.

Fifty yards away, twenty. Finally, we were there. The plane had spun around now, so that the Gannon dummy was on the opposite side. I grabbed onto the float and hauled myself up to the ladder. The side door was ajar. I pulled it open and threw in my coat and the rifle. Vinnie was a few yards behind me. I waited there on the float, shivering like all goddamned hell in the cold wind, until he was close enough for me to grab his hand.

When we were both in the plane, we wrapped ourselves up in our coats. I sat down in the pilot's seat, took the key chain out of my pocket, and started trying all the keys in the ignition switch.

Vinnie reached down into a paper bag and pulled out a couple of energy bars. He opened them up and gave me one. I sat there looking at it for a moment, not quite registering the fact that this was food in my hand. I finally bit into it and it was like eating chocolate-flavored cardboard. But at that moment it was the best-tasting cardboard I'd ever eaten.

When I had finished half of it, I went back to working through the keys with shivering hands, finally finding the right one and turning the whole electric system on. Lights started to glow and when I flipped on the radio and put on the headset, I heard the beautiful sound of live static. I didn't know what to say, so I just started yelling, "Mayday! Mayday!"

Vinnie looked out his window. Then he popped the passenger's side door open. "What are you doing?" I said, and then I thought I heard something break in the static so I went back to my yelling.

For the first time, I started to think about what would happen when we got out of this. All those dead men, and now Gannon. And whatever had happened to Guy and Maskwa. I could only imagine how Constable DeMers would take all this. Three months from retirement and this is what he goes out on.

Vinnie called to me. He was out on the other float.

"Vinnie, what are you doing? Get back in here!"

"Come here," he said.

"For God's sake, I'm calling for help."

"Just come here."

I put the headset down and poked my head out the passenger's side door. Vinnie was down at the front of the float, hanging over the water, right next to the dummy.

"What is it?" I said.

"Look."

I saw the blue pants first. Then the rest of the uniform as Vinnie pulled away the poncho. When he took off the hat, I saw the man's face.

I was staring right into the lifeless eyes of Senior Constable Claude DeMers.

Chapter Eighteen

I sat back down in the pilot's seat, put the headset on, and yelled into the transmitter. "Mayday! Mayday! Come in! Mayday! Mayday!"

The radio crackled with static. Vinnie climbed back into the plane and sat beside me.

"Mayday, God damn it! Mayday!"

"We're too far away," he said quietly. "Sitting down on this lake, with these trees, we'll never reach anybody."

I took the headset off. "There's got to be some other way," I said. "Some kind of distress call. Some GPS thing."

"I don't know, Alex."

"Someone has to know this plane is here," I said. I tried hard to keep the desperation out of my voice. "You can't just fly a plane into the woods and not have someone notice it's gone."

"They were all packing up," Vinnie said. He kept looking out the window, his whole body slumped in the seat like somebody had pulled his plug. "The lodge could have been empty."

"What about DeMers? Somebody will be looking for him."

"Yeah. Eventually."

"Are there any more of those energy bars down there? You should eat something."

"I didn't see any."

I leaned my head back against the seat. As soon as I closed my eyes, I felt dizzy. Bad idea. When I opened them again, the plane had spun around so that we were facing the spot on the shore where we had left Gannon. I could just barely make out his body, lying in the dirt. The plane kept turning slowly, Gannon's body and all the trees moving across our line of sight, the whole world spinning around us.

I picked up the headset again, yelled into the transmitter a few more times, then threw it back down.

"At least I got him," Vinnie said. "At least he'll go down with us."

"Stop it, Vinnie. Stop talking like that."

"I killed him, Alex. At least I did that."

"We've got a rifle now. Hell, we can go shoot that moose."

"You go ahead," he said. "I don't think I can move anymore."

"You rest a while," I said. "I'll take care of it. Don't worry."

Vinnie closed his eyes. I tried to fight it, but my eyelids dropped. I felt dizzy again but then it passed and I was almost comfortable, except for the pain in my gut and the way my feet felt, like they weren't even part of my body. My clothes were still dripping wet, but they didn't feel cold anymore. In fact, I was starting to feel warm. Just a few minutes with my eyes closed, in this warm, comfortable seat—

I stood up and hit my head on the plane's low ceiling. "Vinnie," I said. I touched his face, the red and black stripes on his cheeks, now smeared by the water. "Vinnie, you gotta hang in there."

He didn't move.

I pulled his coat tighter around his neck. I climbed back over the rear seats, looking for something else to keep him warm. There was a metal box in the very back of the plane. Inside it were a polar fleece blanket and a first aid kit.

"This is great," I said. "We could have used these two days ago."

I took the blanket back up to Vinnie and wrapped it around him. I was about to break out some bandages, then thought better of it. Let him sleep for a little while. In the meantime, I'm gonna go get us some food.

I picked up Gannon's rifle, opened the door, and climbed down the ladder to the float. I looked under the belly of the plane, across to the other float. DeMers's body was still lying there. One boot was in the water, and the stain was rising up his pant leg.

"What the hell happened, DeMers? How did you get mixed up in this?"

I looked down at the cold water. Just the thought of jumping back in made me start shivering again.

"You're not talking, eh? I don't blame you."

The shadow of a cloud passed over us.

"God damn it, DeMers. I think I know what happened. You got yourself killed trying to get us out of here."

A wind picked up in the trees. I could hear it rattling the branches.

"Am I right?"

The wind moved out and rippled the water.

"I'm sorry, I can't even think about that right now," I said, "I've got a moose to kill."

I wasn't looking forward to that, either. All we had was Vinnie's little pocket knife. We'd have to make a fire somewhere, and cook the meat. None of which would happen if I kept standing there talking to a dead man.

I was just about ready to jump in when I heard the noise. In the distance, it sounded like—

A plane.

The buzzing grew louder and louder. My first thought was, here's more horror coming from the skies, another planeload of killers. My second thought was thank God, it's Guy and Maskwa, coming to get us out of here at last.

It was neither.

A blue Cessna finally appeared over the tree line, heading north. I stood there on the float, watching it. I didn't hide. I didn't wave at it. I just stood there with Gannon's rifle in my hand, watching it bank and circle around and begin its descent onto our lake. The pilot had spotted us. There was no way he could have missed us. When the plane was low enough, I saw the official markings and emblem of the Ontario Provincial Police. That's when it occurred to me.

Constable DeMers was dead. His body is hanging off the other side of this plane.

And I'm holding the rifle that probably killed him.

By the time they hit the water, I had thrown the rifle back into the plane. Vinnie was still out cold. As the plane got closer, I saw somebody leaning out the window with a megaphone. I couldn't hear a word over the engine noise.

Finally, when the plane was thirty yards away, I could make out what he was saying. "Did you hear me? I said, put your hands in the air! Right now!"

I put my hands up. As the plane drew close, it kicked up enough turbulence in the water to make me lose my balance. I grabbed on to the ladder, and spent the next minute or two listening to the man yell at me while he climbed out of his own plane and tried to jump onto ours. It's a tough maneuver, and this man obviously didn't have the knack for it. He ended up with one leg on the float and one leg in the water, all the way up to his crotch. It was the constable with the boxer face, one of the men who had shown up when we had found the Suburban in the woods.

"Son of a bitch, that's cold," he said. I was about to tell him he didn't know anything about how cold the water was, but I held my tongue. I knew the scene was about to go from bad to worse.

"That man on the other float," I said. "That's DeMers. He's dead."

That's when I noticed Reynaud getting out of the plane. "McKnight, what did you just say?"

It all went to hell in the next few minutes. It didn't matter whether we were in America or Canada—cops are cops, and they're supposed to stay in control of everything around them, but this was something they'd never had to deal with before. I kept my mouth shut while they piled out of their plane and climbed aboard Gannon's. The other constable we had met, the one with the suntan, was the pilot. Reynaud jumped out first, landing light on her feet. She climbed up the ladder and down the other side, making her way out on the far float to her partner's body. I didn't see her reaction. I was too busy cooperating with the other constables, putting my hands behind my back so they could cuff me.

Of course, once they cuffed me, they couldn't get me into their plane. On another day it would have been funny.

"This other man in the passenger's seat," Boxer Face said to me, "is he dead, too?"

"That's Vinnie LeBlanc. You met him before. We need to get him to a hospital right away."

She came back through the plane, looked at Vinnie, put her hand on his neck, and then came down to me. She looked at me for exactly one second and then backhanded me right across the face.

"I'm sorry about DeMers," I said. "But I didn't do it. He was dead when we got here."

"Who killed him?" Her face was red, and she was rubbing her hand.

"As far as I can tell, Hank Gannon. He's over there on the

shoreline." I nodded my head in the general direction.

"Where?"

"Up in the trees. He's dead, too."

I felt one of the other constables squeezing my shoulder.

"We did kill Gannon. He was trying to shoot us."

"We saw you with the rifle, McKnight. You threw it back in the plane when we landed."

I took a deep breath. It was probably a good time to stop talking. That would have been the smart thing. But nobody's ever accused me of being smart. "Look," I said, "we've been up here for two days. Guy Berard and his grandfather flew us up here."

"I know," she said.

That stopped me. "Where are they now?" I said. "Are they—"

"They're at home," she said. "Why did they fly you out here?"

"It's a long story, okay? We need to get Vinnie back to a doctor. I'll tell you the rest on the way."

She looked at the two men, then at me. "My partner is dead, McKnight. The best cop I've ever known. The best . . . human being. He's dead."

"So are the other men," I said. "Okay? I should tell you that much right now. We found them."

"What men?"

"Vinnie's brother, Tom. And Albright, and the rest of the men who were missing."

"What are you talking about? They flew back out on Saturday."

"No," I said. "We found them. A couple of miles north of the cabin."

She didn't know what to say to that. Not that I blamed her. A dead partner, that was more than enough. That's one thing I knew all too well.

"I'll tell you everything I know," I said. "Please, we've got to get Vinnie out of here. He's been shot in the face, for God's sake."

That woke her up a little bit. "Jim, you better get on the radio."

"I don't think we'll get through," he said. "Not sitting down here on this lake. We need to get up in the air."

"All right, you better take these men back, then. I'll stay here."

"Natty, you can't do that," he said.

"I'm not leaving my partner," she said. Her face was like stone now. "Get in the air and call for backup."

They had to drag Vinnie out of his seat and carry him to the other plane. After all we had been through, he just about drowned right there. They took my handcuffs off, let me jump across, then put the handcuffs back on when I was in my seat. The pilot spun the plane around and gave it the gas.

"Smallest damned lake I've ever taken off from," he said. He pulled back on the yoke and the plane fought its way up into the air.

As we climbed over the trees, I looked down at Gannon's plane. Reynaud stood there on the float, holding on to the ladder, watching us fly away.

Chapter Nineteen

When we were in the air, the pilot called in the basics. A constable dead on the scene, another man, the owner of the plane, dead on the shore. Five men in a shallow grave north of the cabin site. At least according to me. Boxer Face sat in the passenger's seat, looking back at me every few minutes. It was hard to read his expression. He was probably thinking twenty different things at once. I was sure one of those things was just how good it would feel to open the door and toss us right out of the plane.

They didn't ask me to tell the rest of my story, as I had promised. They were saving that for the ground.

We flew for an hour and a half. The drone of the engines eventually got to me, and I drifted in and out of a trance as we bounced and buzzed our way all the way to a small airport. It was a true amphibian plane, one that could land on pavement as well as water. When we got out, three OPP cars and an ambulance were waiting for us.

They put Vinnie in the back of the ambulance and me in the

back of one of the cars. About a half hour later, I was sitting in a bed in the clinic with an IV in one arm and the other arm handcuffed to the bed rail. A doctor was cutting the laces off my boots with scissors while the two constables stood by watching.

"How long were you out there?" he asked.

"Most of two days."

"Immersion foot," he said. "Let's see how bad."

"What about Vinnie? How's he doing?"

The doctor looked up at the officers. "I don't know," he said. "Someone else is working on him."

When he finally slipped the boot and sock off, the foot was purple. It looked and felt like some alien thing. "Not good," he said.

"What do you have to do now?"

"We have to let them warm up slowly," he said. "And then it's just a matter of keeping them dry and elevated." He went to work on the other boot.

"Can one of you guys go see how Vinnie is doing?" I said.

Neither of them moved. They both stood there and looked at me with their hands folded across their chests.

"Thanks a lot," I said.

Another man, vaguely familiar to me, came in while the doctor was getting my other boot off. That foot looked just as bad. "Nice case of trench foot," he said. "You're gonna be hurting for a long time."

"Can you tell me about my friend?" I said.

"They're cleaning out his wound right now. That duct tape probably saved his life. Was that your idea?"

"It's all we had to work with."

"That spear that killed Mr. Gannon, was that yours, too?"

"Yes."

"Who actually killed him?"

"We both did. We had to."

"Mr. McKnight, who physically ran the spear through Mr. Gannon's body?"

"Vinnie did."

He let out a long breath, closed his eyes, and pinched the bridge of his nose. I realized where I had seen him before. He was the staff sergeant we had seen at the station. This was obviously supposed to be his day off, because he wasn't wearing his uniform.

"Your name is Moreland," I said. "You're the detachment commander."

"Yes."

"You've got to understand something. We didn't kill Constable DeMers."

"He was three months away from retirement. Did you know that?"

"He mentioned it, yes."

He opened his case and took out a tape recorder. "So start at the beginning."

That's what I did. I told him everything, from the first time we came up to the lodge, to meeting Guy and his grandfather, flying up to the lake, finding the dead bodies, and then the other plane landing. I told him the whole thing from start to finish, and then I told it to him again, this time with some other men standing around listening to me. The doctor took out the IV and gave me some water. He asked me what I thought I could eat. I said anything they had. While I was waiting for the food, some men from the Royal Mounted Canadian Police came in and I had to tell the whole story one more time.

The food came right in the middle of my story. It was turkey and mashed potatoes with gravy. I asked the men to forgive my bad manners as I dug into my own little early Thanksgiving.

When they were all gone, a new constable I'd never seen before stayed to watch me. He looked like he had just started shaving, and he sat in a chair and never took his eyes off me once, like he was expecting me to hop up at any second and try to escape. I lay there, still cuffed to the bed, with my legs propped up with pillows, my feet in the air.

I must have passed out for a while. When I woke up, the constable had been replaced by Boxer Face. The room was in shadows. I asked the man about Vinnie, but he had nothing to say to me.

"You've got to uncuff me," I said. "I need to use the bathroom."

Nothing. He didn't even blink.

"Look, if I was told to sit in a chair and watch somebody who I thought might have killed one of my fellow officers, I'd be acting the same way. Hell, I'd be tempted to do a lot more than just give him the silent treatment."

He stared at me.

"But you need to know something," I said. "I didn't kill him. Okay?"

"If you need to take a piss," he finally said, "then use the bottle."

"You're a real pal," I said. Then I proceeded to attempt the impossible—urinating into a urinal bottle with one hand cuffed to the rail.

"I don't suppose you'd feel like taking this away," I said.

"What do you think?"

I rang the nurse for some help, then I settled back and tried to sleep a little bit. It didn't work. I couldn't stop thinking about Vinnie, wondering where the hell he was and how he was doing.

And more than anything, I couldn't stop wondering what had really happened up there. And why. I couldn't stop thinking about it.

Hours later, when it was dark in the room and the constable had been replaced by yet another, I finally drifted off into a hazy half sleep. In my head I saw pine trees, and a plane turning slowly in the middle of a lake, and the wide-open eyes of a dead man.

And bears.

* * *

The doctor looked at my feet again in the morning. He told me the color was a lot better, and asked me how they felt.

"Like hell," I said. "They itch like crazy."

"That's to be expected," he said.

"Any chance I could get some socks? I feel like Frankenstein's monster lying here."

"I'll see what I can do," he said. "I hope you like white cotton socks, because that's all you'll be wearing for the next few weeks."

"Fine, whatever. Now can you tell me how my friend is doing?"

"Not too bad, considering. He did lose part of his right ear."

"I figured that. Can I see him?"

The doctor looked at the constable who was lucky enough to draw chair duty that morning. "That's not up to me," the doctor said. "There are a couple of men in with him right now, asking more questions."

"I'm sure I'm next," I said.

I was right. About an hour later, two men came in the room. They were wearing dark gray suits and expensive hair, and I wasn't surprised when they told me they were from the FBI. It made sense they were there, with five dead men out of seven being Americans. They asked me all the same questions. I gave them the same story. They promised me they'd be speaking to me again if and when I got back to America. If and when, they said.

I ate some more. I lay there in the bed, quietly going insane.

Then Constable Reynaud walked in the room. She looked like hell. She looked like she was having almost as bad a week as I was. She told the constable on duty that he could leave, and then she unlocked my handcuffs.

"We found the bodies," she said. "Right where you said they'd be."

"And Gannon, I assume." I rubbed my wrist, where the cuff had been.

"Yes, of course. I could see the body from the plane. I waited there for a couple of hours until they came and got me."

"I'm sorry about your partner." I didn't know what else to say.

"I talked to him while I was waiting. I promised him I'd find out what really happened out there."

"I want to know just as badly as you do," I said. "Have they figured out when Albright and those other men were killed? Tom, I mean."

"They think about ten days ago. Long before you ever got there."

"Yes," I said. "That's right."

"One of the men at the crime scene must have seen your truck go by. Apparently, he mentioned this to Claude, so Claude went up there and saw your truck parked outside the Berards' house."

"And he must have figured—"

"That you didn't go home like we told you. That you got Guy and his grandfather to fly you up to the lake. The Berards told me what happened, McKnight. They said Claude was so mad at you guys, he wanted to fly out there and bring you back, and then kick your asses all the way back to Michigan. He could've called it in, had one of the OPP planes fly up there to pick you up. But he didn't. You wanna know why?"

I had a sick feeling I already knew the answer. "Why?"

"He told them that if he called it in and they had to get a plane up there, then both of you would definitely be charged with felony obstruction, and that the Berards might even be charged, too. As mad as he was at you guys, he still didn't want to see you in serious trouble. Do you understand what I'm telling you?"

"Yes. I do."

"He wasn't about to fly out there in Mr. Berard's plane, though.

Did you know that plane is supposed to be out of service?"

"No."

"He stopped doing fly-in hunts three years ago. He was supposed to get it inspected and recertified before taking it up again. So Claude took Mr. Berard's keys and told them both to sit tight. He said he'd give Hank Gannon a call over at the lodge. His plane was faster, anyway."

"You didn't know anything about this?"

"I was back at the station. He knew I wouldn't have let him go out there. That's the kind of thing he'd do all the time, McKnight. He used to drive me crazy."

She shook her head, almost smiling.

"I don't know if I would have made him call it in or not," she said, "but at least I would have made him take me with him."

"If you had gone," I said, "you'd probably be dead now."

"He wouldn't have gotten both of us."

"If you weren't expecting it," I said, "and if he had gotten both of you in front of him—"

"You guys would have been his out," she said. "Gannon would have made it look like it was all on you."

"It really was just him? Nobody else from the lodge was involved?"

"It doesn't look like it. It turns out Helen and the Trembleys weren't even around last Saturday. That's the day those men supposedly flew back."

"I knew about Helen not being there. Trembley, that's Ron and Millie, right?"

"Yeah. They were all in Timmins that day, buying storage containers, so they could pack everything up and move."

"So you talked to them," I said. "I mean, since yesterday—"

"Three months, McKnight. He was three months away from retirement. This was like the last thing he could do for somebody.

Flying out there like a cowboy, getting you and your friend out of there, saving you from going to jail. That was the last big stupid thing he was gonna do before he retired."

I closed my eyes.

"The Berards waited around all day yesterday. By this morning, when they still hadn't heard anything, they finally decided they had to call us. I went up there, got the whole story from them, drove over to the lodge. The plane wasn't there. Everybody was gone. The whole place was closed up. We tried reaching him on the radio—"

She stopped. She looked out the window.

"The Northeast regional commander himself called me and asked me how I could not know where my own partner was for a day and a half. Then he told me to get over to the airport, because I was going out to help look for him."

She rattled the cuffs around, and then pulled them tight.

"Gannon killed him. He flew him up there and killed him. He shot him right in the back. While I stayed behind, not doing a damned thing."

I let the silence hang there for a moment, not sure if I should say anything. "Do you have any idea what this is all about?" I finally said. "I mean, once it was done, he was afraid of what your partner would find up there. That almost makes sense. But to kill those other men like that in the first place—"

"We don't know, McKnight."

"Those men were all from Detroit. You've got no idea how they figured into this?"

"Not right now."

"This isn't over," I said. "We've got to find out what happened."

She looked at me. "I'm not going to talk about this anymore. You need to go home and get well. And cooperate with whoever you need to, back in Michigan."

"I'm free to go?"

"Yes, you are."

"And Vinnie?"

"Yes."

"I lost my partner, too," I said.

She took a moment to think about it. "When was this?"

"In Detroit, when I was a cop. My partner and I were both shot. He died. I didn't. I spent a lot of time blaming myself."

"So you're saying you know how it feels."

"Yes."

"I shouldn't have hit you before," she said. "But if I don't get out of here right now, I swear I'm gonna do it again."

"I understand."

"Like hell you do," she said. And then she left.

Chapter Twenty

An hour later I was standing. That was my big accomplishment so far that day. It felt like somebody had put needles all over the floor, but I was on my feet and that meant I could move around and maybe even get out of there. I was slowly walking around the bed when Guy and Maskwa appeared in the doorway. Maskwa came right up to me and grabbed both of my arms.

"Alex," he said. "How are you feeling?"

"I'm standing," I said. "That's enough for right now."

He kept studying me. "You look terrible."

"Don't worry about me," I said. "Have you seen Vinnie?"

"Yes. His face—"

"He was actually very lucky. Although I'm sure he doesn't feel that way."

Maskwa looked at his grandson, then back at me, shaking his head slowly. "We are so sorry," he said. "We were trying to do the right thing."

"I know, Maskwa. Nobody could have imagined this."

"The constable wouldn't let us fly back to get you. He told us he was going to go get you himself."

"He may have saved your lives."

He looked at me close. "DeMers. That was his name, right?"

"Yes."

"I still can't believe it."

"At least we found Tom," I said. "At least we did that much."

"You are a good friend, Alex. And now Vinnie needs you more than ever. Time will heal his body, but his spirit . . . It is very sick. You must know that."

"We'll take care of him," I said. "I will, and his family."

"Good, good. And if you ever need anything from us. Anything. You call us."

"There is one thing." I said.

"Anything."

I gave him my keys. "I left my truck at your house."

He laughed. "Of course. We'll bring it over."

While I was waiting for them, I asked the nurse for something to put on my feet. She brought me some slippers that looked like folded-up old newspapers, maybe size 15 or so. They barely fit on my swollen feet. After a couple more minutes of practice, I went padding down the hall at one mile per hour until I found Vinnie's room. Fortunately, it wasn't hard. The entire Hearst Medical Center might have had ten rooms total, and Vinnie's was two doors down from mine.

He was lying on the bed when I came in. The whole right side of his face was bandaged, and his feet were propped up in the air, just like mine had been. He was staring at the ceiling.

"Vinnie," I said.

He looked over at me, then down at my feet. "Nice slippers."

"Are you all right?"

"Never better."

"Vinnie, I'm serious. Are you okay?" If his spirit was sick, like Maskwa had said, I couldn't see it.

He sat up in the bed. "They told me your feet were twice as bad as mine. We're gonna have to get you some better boots next time."

"Next time, eh?"

"I promised to buy you a beer," he said. "Let's get out of here."

We found our clothes, signed some papers, and then waited for a prescription for Vinnie. An hour later, the staff sergeant came to see us one more time. He asked us a couple more questions, nothing he hadn't asked before. He seemed reluctant to let us go, but finally he did. We stood by the front door, waiting for Guy and Maskwa to bring the truck around. It was a decent day for October in Ontario—no snow, no rain. The temperature was even above freezing. It made it a little easier to walk outside in our cheap slippers when the truck showed up. We said goodbye to Guy and Maskwa again, and then we were finally on our way home. It was hard to feel the pedals under my feet, but I made do. As we left the medical center, I couldn't help noticing that the flag was flying at half-mast.

"Do you think you should call home?" I said.

"The constable told me she already called them yesterday."

"She called your mother?"

"Yes, she did. She told her I'd be home soon."

"Wait a minute," I said. "How come they're not here?"

"What do you mean?"

"Your whole family. I'm surprised they weren't camped out in the parking lot."

"I didn't want them to come up here," he said. "I'm not ready to see them yet."

"Well, it was good of her to call your family. Especially after what she went through herself yesterday."

He looked at me. "Are you surprised?"

"No. She just didn't seem very happy with us today."

He looked back out the window. "Can you blame her?"

"That reminds me," I said, picking up the phone. "Remember we had all those messages? As long as we're still in town, with the cell tower..." I turned on the phone and checked the missed calls.

"Twenty-seven calls in all," I said. "They just kept calling me."

"When was the last call?"

"Let's see. Yesterday. Around two o'clock."

"None since then? They just stopped?"

"Yes."

"They must have found out," he said. "That guy who called you, didn't he say he was Red's brother?"

"Yeah, he did."

"So I guess I know how he feels." He kept looking out the window.

"Yes," I said. "I suppose so."

He didn't say anything. I kept driving. I couldn't help thinking about the man's voice, the faraway voice of Red Albright's brother—he had come all the way up here himself, just as we had done. He just wanted to know what the hell was going on. I couldn't blame him for that, despite his lack of manners. He just wanted to know.

And now he did.

Home was eight hours away, down the same roads we had already driven on, through the same trees. It was only a few days before, but now it all felt different. The whole world had changed.

Vinnie slept for a while. He almost looked peaceful, until I'd hit a bump or until his mind would cycle through all the things he'd seen and he'd wake up with a start.

"Alex," he said, more than once, with a sudden panic in his voice.

"It's okay, Vinnie. We're almost home. Go back to sleep."

I stopped at a gas station in Wawa. I got out and pumped the gas, standing there in my cheap slippers and my coat covered with dried mud. I shifted my weight back and forth from one burning foot to the other. When I paid the man, he looked at me like I was a mental patient.

The day dragged on. I kept driving. I was tired, but I'd be damned if I was going to stop anywhere short of home. From Wawa we drove south along the shores of Lake Superior, around Batchawana Bay, into Soo Canada. We were so close to home now. All we had to do was get over the bridge.

"Oh, horseshit," I said. "They're gonna take one look at us and . . . God damn it."

I picked up the cell phone and called information, got through to the OPP station in Hearst, and asked if Constable Reynaud was still around. A minute later, I heard her voice.

"Constable," I said. "You're still there. This is Alex."

"What is it, McKnight?"

"We're coming up to the bridge. Any chance you could call ahead and clear the way for us?"

"You're all the way down there already? You shouldn't have driven so far in your condition. It's not safe."

"I would have thought you'd be happy to get us out of the country."

"Don't get cute with me, McKnight. All right? It's bad enough."

"I'm sorry. We just want to get home."

"I'll call right now," she said. "I'll tell them to expect two men who look like shit."

"That sounds about right," I said. "Vinnie tells me you called his mother personally. I'm glad I got the chance to thank you for that."

There was a silence on the line. "Mrs. LeBlanc sounded like a good woman," she said. "Now if you'll excuse me."

"Good night," I said. "I'm sorry about your partner."

She hung up.

I rolled through town and onto the International Bridge. Vinnie woke up and looked out at the water. "The bridge," he said.

"Don't worry, they know we're coming."

When we pulled into the American customs booth, the man had obviously gotten the message. He looked us both over and whistled. "They said you'd look bad, but good Lord."

The sun was going down when we hit Michigan soil. We had forty-five minutes to go. Forty-five minutes to my own bed.

I drove the roads I knew so well, from Soo Michigan to Paradise, through the Hiawatha National Forest, along the southern rim of Whitefish Bay. It was too dark to see the water now. The sign on the edge of town said WELCOME TO PARADISE! WE'RE GLAD YOU MADE IT! I drove by the sign, stopped at the blinking red light, went past Jackie's place to our access road.

Drop Vinnie off at his house, I thought. Get him inside, make sure he's comfortable. Then go home and go to bed. And sleep for at least three days.

As I pulled onto my road, I was blinded by a pair of headlights.

"Who the hell?" I couldn't imagine who was on their way out. Then I remembered all the hunters who were due to check out of my cabins. I would have been back in plenty of time to see them off, if everything hadn't gone to hell.

I stopped the truck and opened my door. It was a long, black sedan. I didn't recognize it. Two men got out.

They weren't hunters. That was obvious. Then it came to me. The two FBI guys said they'd be in touch. They didn't waste any time.

But I was wrong again. It wasn't the FBI. I realized that as soon as I saw their faces, and the guns in their hands.

They had my cell phone number. With a little work, you could find out my address. And here they were.

They were on top of us before I could do a thing. No time to back up, no time to get out and run—not that we would have been able to run, anyway.

"Out of the truck," the one man said. He said it in a matter-of-fact way, the way you'd tell a mover where to put the furniture. The guy on Vinnie's side, he looked a little more serious about it. He had a big nose, but with all the advance publicity, I was expecting something even bigger.

I looked at my man closely as I got out. He was thick in the neck and shoulders, the way an old football player would look, years after he's stopped playing. My guess was linebacker turned nightclub bouncer. He had a nice leather jacket on, a high forehead with thinning hair on top. I understand steroids are murder on the hair. There was a diamond earring in his right ear.

"Nice and easy," he said. He gave me a quick pat-down and turned me around to face the other man across the bed of my truck. The whole scene was side-lit by the glare of the headlights.

"Which one of you is McKnight?" the man with the nose said. Red's brother. He was smaller, built more like a baseball player. He had a leather jacket on, too—probably a size L to my man's XXL. He was using a gun a lot more, holding it right to Vinnie's temple, just above the tape.

"I am," I said. I looked at Vinnie. He was doing just fine, all things considered.

"And you're the Indian?" He pulled his head back by the hair. Vinnie didn't flinch. "Yes."

"Start talking."

"About?"

"Why did you call Red?"

223

"We were looking for my brother," Vinnie said. "Red hired him as a guide."

"Yeah, I know that."

"Then what do you want from us?"

Easy, Vinnie. I tried to catch his eye.

"What I want from you, you stupid fucking Indian, is the whole story." He got a tighter hold on Vinnie's hair, came closer to him, put his face right next to Vinnie's. "What the fuck happened up there?"

"Did the police call you?"

"They called his wife. They said he was buried in the ground up there."

"They all were. My brother, your brother. All of them."

The man shook his head. "Who did this?"

"We don't know," Vinnie said. "We know a man named Gannon was involved. That's all."

"No. No, that's not good enough. You hear me? That's not fucking good enough. My brother is dead. And I want to know why."

"So do I," Vinnie said. His voice was even, his eyes clear. There was a supernatural calm all over him, and it was scaring the hell out of me.

"So talk," the man said. "Tell me what you know about this. You gotta know something. You were up there, weren't you? Were you involved in this? Was this something you and your Indian brother did?"

"No," Vinnie said. "We didn't. And you can stop talking like that. If you want to kill us, go ahead. After what we've been through, I don't even care anymore. Go ahead and put a bullet in my head if you want, but stop talking about my brother that way."

That threw him a little bit. His eyes got wider, and I was sure he was about to do something stupid. It was a good time to speak up.

"We found him," I said. "We found your brother."

He looked over the truck bed at me. "Where?"

"Out in the woods. Where Gannon had buried him, along with the others."

He took a few hard breaths. Everything else was still, all around us. "You found Red?"

"That man you're holding on to, you see the bandages on his face?"

"Yeah?"

"Gannon shot him. He blew part of his ear right off."

He looked closer. "Okay. Then what?"

If I was gonna do this, I had to sell it all the way. It seemed like our only way out. "You wanna know what this man did to Gannon? You wanna hear what this man did to the man who killed your brother?"

"Yes, I wanna hear it."

"He took a long, heavy stick," I said, "and he sharpened it. I distracted Gannon, so Vinnie could sneak up behind him. We didn't have any other weapons. You understand what I'm saying? All we had were sticks."

"Go on."

"While Gannon was shooting at me, Vinnie came up behind him and ran that stick right through his back. If he had gotten him in the heart, he would have died almost immediately, but that's not the way it happened."

"How did it go?" he said. "Tell me."

"The stick must have gone through his lung. The blood was such a bright color. He was pumping that blood right out of his lungs, all over the ground."

"How long did it take him to die?"

"A long time," I said. "He was bleeding on that ground for a long, long time."

"Were his eyes open? Did he say anything to you?"

"His eyes were open. He tried to say something, but he couldn't. He was drowning in his own blood. He was choking on it."

There were tears in the man's eyes. "You're telling me this man killed the man who killed my brother."

"Yes," I said. "He ran a stick through his chest and he died a horrible, painful death. That's what this man did."

"This man right here." He pulled the gun away from his head.

"He did it for his brother," I said. "And for your brother. And the other men. And me. He saved my life."

The man let go of Vinnie. He bent over and put his hands on his knees, the gun pointing at the ground. He took a few wet breaths through his nose and shook his head. "Is that it?" he said. "Is that all there is? What was this guy's name again?"

"Gannon. Hank Gannon."

"He did all this by himself?"

"We don't know that," I said. I figured, what the hell, go ahead and push your luck. "Maybe you can help us figure it out."

The man stood up straight and looked me in the eye. "What do you mean?"

"We're just wondering. If somebody else was involved, maybe it was one of the other men in the hunting party. Or at least somebody else that you'd know about."

He thought hard. He looked past me, at the big man standing behind me. "What do you think, Jay? Who could it be?"

I sneaked a look at him. He was standing there with both hands on his gun. He was looking at the ground. "I'm just thinking," he said.

"What?"

"You know."

"No, man. Are you serious?"

"What are we talking about?" I said.

The sudden look on his face told me I was pushing it a little too far.

"Never mind," I said. "We just want some answers. As much as you do."

"Well, don't you worry about it," he said. "If we find out there's somebody else still walking around, we'll make that person pay. Believe me, we'll turn them fucking inside out."

He stood there for a long time, breathing hard and shaking his head. The big guy crossed his arms and looked around at the trees. I wasn't sure what to do. Ask them if we could go? Invite them down to the Glasgow for a drink?

"I was supposed to be up there," he finally said. "Those guys never go hunting without me. Until this time."

It made sense. That's why there were five men instead of six.

"I should have been there," he said. "I should be in the ground with Red."

The big man looked at the sky and shook his head.

"I hope you guys understand why we're here," he said. He put the gun back in his coat. "I've been going a little crazy ever since I found out. I just have to do something about it, you know what I mean?"

"Yes," I said. "I understand."

"We drove all the way up there," he said. "And then all the way home. And then when we heard. . . . Fuck, we drove all the way here. We waited around for you. This is some kind of little shit town you got here."

He looked down at Vinnie's feet. "What's with the slippers?"

"It's a long story," I said.

"Yeah, well, we got some things to do now. We gotta go talk to some people. Let's get out of here, Jay . . ."

They went back to their car.

"Hey," he said, standing in the glare of the headlights. His voice caught as he asked us his final questions. "Is it true what they said? Did my brother really get set on fire up there?"

"Yes," I said. "They were burned."

He stood there for a long moment, looking up at the sky.

The big guy spoke up again. "They were burned, Dal."

"Yeah, I heard the man."

"I'm just saying—"

"That's enough. Let's go."

They got in the car and drove it around the truck. Their wheels spun as they edged off the road into the heavy grass. For a moment I thought we'd end up standing in the mud in our hospital slippers, trying to push them out. That would clinch the evening, right there. But then the wheels found purchase and they were free. I watched the glowing taillights as they turned right onto the main road and were gone.

"Are you all right?" I said.

Vinnie stood there holding on to the side of the truck. "Yeah, I'm just fine," he said. "That was actually a good warm-up."

"How's that?"

"Tomorrow will be worse," he said. "That's when I've got to face my family."

Chapter Twenty-One

When I woke up, it was snowing. It was a light October flurry, nothing to get the snowplow out for. The clock said 12:34. I did the math and figured I'd been sleeping for about fourteen hours. It didn't feel like nearly enough.

My feet hurt when I put them on the cold floor. But I could walk a little better. I wasn't ready for the decathlon, but at least I could start getting around again. I took a long hot shower, shaved six days of beard off my face, and got myself dressed. I put on clean white socks and very carefully stepped into a pair of old shoes.

As I fired up the truck, it felt strange not having Vinnie sitting there next to me. When I drove down my road, I noticed that his truck was gone. He must have been over at his mother's house. For a second I thought I should go over there myself, but then something told me I should leave them alone for one day, at least. I hoped it wasn't just me being afraid to face Mrs. LeBlanc.

I went down to the Glasgow Inn. Jackie looked me over like

I was the walking dead and made me a cheese omelet with five eggs. He served it to me with a cold Canadian Molson as I put my feet up by the fire. If he had asked me for everything I owned, I would have given it to him right then.

"I've already heard the basics," he said as he sat down next to me. "Hell, it was on the front page of the Soo *Evening News*. Are you gonna tell me the rest?"

I spent the next hour going through the whole story for him. It felt good to tell him, like maybe I was almost ready to let go of it. Almost. When I was done, he got me another Canadian and I fell asleep in front of the fire.

When I went back home, I still didn't see Vinnie's truck in his driveway, but there was a note from him pinned on my door. "Service for Tom," it read. "1:00 tomorrow. See you there."

I drove down to the end of my road. The blue tarp was still tied tight over the walls we had started. The center post we had stuck in there was doing its job, letting the light snowfall glide off to the ground.

I can't believe it, I said to myself. I actually started building this cabin. In October. That's how crazy I was.

I checked the other cabins on my way back. Two were still occupied, the other two empty. In both cases, the men had left while I was up in Canada. And in both cases, the cabins were spotless and money had been left in envelopes. Bow hunters, I thought. God bless them.

There was a message on my machine when I got back to my cabin. The two men from the FBI were checking up on me, wanted to make sure I was back in the country. I called the number they left, and told them I was here in Michigan and not planning on going anywhere. That seemed to satisfy them for the time being. They knew where to find me if they had any more questions. I tried to ask the man a few questions of my own. He told me they were working hard on the case but didn't have anything to say about it yet.

I went back down to the Glasgow for dinner that evening. I ate sitting by the fire again, and as I sat there feeling a hell of a lot better than the day before, I couldn't help thinking about it. Again. Five men dead, a vehicle moved several miles. Somebody else had to help Gannon do this. But who?

And those men from last night, the big man, Jay, and Red's brother—what was his name? I replayed the whole scene in my mind. Dal, he called him—the man with the look in his eyes like he'd be capable of anything. And the way they were talking. I tried to remember it, word for word.

What?

You know.

No, man. Are you serious?

These men knew something. At least they had an idea. If anyone could lead us to the answers, it was these two men.

So rest up, Vinnie. We've got some work to do.

I went to bed early that night, and slept in again the next morning. I almost felt human. I was able to put shoes on my feet without incident, and I could even walk around a little bit without feeling like I was ninety years old. I put on my old black suit, spent a few minutes tying my tie, and then drove down past Vinnie's house. He wasn't there, so I headed over to the reservation. There were a lot of cars at the Cultural Center, so I knew I was in the right place.

When I went inside, I saw that everyone had gathered in the main hall. There had to be two hundred people there. They were all dressed nicely, but nobody was in black. The room itself was simple, with a high ceiling and drawings of animals and mountains and trees, along with the Bay Mills crest of four feathers. A great fireplace stood in the center of the room. The fire was going strong, and the sweet smell of burning tobacco hung in the air.

Vinnie came to me and took my right hand. His face was still taped up. "Alex," he said. "You look a lot better."

"So do you," I said, although it felt like a lie. He still looked totally worn out, even worse now than before, like something had been taken from inside him.

He took me to his mother, the moment I had been dreading all along. But she took my face in both hands and kissed me. "Thank you," she said. Her face was red with grief. "Thank you for everything you've done."

I didn't have any words for her. I took her hands and held them.

"You're my son now," she said. "I hope you know that. You are my son."

I shook hands with the rest of Vinnie's family, losing count around thirty. I couldn't help noticing there was no coffin in the room, and then it hit me. Tom's body was probably still up in Canada, in some forensics lab. I wondered how they could be having his funeral without him. Then I found out. A traditional Ojibwa funeral lasts for days. You go, you spend time with the family, you offer tobacco in the fireplace, you eat, you go home. And then you come back the next day.

A man stood up to speak. The room went silent as he talked about the Path of Life, and what a man must do to live in peace, and how when a man's time on this earth is over, he must follow the setting sun to the west, crossing over the Path of Souls to the Land of Souls. It made me think of Mrs. LeBlanc and what she had said about Tom's Ojibwa name—how being named for the western sky was a bad omen. It turned out she was right.

I ate with the family, sitting at the long table with cousins and aunts and uncles all around me. I wondered if me being there was painful for them. It must have made them think about what had happened to Tom. The flames burned in the fireplace as we sat there together.

After the dinner I said goodbye to Vinnie and his family. Vinnie followed me outside into the cold night air and stood there breathing it in with me. "I appreciate you coming," he said.

"Least I could do, Vinnie."

"You don't have to spend the whole time over here, but I'm sure my mother would appreciate it if you stopped by again."

"I will," I said. "And we've got some other things to talk about."

He looked at me. "I can't even think right now, Alex. Give me some time, okay?"

"Okay." Then I said good night and went home to bed.

When I stopped in at Jackie's the next morning, he asked me where I had been the night before. I told him about the funeral, how it would go on for days. He told me to wait while he went upstairs to put his suit on. He put a sign on the front door, reading GONE TO A FUNERAL, and then he went with me and met all of Vinnie's family.

Some people stood up after dinner and told stories about Tom, about all the funny things he had done, about all the times he had gone out of his way to help somebody. Vinnie stood up toward the end and tried to say something. He started to tell a story about the first fishing trip he and Tom had gone on, when they were little kids. Vinnie couldn't bring himself to stick the hook through the worm, so Tom had told him to stop acting like a *chimook,* which is Ojibwa slang for a white man. That got a laugh, but Vinnie couldn't continue the story. He sat down next to his mother and she rubbed his back.

When Jackie and I were about to leave, Vinnie came to us and thanked us for coming.

"You don't look so good," I said. I had been wanting to talk to him about the men from Detroit, but now that I saw him I knew it would have to wait.

"I can't sleep," he said. "Every time I close my eyes, I see the same thing." He didn't have to tell me what.

That was the second day of the funeral.

On the third day, I came around dinnertime again. I heard some more stories about Tom. Vinnie didn't try to speak this time. I was walking almost normally now, and feeling like I had most of my energy back.

Vinnie looked even worse than the day before. I didn't try to talk to him at all. I went home, wondering what in the world I could do for him.

Maskwa was right. His spirit was sick. Even I could see it now.

That was the third day.

On the fourth day, Vinnie collapsed. I picked him up off the floor, with some help from his cousins. We sat him down, fanned him, and tried to make him drink some water. Like a prizefighter, he tried to shake us off and get back on his feet.

"I'm all right," he said. "Come on, guys. I just blacked out for a second. I'm all right."

He wouldn't go home. I offered to take him there myself and stay with him. But he refused. I went home by myself.

On the fifth day, Tom's remains finally arrived from Canada. The last day of the funeral moved from the Cultural Center over to the Blessed Kateri Tekakwitha, a Catholic church located right on the reservation, between the two casinos. They did a Catholic funeral mass and then drove Tom's coffin up to the top of Mission Hill. It was a cold day, as gray as only a Michigan October day can get. They buried Tom in the reservation's graveyard, facing west.

When they were done, Vinnie went off by himself and looked out over the cliff. I went and joined him and looked down at the scene below—at Spectacle Lake and the new golf course, at all the pine and birch trees and Waishkey Bay and beyond that the heart of Lake Superior. There was a wooden shelter there on the overlook, with a couple of benches underneath. I had heard this was a party spot for young men on the reservation, but I didn't see any trash lying around. Someone had taken some yellow paint and carefully written a message on the shelter. PLEASE RESPECT THE LAND. THE SPIRITS OF OUR ANCESTORS LIVE HERE.

"It's a nice view up here," I said. "It's a good place to end up." I felt stupid as soon as I said it, but Vinnie turned to me and gave me a weak smile.

"It's a good place," he said.

"Your mother told me I'm her son now," I said. "Does that mean we're brothers?"

"Of course it does."

"I never got to ask you," I said. "What does that word mean? The one you called me at the lodge?"

"I don't remember that."

"When we first got there, and we were stuck in the mud. You said my Ojibwa name would be Mada-something."

"Oh, now I remember. Madawayash."

"That's it. What does it mean?"

"Well, you have to remember what we were going through at the time."

"Yeah, yeah," I said. "Just tell me."

"It means 'chattering wind.'"

"Good thing you're my brother now or I'd have to smack you."

"If you're my brother, that means you have to come to the sweat with me."

"A sweat? Is that part of the funeral?"

"No, it's something they're doing for me," he said. "It'll be good for you, too."

"I've been wanting to talk to you about some things I've been thinking about," I said. "About Red's brother and that other guy, and some of the things they said. I promised myself I'd wait until you felt better."

"I appreciate that."

"The problem is, I don't want the trail to get cold. You know what I mean?"

"I don't want you to do this, Alex."

"What are you talking about?"

"Tom is gone. We can't change that."

It took a moment for it to sink in. "Vinnie," I said, "are we going to find out what really happened, or not?"

"Come on," he said. "We'll talk about it later." He turned to go.

"Vinnie—"

"Later, Alex. I promise."

I watched him get into one of the cars. I stood there for a while, breathing in the cold air, and then I finally went to my truck and followed them.

We ended up over at the home of his cousin Buck, just down the street from his mother's house. Buck had built a little sweat lodge in the backyard. It was a half sphere, about ten feet in diameter, made by lashing saplings together and covering them with canvas and old rugs. The men already had a fire going, several yards from the lodge. They were heating rocks in the fire, and then moving them into the lodge with a long shovel.

There were eleven men, counting me. The others stripped down to their underwear, piling their clothes on the ground. They waited patiently until everyone was standing there together, these mostly naked men of all ages, with long dark hair over their shoulders. I couldn't imagine doing the same on a day like this, but I figured what the hell. I'd certainly done worse things on days even colder than this one. Like jumping into a lake so a madman could shoot at me.

I almost choked on the steam when I went into the lodge, but it was warm and made every muscle in my body go loose. There was a faint light from the sparks and from the glowing rocks in the center pit. I felt my way over to the edge and sat down with the other men, closing my eyes and letting the steam fill my lungs. Someone dipped a large ladle into a bucket of water and poured it on the rocks. Then he added some sage. One of the four medicines, that much I knew. I sat there hoping that the medicine would work and that it would make Vinnie start feeling like himself again.

That little scene up on the cliff. Vinnie not wanting to talk about it, or to even think about what to do next. That wasn't the Vinnie I knew.

We sat in the lodge for at least an hour. It was better than any sauna I had ever been in. The sweat rolled down over my face, as if every poison in my body and every bad thought in my mind were being drawn out by the heat. Nobody said a word.

Finally, one man opened a flap and we all crawled out. The air felt as cold as the water had been in that lake, but I didn't shiver. Instead I felt a tingling all over my body, and a lightness in my chest. I put my clothes back on, moving in slow motion. When I was dressed, I looked around for Vinnie, but didn't see him. He was still in the lodge, fast asleep.

I helped a couple of his cousins carry him out of the lodge and into one of the cars. He didn't wake up, and we didn't bother dressing him. We just wrapped him up in blankets.

"Just take him to his house," I said. "I'll take care of him."

"We'll take him home," Buck said.

"Good, I'll follow you."

"No," he said. "I mean we'll take him to the reservation." He stood there in front of the car door, his body between me and Vinnie. He was four inches taller than me. The other cousins were all looking at me.

This was the look. I'd seen it before. Between one moment and the next, my welcome among them had ended. I was an outsider again.

"Thank you for everything you did," Buck said. "We'll take care of Vinnie now."

Thank you, he says. The man says thank you and they'll take care of him now. I had a sudden urge to fight them, all of them at once. They would have taken me apart, but what the hell.

"He's my brother now," I said. "You understand? Vinnie's my brother."

Nobody said a word.

"You can't change that," I said. "This time you're not going to come between us."

Buck didn't move.

There was nothing else to do. I shook my head and left. As I looked in the rearview mirror, they were all still standing there, watching me drive away.

I headed back home. I pointed the truck straight down the road and I drove. I was tired and used up and empty. Finally, I pulled off the road. I sat there for five or six minutes, staring off into nothing. The wind kicked up and whistled past the windows. I thought about how good it would feel to go sit by the fire at Jackie's place. Put your feet up and forget about it.

Then I turned the truck around and went back the way I came. I drove due east, straight toward Sault Ste. Marie.

If I was going to do something stupid, I couldn't do it alone. And if Vinnie couldn't help me now, then I knew there was only one other choice.

It was time to talk to my old partner, Leon Prudell.

Chapter Twenty-Two

I found Leon Prudell at the big custom motor sports shop on Three Mile Road. It was the kind of place that'll sell you a snow-mobile in the winter, an outboard motor in the spring, and a four-wheel all-terrain vehicle for hunting season. I found Leon in the showroom, pointing out the features of an Arctic Cat to a pro-spective buyer and his young son. "This is a hell of a sled," I heard him say. I knew that's what the real riders call them. They're sleds, not snowmobiles.

When he spotted me, he stood up straight and switched off the sales pitch. "Excuse me," he said, and then he came over to me and took my right hand.

"Leon," I said. He was the same old Leon, 240 pounds of nervous energy and wild orange hair—the Leon who had always wanted to be a private eye, the Leon who introduced himself to me by trying to take me apart in Jackie's parking lot, and who would later talk me into becoming his silent partner in the short-lived Prudell-McKnight Investigations. He tried to go it alone after that, but it didn't work out. Sault Ste. Marie just isn't the right market for a private investigator, especially when everybody in town remembers you as the goofy fat kid in the back of the class. That's why he was selling snowmobiles now. He wore a black windbreaker with the name of the business on one side of the zipper, and "Leon" on the other.

"Alex, my God. Are you all right?"

"You must have heard—"

"Of course I did. You were in the paper. You and Vinnie. I'm sorry I didn't get out to the funeral."

"Don't worry about that," I said. "Listen, I hate to bother you, but I don't know who else to ask."

"Hey, once a partner, always a partner," he said. "What's going on?"

"It's about what happened," I said. "I'm trying to find some things out."

"Oh yeah?" The way he said it, the way his eyes came alive, I knew I had him hooked. It made me feel even worse.

"I'm sorry, Leon. It's just—"

"I'm almost done here, all right? You hang tight for a few minutes. We'll go somewhere and talk."

When he turned around, the man and his son had disappeared.

"I blew your sale," I said.

"Nah, they weren't buying. I could tell. Come on, let's get out of here."

"Can you just leave?"

"It's slow today," he said. He went in the back for a moment. I heard him talking to somebody, and then he came back out. "Where do you want to go?"

"You still have your computer at your house? You see, I just wanted to look up a couple of names."

"Say no more," he said. "Let's go to my house. I'll drive. Just leave your truck here."

"But then you gotta bring me back."

"It's all right, Alex. Come on. You can brief me on the case in the car."

Brief me on the case, that's the kind of thing Leon would say. Two minutes around me and he was already talking like a private eye again.

He opened the car door for me and got in the driver's seat. It was the same old red Chevy Nova he'd had forever. How he could drive this piece of crap in the snow was a mystery to me. "It's good to see you," I said. "Everybody at home okay?"

"Yeah, Eleanor's a lot happier," he said as he pulled out of the parking lot. "Now that things have settled down a little bit." Settled down meaning he didn't have his little office in town anymore, and he wasn't buying any more high-tech listening devices or hidden cameras.

"I feel bad," I said. "I haven't even seen you since the last time you saved my ass."

"Alex, stop apologizing and tell me what's going on."

"All right," I said. "Here's the deal." I ran through the whole story again, just as I had done for Jackie. A few more days had passed since the last time I told it. I should have felt more distance from it, but I didn't. It still felt like something that had just happened to me.

"The funny thing is," I said as I got toward the end of the story, "every time I say that name, Red Albright, it gets more familiar to me. I'm starting to think I've heard that name before, somewhere."

"Well, you said he lives in Detroit, right? You were a police officer down there, when?"

"For eight years. Up until 1984."

"When you were shot."

"Yes."

"Do you think you ran into him when you were on the force?"

"It's possible," I said. "I can't remember."

"Well, we'll work on that name," he said. "I still have access to my databases."

"Doesn't that stuff cost you money?"

He hesitated. "Yeah, a little bit."

"You're not thinking of going back into business, are you?"

"No," he said. "I'm done with that. Really."

I wasn't sure that I should believe him. But on this day I was glad he could still think like a private investigator.

When we got to his house, I gave his wife Eleanor a hug. She was still just as big as her husband, and she still looked strong enough to bench-press me. If I had any doubts, she gave me a squeeze that almost broke a few ribs.

But as happy as she was to see me, there was something else in her eyes when she looked at me. She had always humored Leon with his private-eye dreams, until those dreams almost got him killed. Now that he was making a safe and steady living selling snowmobiles, his old partner Alex was probably not the most welcome sight.

"I'm helping him with something," Leon said. "We're just gonna look somebody up."

She gave us a weak smile and a nod of her head as he took me into the guest room. He had his computer in there, along with a printer. "Have a seat," he said. "We'll get this thing going. Tell me the name of the individual in question."

There he goes again, I thought. Individual in question. "The man's name is Red Albright," I said.

"He's one of the deceased."

"Yes."

"I'll try a P-search," he said. "It's a standard person search, using most of the public databases. You say he lives in Detroit?"

"DeMers said he came from Grosse Pointe."

"I'll try all of Michigan," he said.

I sat there and watched him type.

"This won't take long," he said. "Let's see what comes back."

A few seconds later, he had exactly one hit to show me. "Here's a Red Albright in Port Huron."

"No, that can't be it," I said. "I mean, Red is obviously a nickname, don't you think?"

"I'm sure you're right. If I try Albright, though, we're gonna get a lot of names."

"How about his brother?" I said. "His name is Dal."

"Probably short for something," Leon said. "But that's okay. We'll look for any first name that begins with those letters."

He typed that in and waited a few seconds. A few names came back. "Here's one," he said. "Dallas Albright, in Grosse Pointe."

"That's gotta be him," I said. "Can you give me that address?"

"Done," he said. He hit a button and the printer came to life. "What else can we find out about him?"

Leon smiled at me. "What else? How about his whole life? Employment history, court records . . . It's all out there, Alex. Yours is, too."

"How long will it take?"

"Well, there are a couple of things we can try right now," he said. He was off and running. Within the next hour, we had found out that Dallas Albright was a part owner of Albright Enterprises in Detroit, and that one of the other owners was named Roland Albright. We assumed Roland was Red. We found his home address, too, and an address for Albright Enterprises on the east side of Detroit. The one thing we didn't find was any mention of either man in the criminal justice system. They were both clean.

We tried Hank Gannon, too. There was nothing to find, outside of his off-season address in Sudbury and his pilot's certification.

"I've got a friend over at the newspaper," Leon said. "He'll run a LexisNexis on them if I ask real nice."

"That's the one that searches the newspapers, all over the country?"

"Yeah, it goes back about twenty years."

"This is really great, Leon. I don't know how to thank you."

That sparkle in his eyes faded away as he stood up. "Yeah, well . . ." he said, looking down at his computer. "It's no problem."

"You miss it, don't you."

"It was nothing but trouble."

"You're good at it," I said. "Better than I ever was."

He laughed at that. "That's not saying much, Alex. You always hated it."

If only he knew, I thought. But today, what I hated was seeing him like this, trying to live a certain kind of life instead of doing the one thing he loved. I never thought I'd admit it, but I missed being his partner.

And here was another friend, come to think about it, who I hadn't seen much of lately. Another lost connection. But this one was mostly my fault.

"I should get out of here," I said. I looked out his window. The sun had gone down. "I think your family ate dinner without you."

"Let's take you back to your truck."

I gave Eleanor another hug on the way out. The two kids were sitting at the kitchen table, doing homework. They gave me the same look their mother had given me. When Alex is around, it usually means trouble. Leon stood there putting his coat on, which made the whole scene look even worse. I was obviously dragging him out into the dark night.

"I'm just gonna run Alex back," Leon said.

Nobody in the room was buying it.

"I'm sorry," I said, as we got into his car. "Your family's all worried now."

"They'll be all right. When I get back, they'll see it was no big deal."

"I shouldn't be putting you through this," I said. "Or them. This was a mistake."

He drove out to the highway and headed north, back to the motor shop. "You know, I've been thinking," he said. "You say Vinnie's brother was on parole."

"Yeah?"

"I'm not trying to convince you he was getting in trouble again, but hear me out, okay?"

"I'm listening."

"You've got a convicted drug offender, some men with money, and a bush pilot. Doesn't that sort of add up to something?"

"Of course it does. If I didn't know anything about Tom, I'd say the combination looks pretty bad."

"Do you really know him? I mean, you know Vinnie—"

"And if I'm seeing Tom through Vinnie, I might not be seeing a very clear picture."

He shrugged. There was nothing to say.

"What am I gonna do? Go hang around the rez and ask about Tom? Find out the real story?"

"You wouldn't get very far with that," he said. "You probably need to talk to Vinnie about this."

"He's kind of unavailable right now. Maybe in a couple days." I didn't feel like talking about it.

He kept driving. The road was empty. It was a lonely October night in the Upper Peninsula. Firearm season was still a week away.

"Just watch yourself, okay?" he said after a while. "I don't have to tell you, these might be some pretty bad people."

"I know."

"Is your gun loaded?"

"I don't have one anymore," I said. "I threw it in the lake, remember?"

He shook his head. "I can't believe it."

"I don't need a gun."

"You just want to find out what really happened."

"Yes."

"And who did this to Vinnie's brother."

I thought about it. "Yes."

"Okay," Leon said. "Whatever you say."

I looked at him. "Don't do it," I said.

"What?"

"Don't get me a gun."

"Who said I was going to get you a gun?"

"I know you."

"Obtaining a handgun for someone else is illegal in the state of Michigan," he said, as only Leon Prudell could manage with a straight face. "I'd lose my license."

"You don't have a license anymore," I said.

I wasn't sure, but I thought I caught a little smile.

A few minutes later, Leon dropped me off at my truck. I thanked him again and sent him on his way. On the way home, I stopped in at the Glasgow and had a late dinner. Vinnie's cabin was dark when I drove past on my way home. It looked small and lonely.

I went to my own cabin. Since coming back home, this was the first night that sleep didn't come easy.

I had some more bow hunters leaving the next day. When I was done with them I drove down to the Glasgow for lunch, passing Vinnie's empty cabin. I passed it again coming back.

You're gonna drive yourself crazy, I thought. You're gonna make yourself absolutely insane.

I thought about giving Leon a call. I decided not to. If Eleanor answered, I'd just upset her again. So I decided to do something even worse. I called the Hearst OPP Detachment and asked for Constable Reynaud.

It took a minute for somebody to find her, and then I heard her voice. The distant static on the line made it sound like she was on the moon. "McKnight? What's the matter?"

"I just wanted to ask you something," I said. "Tom's body came home yesterday. I assume that means you're done with the forensics."

"Is there a question in there?"

"Constable, please. Can I call you Natalie?"

"I'd rather you didn't."

I held the phone away from my mouth and counted to three. "Look," I finally said. "Have you ever been to an Ojibwa funeral?"

"No, I haven't."

"It lasts four or five days. So I've had all that time to think about it. Isn't there anything you can tell me?"

"McKnight, I suppose there's one thing you might want to know. This is something you can share with the family, when the time is right. Tom was shot first, and then burned. He wasn't alive when they set him on fire."

"What about the others?"

For a moment there was nothing but the faraway static. "The others weren't so lucky."

"He must have struggled," I said. "They had to shoot him."

"Is there anything else?"

"Do you have any more information on why this happened?"

"I can't really say, okay? I will tell you that we're not close to anything."

"And how are you doing?" I said.

"I'm just fine, McKnight. You don't have to ask."

"I told you before, I've been there. I know how it is."

247

"Yeah, you told me. Thank you very much. Now if that's all . . ."

"Nobody's looking you in the eye, are they," I said.

She didn't say anything. More static, humming on the line.

"Your partner was killed," I said. "Nobody is gonna come right out and say they blame you."

"Is this supposed to be helping me, McKnight?"

"There's nobody else you can talk to about this, okay? Trust me, nobody else is gonna understand what you're going through."

"But you do."

"Yes, I do."

"Well, aren't I lucky then? If it gets to be too much for me, I'll give you a call. My own personal psychiatrist."

"Constable, come on. I'm just trying to—"

The phone went dead.

"Well, that was brilliant," I said. "I'm such a big help."

I tried to forget about it, but it put me in a bad mood that lasted the rest of the day. I didn't even go down to the Glasgow for dinner. As if I didn't have enough problems—for whatever reason, whether I wanted to admit it to myself or not, Natalie Reynaud had gotten under my skin.

Another day passed. Vinnie was still with his family. I thought about going over to the rez and finding him. But I didn't do it.

Leon finally called me back. His friend at the paper had run Hank Gannon and the Albright brothers through LexisNexis. "He got nothing at all on Gannon," Leon said. "On the Albrights, he found a few things. Some civic awards, something else about a car dealership Red had owned for a while, then sold. Oh, and a ballpark they both rededicated. I guess it was named after their father."

"Albright Field," I said. "Of course. That's where I've heard that name before. It was over on the east side."

"It sounds like an old Detroit family with a little bit of money," he said. "Nothing out of the ordinary."

"I don't know, Leon. Dallas and one of his buddies came all the way up here to stick guns in our faces. Does that sound like an ordinary businessman to you?"

"Maybe he's done a real good job keeping his name clean," he said. "Either that or he just went a little crazy."

"Who knows? I don't think we're getting anywhere."

"Well, I'll let you know if I find out anything else."

"No, Leon. You don't have to do that. You've already done too much, believe me. Your wife probably wants to kill me."

He laughed at that. "She loves you, Alex."

"Give her my best," I said. "And tell her I'm sorry. Thanks for everything, partner."

I hung up the phone and sat there looking out the window. At that point, I wasn't even sure what I was doing. Maybe it was just the fact that I was doing something. After having to fight so hard in the woods, I couldn't just sit still now and relax.

Reynaud was right, I thought. I sound like a psychiatrist.

I headed down to the Glasgow. A couple of hours with Jackie and I'd be myself again. I passed Vinnie's empty cabin yet again. I never had a brother before. That's what I thought as I drove by. I never knew what it felt like.

I spent the rest of the afternoon with Jackie. It was a Sunday, so that meant football games on the television above the bar. We sat by the fire and watched the Lions find another way to lose a game. I finally read the newspaper Jackie had saved for me. The story had made the AP wire—five bodies found on a remote fly-in lake, way up in the wilds of northern Canada. A constable from the Ontario Provincial Police dead on the scene. The apparent killer also dead, with two men from Michigan the sole survivors. It surprised me that nobody had called me, looking for the inside story.

"How's Vinnie doing?" Jackie asked.

"I'm not sure. He's with his family."

"Tell him I'm thinking about him."

"I will," I said. "If I ever see him again."

"Alex, what's going on?"

"It's nothing, Jackie. Just a little disagreement."

"Disagreement, my ass. They're taking care of him and you're feeling left out. Am I right?"

"There's more to it than that."

"Yeah, I bet. Why don't you just go over there and find out how he's doing? Instead of moping around here, making me miserable."

I didn't have much of an argument. Deep down, I knew he was right. So what the hell, I thought. I'm going over there. I drove down to the reservation, taking Lakeshore Drive around the bay. The wind was kicking up, just in time for the change of seasons. November would be here soon, and Lake Superior would turn into a monster.

I felt the truck rocking, saw the whitecaps on the water in the dying light. When I got to the reservation, the snowflakes were flying through the air like tiny bullets. I pulled up in front of Vinnie's mother's house.

Vinnie's truck wasn't there.

I got out of the truck and rang the doorbell. Mrs. LeBlanc opened the door. Her eyes were red and she looked like she had aged twenty years.

"Alex," she said, letting me in.

"I was just stopping by," I said. "I wanted to see how Vinnie was doing. But it looks like he went home."

She frowned. "Vinnie went home a couple of days ago," she

said. "He went home the day after we buried Tom."

"That can't be," I said. "His truck's not there. You mean you haven't even heard from him?"

She shook her head. "I just thought he needed some time to himself. You know how he is. He's always been that way."

I stood there watching a dark cloud pass over her face, this woman who had already been through so much.

"Mrs. LeBlanc, I'm sure you're right. After all that time at the funeral, he probably doesn't want to be around anybody for a few days. Even me. Or even—"

"What is it, Alex?"

"His cousins," I said. "Could he be with them somewhere?"

"I don't think so. Most of them were here today."

"They didn't say anything about where he might be?"

"No, they didn't. They thought he had gone home, too."

"You know what? I bet he's at the casino. He's either back on the job, or maybe he just got a room for a couple of days. I'll go check on him, okay?"

"Yes," she said. "Please check, Alex. Will you call me?"

"Of course I will. You just relax."

I gave her a quick kiss on the cheek and left. When I was back in my truck I fired it up and pulled out hard, ready to bury the accelerator. The only problem was I had no idea where I was going. I had told Mrs. LeBlanc he was probably at the casino, but it sounded weak even as I was saying it. But what the hell. I drove over to the Bay Mills Casino and looked for Vinnie's truck in the parking lot. It wasn't there. I doubled back and hit the Kings Club. No luck there, either. So I gunned it down Three Mile Road into the Soo and checked the Kewadin. It was a bigger casino with a much bigger lot, so it took me a few minutes to cover the whole thing. There was no sign of Vinnie's truck.

I drove over to the Big Bear Arena, thinking maybe he was there playing some hockey or just skating. It seemed like the kind of thing he'd do to clear his head. But he wasn't there, either.

I didn't think I'd find him at a bar. Not with eight years of sobriety under his belt. But I couldn't help taking a look through the couple of parking lots I passed on my way back to the reservation. I rolled past his mother's house again, hoping he'd be there now. He wasn't.

I was running out of ideas. It was getting dark. I drove past the road that led up to Mission Hill, turned around and went up. I wasn't even sure why. Maybe he was up there, I thought, sitting next to his brother's grave. At this point, it was about all I had left.

It was a steep climb up that road, and the wind and the snow racing around in the air didn't help me. There was no guardrail on the road. It just snaked up to the top of the hill, with nothing to the right but a long drop into Waishkey Bay. I put the truck into low gear and ground my way up, swearing at the wind. When I got to the top, I didn't see Vinnie's truck anywhere. It was just an empty graveyard and the overlook. I was about to turn around when something came back to me. A memory of Vinnie looking out over the cliff the day he buried his brother, that beautiful high view where you could see forever.

And then another memory, something he had said to me before, when he was telling me the story about Tom, about finding him as he was about to hang himself.

"If you're gonna kill yourself, you go up to the old graveyard on Mission Hill, you say hello to your ancestors and then you jump off the cliff. Just walk right out into the sky. That's how you kill yourself."

That's what he said.

I parked the truck. I got out and walked over to the edge of the overlook. This was where he stood, right next to the little shelter, with the message painted in yellow about respecting this land where the spirits of your ancestors live. I went up to the very edge of the cliff and looked down at the rocks and trees far below. It was too dark to see. I couldn't tell if Vinnie's truck was lying down there in a broken heap. Or his body. My friend. My brother.

"God damn it all," I said. "You didn't do it. I know you didn't."

The wind caught me. It almost took me right over.

"How could I even think it? There's no way, Vinnie. I know you're not down there."

I put one knee down on the ground. I looked out at the few lights scattered along the shoreline. Beyond that there was only the dark mystery of the lake.

"So where the hell are you?"

Chapter Twenty-Three

I had a tough call to make. The last thing I wanted to do was get Mrs. LeBlanc even more worried than she already was, but if I was going to figure out where he was, I'd have to start with her. I had no other choice.

She looked surprised when I showed up on her doorstep again. "Alex?" she said as she let me back in. "You found him already?"

"No," I said. "Mrs. LeBlanc, I have to talk to you."

"What's wrong?"

"Nothing's wrong. I think Vinnie went somewhere to be by himself for a while. I'm sure he's okay." It sounded reasonable. Hell, for all I knew, it was the truth. Maybe I was totally wrong.

When she let me in the house, I saw Buck sitting at the kitchen table. He stood up and came into the front room.

I looked him in the eye. "Do you know where he is?"

"If I knew he was going to leave, do you think I'd let him go alone?"

"What about his other cousins? Could somebody else be covering for him?"

He was staring right back at me. "Of course not."

"You said you were gonna take care of him."

"You can blame me for this later," he said. "Right now we've got to find him. You got any ideas?"

"Yeah," I said. "I've got one idea. Does Vinnie know anybody in Detroit?"

"Why would he go down there?"

"There are a couple of men down there. They might know something."

He thought about it. "There's the casino. A lot of Sault members go down there to work."

Of course. Detroit had three casinos, and one of them was partially owned by the Sault tribe. There was a busload of Sault Ojibwas going down to Detroit every week.

"Can you find out if he contacted any of them?"

"I will."

"Will you let me know if you get anything?"

"Yes, Alex. Give me your number."

He gave me a piece of paper, and I wrote down my cell phone number.

"I'm gonna go do that now," he said. "I'll call you." He put one big hand on Mrs. LeBlanc's shoulder, then he stepped in front of me, hesitating for one instant, and then he opened the door.

Mrs. LeBlanc watched him go out into the night. Then she looked up at me. "I don't understand any of this."

"Please don't worry," I said. The expression on her face was enough to turn my stomach inside out. "I'll find out where he is. I promise."

She looked back out the door. A car rumbled by. It was Buck on his way home to make phone calls, or maybe over to the Sault Reservation to make the rounds in person.

"His cabin," I said, an idea coming to me. "Do you have a key?"

She nodded her head, turned and went down the hallway. A minute later, she came back with a single key.

"Here," she said. "I've never given it to anyone before."

"Thank you, Mrs. LeBlanc." I kissed her on the cheek again and left. For the second time that month, I went out to find one of her sons.

Detroit. I said it over and over in my mind as I drove back to Paradise. It was once my hometown, at least in the sense that I lived right next to it and grew up rooting for the Tigers and Lions and Pistons and Red Wings. People ask you where you're from and you say Detroit, because that's the simple answer. You don't tell them that you never actually lived in the city itself, that hardly anyone lives in the city itself if they can help it.

Later, I worked in Detroit as a police officer. Eight years of my life. And even then I didn't live there, which was technically illegal. But I knew the city inside and out, through hot summer nights and cold winter mornings.

There is crime in Detroit. There is crime in Detroit like there are fountains in Paris, like there are canals in Venice. People all over the world know this about Detroit. It might not be fair to think that way. You can look at the art museum and the new ballpark and the casinos and restaurants and believe it's all part of the Detroit Renaissance, and maybe you'd be right. You can even love the place like I do. But it's still Detroit, and always will be.

That's where Albright came from, Red and his men, driving twelve hours due north to go hunting for moose in Canada, or whatever the hell they were doing. That's where his brother came from, days later, driving up the same way, looking for some answers. The way it sounded, he went right back home thinking maybe the answers were all down there to begin with, that he didn't have to leave town to find out the real story.

Now that Vinnie had buried his brother, it looked like he had gone down there, too. If he was looking for his own answers, it was the best place to start.

And also the worst place.

Which reminded me—I already had Dallas Albright's address and phone number, courtesy of Leon and his computer. They were right here in the truck, in the manila folder Leon had given me. While I circled around Whitefish Bay, I pulled out the piece of paper and dialed the number. I got a recorded voice from the cell phone company—the party was not available and I could leave a message. I hung up.

I drove past the Glasgow. The lights looked warm and inviting, but I had something else to do that night. I turned onto the access road, and then into Vinnie's driveway. I kept the headlights on for a moment, got out, and looked at the ground. I would have had to see it in the daylight to be sure, but it looked like Vinnie had driven his truck around the side of his cabin.

God damn you, Vinnie. You didn't even want me to know you were here? Wherever you are, you better be in one piece, so I can personally kick your ass all the way home.

I turned the truck off and used the spare key to open his front door. I felt bad about letting myself in for exactly half a second. "Okay, Vinnie," I said out loud. "I hope you left something lying around here to let me know what you're up to."

I picked up Vinnie's phone to call Dallas Albright again. I stopped myself just in time. Instead, I hit the redial button to find out where Vinnie's last call had gone. I got another recording. This time it was the Archive and Reprints Department of the *Detroit News*. Their regular business hours were 8:30 to 4:30, and I needed to either call back then or leave a message.

I kept looking around his cabin. It was a great-looking place, small but perfectly put together. The bed was made, one of his mother's quilts folded tight on top. The wood stove looked as clean as a rifle barrel, and the wood was stacked next to it in a perfect triangle. A copper kettle gleamed on the cooking plate. His place made mine look like a henhouse.

This is why he moved off the reservation, I thought. This is why he left all that heat and noise behind, even if it was happy heat and noise. This is how he wanted to live—straight and sober and clean, and alone, with everything in its place.

The one thing that surprised me was the computer on his desk. I didn't even know he had one, yet here it sat next to a printer. I stood there looking at the dark screen on the monitor. I knew it was my best hope. I also knew there was no way I could make it talk to me.

It was 8:30 at night. I pictured Leon at home, maybe putting his kids to bed. The phone ringing, and Leon telling Eleanor he had to go out again, to go help Alex with one more thing. The look on her face.

I picked up the phone and dialed the number.

Leon told me he'd be right over. Just like I knew he would.

While I waited, I kept poking around the place. I found only one more interesting thing in the whole cabin—a piece of crumpled-up paper in the wastebasket. When I smoothed it out, I saw that it was a fax cover sheet. It told me that Vinnie had received a fax from the *Detroit News,* which made perfect sense. But whatever the *News* had faxed to him, he had apparently taken it with him.

I tried calling Dallas Albright again. I got the same message.

Leon showed up about twenty minutes later. "What did you do?" I said as I let him in. "Drive a race car over here?"

"I may have flexed the speed limit a little bit." He looked around at Vinnie's cabin.

"I know what your wife said, so I'm not even going to ask."

"This is a nice place," he said. "What have you found so far?"

"Just one thing," I said. I told him about the redial and showed him the paper I had found.

Leon read the cover sheet and ran his free hand through his orange hair. "He found something in the newspapers. Something we didn't find."

"He went right to the *News*," I said. "Maybe he found somebody down there to help him out. They might have tried looking up some other combination of words."

"Or they might have looked further back into the past. Beyond what LexisNexis could find. You think he's down in Detroit right now?"

"He's gotta be. I tried calling the number you found for Dallas Albright, but I keep getting a recording."

"Did you leave a message?"

"My gut tells me not to do that yet. If Vinnie hasn't gotten to him yet, or even if he has and he's just lying low, I don't want to give him away."

"You think he went down there to find out what really happened," Leon said.

"And why it happened," I said. "And who else might still be around who Vinnie could blame for it."

"If anybody."

I shook my head. "It's not a good state of mind to be in, all by himself down there. He's gonna do something crazy."

"Let's try his computer," Leon said. "See if that tells us anything."

He turned it on. While he waited for it to come up, he looked at Vinnie's printer. "It's an all-in-one," he said. "With a fax machine. Very nice."

"I had no idea he was into all this stuff."

"Most people have computers now, Alex."

On another night I would have smacked him, but tonight he was doing me a big favor. "That fax," I said. "There wouldn't be like a copy of that on his computer, would there?"

"No, not with this external fax machine. An online fax, that's another story."

"Well, what are you gonna be able to find out then?"

"I can't log on to his ISP, but let's see . . . Yeah, I can log myself on as a guest. If he was using an outside browser, I might be able to follow his tracks."

"You're kinda losing me, Leon. But go ahead."

"I'll bring up the browser," he said. "See, if I click right here, it shows the last few Web sites he went to." He showed me the small window under the address line.

"I see the *Detroit News* there," I said. "What are those other things?"

"Ah, just general stuff. Yahoo and Amazon, and something for the casino, it looks like. A real hacker could maybe get into his actual history file and really see where Vinnie was going. But I can only do the basics. I'm sorry, Alex."

"Don't be sorry. I dragged you all the way over here."

"Let me try one more thing," he said. "I can search on every file that's either new or changed in the last couple of days."

While I waited I picked up a pot holder decorated with the four Ojibwa colors. Yellow, red, black, and white. They represented the four points of the compass, the four races of man, the four medicines, the four seasons. I knew Mrs. LeBlanc had made this for him. "God damn it, Vinnie," I said. "Did you think about your mother? Did you think about what this would do to her?"

"I see some cookie files here, Alex. Web sites will set them, and usually the site will be in the file name. Wait a minute, what's this?"

"What is it?"

"It's a map program. You know, you give them an address and it draws you a map with driving directions."

"Can you tell what addresses he looked up?"

"No, not from the cookie. But maybe if I go to the Web site itself." He typed in the name and waited. "God, when are we gonna get DSL up here?"

A good minute later, he was in the site. "Now, if this lets you recall the last few addresses..." He clicked the button for the saved addresses.

"We got something," he said. "I see a couple here."

"Don't tell me," I said. "They're in Detroit. I bet one of them is Dallas Albright's house."

"No," Leon said. "They're not in Detroit."

That stopped me cold. "Where are they?"

"They're in Canada," he said. "In Sudbury, Ontario."

"Sudbury..."

"Do you know who lives there?"

"Yeah," I said. Two addresses. Three people. "Yeah, I do."

Chapter Twenty-Four

"What about the phone numbers?" I said, looking over Leon's shoulder. "Are they listed on there?"

"No," Leon said, "just the addresses, with the maps."

"Can you print those out?"

"Sure." He hit the print button. Vinnie's printer woke up and started working. "Who are we talking about, anyway? I can look them up."

"Helen St. Jean," I said. "If it's Sudbury, that's got to be one of the addresses. The other is Ron and Millie something." I thought hard, trying to remember their last name.

"I'll try St. Jean." He went to another Web site and typed in the name.

"Trembley," I said. "Ron and Millie Trembley."

"I'm not getting anything on Helen St. Jean," he said. "Not in Sudbury. Of course, it's not unusual for a single woman to be unlisted. I'll try the Trembleys."

"I don't get it," I said. "Why would he go up there to see them?"

"Those were the other people at the lodge, right?"

"Right."

"I'm not getting the Trembleys' phone number, either," he said. "I can get them, but I'll have to go home and use my database. We'll stop there on the way."

"What are you talking about?"

"We're going to Sudbury, aren't we?"

"Leon, I'm already in enough trouble with your wife. If I take you to Canada in the middle of the night, she'll have my head on a stick."

"You can't go up there alone."

"Sure I can. I'm just gonna find Vinnie and bring him home."

"If it's that simple, why don't you just go in the morning?"

"Maybe I will," I said. I didn't want to tell him how worried I was—how confused and shook up, and how much I wished I was already on the road that second.

"You're a terrible liar, Alex. Just get going. I'll go home and find the phone numbers and call you on your cell phone."

"Thanks, Leon. Once again."

He gave me the two maps he had printed out, and sent me on my way. He drove home, and I headed straight for the bridge. It was after ten when I reached Canada. The man in the customs booth gave me a quick once-over, asked me what I would be doing in his country. I told him I was hitting one of the clubs in the Soo. He asked me the standard questions about drugs or firearms in the vehicle. I answered no to both. He told me to drive safely.

I took the Queen's Highway east this time, instead of north. It ran through downtown Sault Ste. Marie, then out along the shore of the North Channel, passing through small towns like Bruce Mines and Iron Bridge. The phone rang just after eleven.

"It's Leon. Sorry I took so long."

"Don't worry about it. Did you get the numbers?"

"Yeah, finally. Here they are." He read me two phone numbers. I wrote them down on my pad, keeping one hand on the wheel.

"Thanks, Leon."

"Where are you now?"

"I'm coming up to Serpent River," I said. "I've got another couple of hours to Sudbury."

"You're making good time," he said. "You gonna try calling them now?"

"Might as well. If this is all a big mistake, then I guess I'll just be waking them up."

"Well, just in case it's not a mistake, I left a little present for you in your truck."

"What?"

"You'll have to reach inside your rear bumper, toward the driver's side."

"Leon, you didn't."

"I'm just taking care of my partner," he said.

"Is it your Luger?"

"No, that gun's just for show, Alex. I gave you my Ruger P90."

"Luger, Ruger. How did you even get it in my truck?"

"When I came over to Vinnie's cabin. You were parked outside, remember?"

"I assume it's loaded."

"No, it's empty, Alex. I put an empty gun in your truck."

"Leon, I swear to God . . ." I thought about the customs booth I had just rolled through, the lie I had told the man about not having a firearm, and then about all the other crazy things Leon had done in the short time I'd known him.

"Take care of yourself, Alex. I'm sorry I'm not there to cover you. Call me when you're on your way home."

He hung up before I could say anything else.

I put the phone down for a moment, shook my head, then

picked the phone back up and called the two numbers Leon had given me. I got a recording on the first number—Helen St. Jean's voice telling me she couldn't come to the phone. The machine beeped and I froze for a second. "Helen," I finally said, "this is Alex McKnight. Remember me? If you're there, please pick up."

I waited a few seconds. Nothing.

"I'm sorry I'm calling so late. This is an emergency."

Nothing.

I gave her my cell phone number and asked her to call me. Then I dialed the second number. The phone rang seven times. The Trembleys apparently didn't have an answering machine. I let it ring a few more times, then hung up. I kept driving.

It was almost one o'clock in the morning when I saw the Super Stack looming in the distance. It was over twelve hundred feet high, the tallest freestanding smokestack in the world, with the lights at the top so planes wouldn't hit it. I drove through the great slag heaps that dominated the western part of town. In the eerie light it looked like the surface of the moon. I had read that Sudbury was coming into its own lately—it wasn't just a big hole in the ground anymore, but it looked like it still had the heart of a mining town. Most of the new houses were being built to the north, up by the lake, but down here by the highway it was still mostly working-class neighborhoods with small houses and a bar on every corner. I cut in off the highway, passing a big ice arena, and then off that road to another, leaving any traffic behind me.

I rolled down a residential street, past dark, quiet houses. I saw two men walking on the sidewalk. They opened the door to a bar and the light made a long fan on the street and then it was gone as they stepped inside.

I stopped for a minute, switched on my interior light, and looked at the maps. The Trembleys' house was closest. I hit the light and kept going south, looking for a street on the right. A streetlight was out and I almost missed it.

When I turned, I started looking for the numbers on the houses. It was after one-thirty now. The street was deserted.

Two-twelve, two-fourteen, two-sixteen.

I pulled over in front of the house and got out. The air was cold, and it had a slight metallic taste. Around here you probably got used to it.

The house was dark. I went up to the front door. Why the hell not, after driving all the way up here. A dog barked in somebody's backyard, a few houses away.

The front door was slightly open, just a couple of inches. I knocked lightly.

Nothing.

"Hello," I said. "Anybody home?"

Silence.

Why was the door open? I pushed on it. It swung open a few more inches. There was a light on inside, in the back of the house.

I smelled gasoline. And something else. A smell I knew.

I should have left then. I should have turned and gone back to my truck and driven all the way home.

I didn't. I stepped into the house. A small table was turned over on its side. A plant was lying sideways on the floor, dirt all over the carpet. I walked through the room, saw a single tiny red light in the kitchen. A coffeemaker, sitting there keeping the time as if everything was quiet and normal in the house. My eyes were adjusting to the dark. A hallway. A thin stream of light under a door.

The smell.

Where are you, Vinnie? Are you here?

I went down the hallway. Quiet and normal.

Vinnie, please.

I stopped at the door. The smell, the smell.

I put my shoulder against the door and slowly pushed it in. It opened a few inches and then stopped. I pushed a little harder, felt something give way. It was something heavy, leaning against the door.

There was just enough room to poke my head through the door. I knew what I was going to see in that room. The second I had opened the front door, the second that smell had hit me, I knew what I'd find. So why did I go in?

"Oh, sweet God," I said as I looked around the door. "Oh, no, please." If I thought I was ready for the sight, I was wrong. Not in a million years.

It was a bathroom. The lights were on. It was so bright it hurt my eyes after the dark hallway, the cruel whiteness of it all, the unholy sight of burned flesh on the white, white floor.

I saw the wallpaper half burned off the wall, hanging in strips. The scorch marks on the ceiling. The remains of draperies, thin as spider webs. Smoke in the air.

Two bodies. One in the bathtub, the woman, her head on the edge, one arm hanging. The other body right below me, by the door. I was pushing against his legs.

He had been trying to get out. He had made it this far.

I backed away from the door. It closed slightly, not all the way. I turned and went down the hallway, to the front door. I was blind now, after the brigll niht light in the bathroom. I walked into one wall, and then another.

Careful, Alex. Take it easy. The door is this way. Get to the door.

I made it to the front room. I felt the dirt under my feet, from where the plant had tipped over. I kicked something hard, then I was out the door and onto the front walkway, stumbling over something else I couldn't see, then finally to the truck, opening the door, the light coming on, closing the door, putting the key in the ignition and turning it. The engine came to life with an explosion of noise. I dropped it into gear with a heavy clunk, lurched away from the curb.

Drive. Drive slowly. And breathe. I kept the lights off, driving by the dim light of a half-moon covered by clouds, a street lamp burning in the distance. I drove straight to it. Breathe, Alex.

Dead end.

"Shit shit shit shit," I said, turning in the cul-de-sac and going back the way I had come. I passed the house again, that evil house. I tried not to look at it as I rolled by it one more time.

God, get a hold of yourself. What do I do now? Do I call 911? Do I call them anonymously and tell them what's in that house? Can they trace 911 calls from cell phones? Fuck, do they even have 911 in Canada?

I can't call it in. What's the use, anyway?

Yes, I've got to. I can't let somebody find that by accident.

I'll go to Helen's place first. Then I'll call it in.

When I got back to the main road, I stopped the truck and sat there for a moment. I pulled out the other map and turned on the light. My hands were shaking. Helen's house was on the other side of town, maybe five or six miles away. I knew I had to go there. Instead of taking a left and driving back to the highway and all the way back to Michigan, I took the right.

Finding her house gave me something to do, at least. It was something real and almost mundane, looking for the street signs, instead of thinking about what I had just seen in that house.

Ron and Millie. Together they had said maybe ten words to me. But I could see them at the lodge, standing out on the dock, Ron putting his arm around his wife's shoulder.

Somebody made them get in the bathtub. He soaked them with gasoline and set them on fire.

Take this street, Alex. Watch for the next one. Keep watching.

No, they didn't just get in. Who would do that? They had to fight back.

Where is the street? Where is it?

Blood. There was blood on the floor. I had seen it, but it didn't hit me until now. Were they shot first? Were they cut?

Another street. Not the right one.

Ron tried to get out of the tub. Or maybe not. He was facing the other way, away from the door. The door hit his feet.

Is this the street? No. Keep going.

A towel. There was a towel on the floor. Another detail. Something else my mind didn't have time to process.

This street. Turn here. I'm getting close.

A towel on the floor, under his hand. He tried to get out and grab a towel. He tried to save her. He tried to grab that towel and wrap it around her burning body.

I rolled the window down, let the fresh cold air slap me in the face. I was in a little better neighborhood now. The houses were a little bigger, with longer driveways and more dead grass between the houses and the street. I passed the Beer Store. The red sign glowed in the dark, although the store was closed. It was coming up on two in the morning now.

Where are you, Vinnie? Where are you right now? I know you didn't kill those people. No matter what happened to your brother, you are not capable of doing something like this. But where are you?

One more left. Then a right. I turned my lights off again, rolled slowly down the street, looking for house numbers. Seventy-one, seventy-three, seventy-five.

I stopped in front of seventy-seven. It was a ranch house with tall, barren trees on either side of the walkway. It would have been a nice house on a normal day. I slipped out of the truck and pushed the door closed. I looked both ways down the street as I went to the front door.

There were a lot more porch lights on in this neighborhood. I felt exposed standing there at the front door. I didn't bother to knock this time. I tried turning the doorknob, but it was locked.

I rang the doorbell. I heard it chime two notes, somewhere deep in the house. Nobody answered.

If somebody was going to break into this house, they wouldn't stand here at the front door and do it. It wasn't nearly as dark as the last house. So I went around to the side door, hidden from the street by a tall wooden fence. There was a metal storm door that had been practically torn off the hinges. The door inside that was open.

I stepped inside. The smell of gasoline came to me again.

But no, it wasn't like before. I could just barely smell it. If it happened here, it was somewhere in the back of the house.

I walked through the house. The only sound was my own breathing. There was a sudden flash of light as a car drove by outside. The headlights swept across the wall and then they were gone.

The front room had bookshelves on every wall. There were thousands and thousands of books. I walked through to the back hallway, poked my head around each door. In the darkness I could barely make out the shapes of beds and dressers and tables.

I went into what had to be the master bedroom. There were framed pictures all over the room, but it was too dark to see the faces. I could make out a faint light from another door. It had to be the master bathroom.

I went to the door and slowly leaned against it. It creaked open. There was a small night-light glowing above the sink. No bodies to see. No horror in this bathroom.

I left the master bedroom, walked back down the hallway, through the room with all the books and back into the kitchen. The smell of gasoline got stronger.

There was another door I had walked right by. I shouldered it open. It was a small guest bathroom. It was empty.

I stood in the darkness, in the middle of the kitchen, trying to figure it out. Then I noticed a piece of paper on the table. I bent down and tried to read it. I could barely make out the letters.

"Millie, I've gone to the lodge, back in a couple of days. Helen."

It made no sense to me. I was there when she was packing up. I heard her say how much she wanted to get out, how much she hated that place. Like a sickness, she said. Why would she go back up there?

I didn't have an answer for that. But I knew one thing. It came to me all at once. Whoever killed Ron and Millie came here next. That's why I smelled the gasoline. They brought the smell with them, into this house. But Helen wasn't here. I didn't know why she'd gone to the lodge, but whatever the reason, it had saved her life.

At least for now. If they knew where the lodge was, they'd go there. They'd find her.

They. Who were "they"? The same people who burned the men at the lake? Was this more of the same?

I went back out to the truck and picked up the cell phone. As I drove away, I dialed the Hearst Detachment. A man answered the phone on the second ring.

"I need to know when Constable Reynaud comes on duty," I said.

"She comes on at seven," the man said. "Can I help you with something?"

"Please have her call Alex," I said.

"Just Alex? Can I have a last name?"

"She knows my last name."

"Can I have your number, please?"

"She knows my number." Or if she doesn't, I thought, she can find out.

"Sir, are you sure I can't help you with something?"

"There's one thing you can do," I said. "I'm going to give you an address in Sudbury. You need to send someone over there." I gave him the Trembleys' address.

"Sir? Can you tell me what happened?"

"Tell her to call me," I said. "Tell her I didn't do this. And neither did Vinnie."

I hung up the phone and kept driving.

Chapter Twenty-Five

I left Sudbury and headed north. It was three hard hours to Timmins, Ontario. I crossed the Canadian Pacific Railway just north of Onaping, and then the Canadian National in Gogoma. The road was empty, which was a damned good thing. I would have run over anything that got in my way.

Timmins was another old mining town. They had struck gold up here, a long time ago, and you could still see the traces in the names of the streets and the businesses. Prospector Street. The Gold Rush Café. A sign on the highway advertised tours in one of the old mines.

It was five in the morning when I stopped to gas up and grab some coffee. This time of year, it was still dark. Sunrise was two hours away.

I drove out of town and it was all wide-open spaces and potato farms for a while, and then it was back into the trees. I finally hit the Trans-Canada Highway and headed west through Smooth Rock Falls and Kapuskasing. The sun was just starting to come up when I hit Hearst. I drove right by the OPP station. It was just after 6:30 at that point, so Reynaud wasn't there.

I slowed down as I passed the station, then sped back up when I was clear. I drove west, with the sun coming up behind me. I was still half an hour from the lodge.

I passed the turnoff to Calstock and the Constance Lake Reserve. Being up here again, it had to be either a bad dream or a bad joke. I rubbed my eyes with one hand. When I opened them, I was drifting right off the road. Drive off the road and hit a big tree, I said to myself. That would be perfect.

I drove past the turnoff for 631, the road down to Wawa. I had spent the whole night making a big circle through Ontario, from the Soo to Sudbury to Timmins and now back on the Trans-Canada, all the way up here. A few more miles and I saw the little dirt road that led up to the lodge. It was the road Vinnie and I found the first time we came up here, when we weren't even sure it was the right one. How much had changed since then?

There was a heavy mist hanging in the air as I turned off the highway. The early sun hadn't burned it off yet. As cold as it was, that mist might have hung around until noon. That last morning, when we were up in the woods, the air had felt exactly the same way. It was just as wet, and the chill was just as penetrating. Even with the windows rolled up, I could feel it.

I took it easy going up the road. I couldn't see where the hell I was going in the mist, and I didn't want to end up in the mud again. That plus the fact that I really didn't know what I was getting into. I had no idea what I was going to find when I got to the lodge.

My cell phone rang. I picked it up. "Is this Reynaud?"

"McKnight, what the hell's going on? Where are you?"

"I'm at the lodge. I think Helen's here."

"Don't move. We'll be right over."

"Vinnie might be here, too. I have to find him."

"McKnight. Do not do *anything*, do you hear me?"

"Did somebody go over to the Trembleys' house?"

There was a brief silence on the line. "Yes," she finally said. "Alex, please tell me what's happening."

"I don't know."

"Just sit tight. We're on our way."

"Okay."

"Promise me you won't do anything stupid."

"Can't do that," I said. I hung up.

I slowed down as I came up to the sharp turn in the road. I knew the moose probably wouldn't be standing there again, but I didn't want to take any chances. I cleared the corner. No moose. But what the hell—

I slammed on the brakes. There was a car off the road, in the same spot where my truck had ended up. I sat there looking at it for a while. It was a black sedan. I recognized it.

I got out of the truck, leaving the driver's side door open. I took two steps, then turned around and went to the back of my truck. I reached down under the bumper and felt inside for the gun Leon had hidden. It was held in place with tape. When I pulled it out, it felt cold and heavy in my hand.

I went around the back of my truck and approached the car, moving slowly. I couldn't see anybody inside. My boot sank six inches into the mud as soon as I stepped off the road. I leaned on the car and made my way another couple of steps, then bent down and looked through the driver's side window. It was unlocked. When I opened the door, I smelled the gasoline.

I replayed that night in my head. Red Albright's brother Dallas with his big friend Jay along, the way they stopped us on my road. The look in his eyes. He promised us he'd find out who else was involved in his brother's death. What were his exact words? He'd turn them inside out.

I popped the trunk release, then fought my way back through

the mud to the road. When I looked into the trunk, I saw the gasoline cans. It made sense, in a horrible kind of way. If you found out who burned your brother to death, and you had a dark enough mind, you'd be tempted to take your vengeance in exactly the same way.

I noticed one other thing as I closed the trunk. There was a board on the edge of the road. It was covered with mud, so I didn't see it at first, but as I knelt down beside it, I saw a dozen long nails pointing straight up, with three nails in the middle bent over. I looked on the other side of the car, and thought I could make out yet another board half buried in the mud.

That note on the table, it was put there for a reason. "This was a trap," I said out loud.

And then I heard the first gunshot. The sound was deadened by the wet air, but I could tell where it was coming from. I got back in my truck and drove the last mile to the lodge. The mist got heavier as I got closer to the lake.

I heard another shot. I slowed down. I sure as hell didn't want to drive right into the middle of it. There was a turn here, I thought. One final turn in this road and then it ended under those big trees.

I still couldn't see very well, but I guessed I was just about there, so I stopped. I turned the truck off, grabbed Leon's gun again, and stepped out onto the road. I listened hard, but there was nothing to hear but the sound of the truck's engine settling.

I started walking slowly, as quietly as I could. I didn't like the fact that I couldn't see more than fifty feet ahead of me. But I figured what the hell, at least nobody could see me. As soon as I came around that last bend in the road, I saw a truck parked among the trees. The fog was too thick to make out the plate number, or even the color. I had to get closer.

I kept low to the ground and made my way to one of the big

trees. I leaned against it for a moment and then looked around it at the truck.

It was Vinnie's.

All the way up here, it had been an idea, a feeling in my gut, based on a couple of maps on his computer, and a newspaper clipping about God knows what. Now it was real. Vinnie was here.

Another shot ripped through the air. This one was a lot closer. I couldn't imagine who was pulling the trigger or how they could even see where they were shooting.

Another shot. This one took me right down onto the ground. I heard another sound right after it, something long and low, like the air being let out of a balloon.

"God damn it," I said under my breath. "Vinnie, where are you?"

The sound stopped.

The fear started building in my stomach. Hold on, Alex. It's time to do something here. I picked Leon's Ruger off the ground and brushed the dirt away. I knew it was a modern gun, with .45 caliber shells, but it looked like an antique in my hand, like something from the Second World War. If I had to use it, I hoped it would be enough.

I made my way from tree to tree. The mist seemed to be drifting in and out now, circling around me like wraiths. I had to keep moving forward. I didn't know what else to do. The lodge started to take shape, the wooden roof appearing above me. I put my back to the wall of the butcher's shed, holding my weapon with two hands. All the training I had, a million years ago, it all came back to me. Gun up, peek around the corner, draw back. It's clear, lead with the gun, keep low. Move quick without hurrying. I edged around the door to the shed, gun ready. I can shoot in any direction.

I'm coming, Vinnie. You better still be alive.

I moved along the base of the wall, heading for the front of the building. I stopped at the corner, caught my breath, then took a quick look up the stairs. They were empty. I looked around at everything else—another small building by the dock, the dock itself leading out into nowhere, the lake still hidden behind the thick wall of fog. I didn't know where anyone was, or who would shoot at me if I moved, but I felt totally exposed crouching down by the wall. Here goes nothing.

I went up the stairs, swearing at every creak and groan of the wood. When I was on the front porch, I stuck my head up over the windowsill for one second, then back down. Did I see somebody in there? I needed to look again. Just wait a few seconds. Count to five. One . . . two . . .

That's as far as I got. The next gunshot was like an explosion going off inside my head. My legs went out from under me and I started sliding down the stairs, until another blast ripped the wood apart.

They're right on top of me. I'm dead. I'm dead. I'm dead.

Back up I went, scrambling up the stairs on all fours. I threw the door open and rolled inside the lodge as another shot took out the screen window. The sound of it was still roaring in my ears as I lay there, wondering if I was hit and just didn't know it yet.

And where the hell was my gun, anyway?

I looked all over the floor for it. This is great, Alex. This is so fucking great.

Then out of nowhere, a voice. "Don't move."

I looked up. Helen St. Jean was sitting in the corner, her legs drawn up to her chest. The rifle barrel was pointed at me over one knee.

"Helen," I said. "It's me. Don't you remember?"

"Don't move," she said. "Don't come any closer."

I put my hands up. "Helen, where's Vinnie?"

She didn't say anything.

"You've got to tell me where Vinnie is."

She lifted the barrel of the rifle off her knee and pointed it right at my heart.

"Helen, please don't point that at me."

I could see the gun shaking in her hands.

"You need to give me that gun," I said. "Those men outside, they're gonna come up here."

She looked at me. She was breathing hard.

"Helen, you need to give me that gun. Those men will come up here and kill us."

She looked at the window. I kept my hands up as I slowly bent down toward the floor. The big table and all the chairs were gone. It was one big empty room now. "I'm coming over there," I said. "Okay? I'm coming over there so we can fight them together."

She kept looking back and forth between me and the window. As I got down on my knees and started inching over to her, she didn't follow me with the rifle. I took that as a good sign.

"You give me that gun," I said. "I promise you, I'll shoot them if they come through that door. Okay?"

Her eyes kept moving as I got closer. My face, the window, my face, the window.

"I was a police officer, Helen. Okay? Give me the gun."

I got closer. I could almost touch her.

"Helen," I said, and then everything came apart. Another gun blast ripped through the air, right outside the front door. And then another as I grabbed for the rifle. The second shot was even louder, so loud it made my ears hurt, made them ring like I'd never hear anything else again.

There was something hot in my hand. The rifle barrel. And something else. Something falling from the sky. It was raining. My ears were ringing and it was raining.

I looked up and saw what was left of the moose head on the wall. A brown cloud hung in the air. I was covered with sawdust and wood shavings and mouse shit and God knows what else. I shook my head. Damn it, my ears hurt.

Somebody was on the stairs. I couldn't even hear it, but I could feel the slight vibration in the floor. Somebody was coming up to the door.

I put the butt of the rifle against my shoulder. "Get down," I said to Helen. "And cover your ears."

I sighted with my right eye, closed my left. I aimed for the doorway, chest high.

A body. A face. Long hair.

It was Maskwa.

I pulled the rifle up. Maskwa took one step through the door and stopped. For one heart-stopping moment, he kept his rifle trained right at my head. Then he finally lowered it.

"Alex."

I opened my mouth, but I didn't know what to say first. He put his hand up to shush me, came over and bent down next to Helen. Her hands were clamped down hard over her ears. Her eyes were closed.

"Helen," he said. "It's okay now."

She didn't move.

"It's okay," he said. He put one hand on the back of her head and pulled her closer. She collapsed against his chest.

"Maskwa," I said. "Are you gonna tell me what the hell is going on?"

"Yes," he said. "But wait—" He turned and looked at the door. "My God, where's Vinnie?"

"Wasn't he with you?"

"We split up," Maskwa said. "He's still outside somewhere."

Maskwa touched Helen's hair and told her we'd be right back. She didn't open her eyes or take her hands away from her ears.

He whispered something else into her ear and stood up.

When we got outside, I saw a body at the foot of the stairs. The man was lying face down in the dirt, a hole blown right through his back. "Oh God no," I said.

"Alex, that's not Vinnie."

I let out my breath. When I got closer, I could see the man's face. "This is Red's brother, Dallas."

"Whatever you say," Maskwa said.

I saw a Beretta lying on the ground next to the body. It was the same gun he had held against Vinnie's head the night they stopped us.

"The other man . . . The big one. Is he around here somewhere, too?"

"I think he's over behind that shed. By the dock."

"Maskwa, how come you're here?"

"Hold on, Alex. Let's find him first." He stopped for a moment, and stood there looking all around him. He held up his hand to me, like he was working hard on something in his mind, maybe playing the whole thing back, frame by frame. The sun was finally burning off most of the morning fog. Only the lake itself was still hidden.

"Yes," he said. "Yes. Over this way. I never saw him after he shot the other one." He went down to the end of the dock. The big man was on the ground just behind the boat shed. A good piece of his skull had been blown away and the back of the shed was painted red and pink. Maskwa stopped right next to him, his foot an inch away from the dead man's curled fingers. "Where is he?" he said. "Oh, come on, please."

I came up next to him. I didn't say a word.

"There," he said. There were some thin trees scattered just a few yards from the shed, then some thick, tall weeds as the shoreline gave way to the forest. He ran into the slight gap he had spotted. I was right behind him. When he stopped, I almost ran over him.

Vinnie was kneeling on the ground. He was holding himself up with both hands on the barrel of his rifle, his head hanging like he had gotten this far and then given up. Maskwa put his hand on his shoulder. Vinnie picked his head up, shaking his hair away from his face. The tape on his right ear was torn away and a fresh stream of blood ran down his neck.

"Did you get the other one?" he said.

"Yes," Maskwa said. "I did."

"Alex," he said, as he stood up slowly. "You're here."

"Yeah, I'm here. I went to Sudbury first."

That stopped him for a second. Then he picked up his rifle and brushed off the leaves. "You saw what happened," he said.

"Yes."

"How did you know to go there?"

"I was in your cabin," I said. "Leon helped me find the maps you printed out."

"Okay."

"What was the article about?"

He didn't say anything.

"From the *Detroit News,*" I said. "Whatever it was, it brought you all the way up here again."

"We need to go see how Helen's doing."

"Vinnie, the police are coming."

"What?"

"The OPP are on their way. I called Reynaud."

"Come on," he said. "We've got to figure out what to do."

The three of us went back to the lodge. We passed the dead man, the ruin of his skull and blood and gore on the shed, the mist finally retreating from the dock and the lake as the sun came up. We passed the other dead man. We stepped over the blood and went up the stairs. Helen hadn't moved. She was still huddled in the corner. High above the fireplace, the moose head was half obliterated, one antler lying on the floor.

284

Maskwa went down on his knees and spoke to her in a low voice. "It's over," he said. "It's over."

She looked up and scanned our faces, all three of us, one by one. She didn't look surprised. She was probably incapable of surprise at that point. She was way beyond it.

"We have to get you out of here," Vinnie said. "You can't be here when the police come."

"Vinnie," I said, "what are you talking about?"

"We'll explain later, Alex. Right now we've got to get her out of here."

"Vinnie, you should go with her," Maskwa said. "Go to my house."

"I can't ask you to stay here," Vinnie said.

"If you're here, they'll ask you why you came looking for Helen."

Vinnie thought about it. "Okay, you're right."

"Do you guys know what you're doing?" I said.

"You've got to trust us, Alex. Okay? Just trust us for now."

I took a long breath. "Okay," I said. "Get going. Give me your rifle."

"When you hit the main road, head west," Maskwa said. "Give them a chance to come up the service road, then double back. We'll meet you at my house."

"We'll see you there," Vinnie said. He threw me his rifle, pausing just long enough to notice my muddy shoes. "What did the doctor tell you, Alex? You gotta keep your feet dry." Then he and Helen were out the door.

I waited with Maskwa while Vinnie fired up the truck and took off. It was about a four-minute ride out to the main road, maybe three and a half if you were flying. I wasn't sure if they'd make it.

"Maskwa, can you tell me what's going on now?"

"It's Helen's story," he said. "She'll tell you."

"Okay, fine. So what do we say when the police get here?"

"You came looking for Vinnie, and you picked me up to help you."

"I talked to Reynaud just before I got here. I didn't say anything about you being with me."

"So you didn't say anything. It doesn't mean I wasn't with you."

"Maybe," I said. "We might be able to sell it."

"We split up and searched the place, looking for Helen and Vinnie. Then those men got here. They started shooting at you, so we had to kill them. It was self-defense."

"That's it?"

"That's the story, Alex. We never saw Vinnie, and we never saw Helen. We have no idea where they are."

A few minutes later, we heard the police cars coming down to the lodge.

"As soon as we're done here, I get all the answers, right?"

He gave me a tired smile. "You and me both. They still haven't told me."

I stood there looking at him. The police cars got closer.

"Okay," he said. "It's showtime."

Chapter Twenty-Six

Maskwa and I spent the next four hours at the lodge, telling our story over and over to several different constables. Staff Sergeant Moreland was there, of course, and as he listened to me go over the whole thing one more time, he had a look on his face like he wished I had never set foot in Ontario. Not that I could blame him. As I watched him standing over the body by the stairs, it occurred to me he was probably near retirement himself. For all I knew, he and DeMers had been making plans to go fishing together when they had both hung it up. Now DeMers was dead. DeMers and Gannon and Tom LeBlanc and four men from Detroit were dead, and now there were two more.

I saw Boxer Face and Suntan standing there for a moment, looking down at the other body, the one by the shed, and I saw a couple other constables who had kept guard over me in the medical center. The one person I didn't see was Natalie Reynaud. When I asked the sergeant where she was, he told me she was back at the detachment and left it at that. Then he told me to go home and to wait by my phone in case he needed me for more questions. Aside from that, he didn't want to ever see me or hear from me again.

When we were finally in my truck, I took my last look at the lodge and then turned the ignition. "Come on, Maskwa," I said. "Let's get the hell out of here."

I turned the truck around and headed out the gravel road. A minute later, we passed the sedan, its front wheels off the road.

"This wasn't the best way to do this," I said.

Maskwa looked over at me. "What do you mean?"

"Setting the trap so far from the lodge. You gave them a chance to regroup."

He looked back out the window. "It wasn't supposed to happen that way. We were going to take Helen to the lodge, get her settled in there, and then come back out. Those guys would have never made it out of the car."

"Did they get here too soon?"

He shrugged. "Vinnie misjudged how much of a lead we had."

"Why not just leave her at your house?"

"She wouldn't let us do that."

"I wouldn't have given her the choice."

"You weren't there, Alex."

I shook my head and kept driving. We hit the main highway, took a left, and headed east, toward the reserve.

"You saw what they did to Helen's friends," Maskwa said. "I didn't see it myself, you've got to understand that. Vinnie just told me about it. But you were there in the house."

"Yes."

"Did they really burn them alive?"

I hesitated as the scene came back to me. "It looked like they were still alive, yes."

"They would have done the same to Helen. They were coming for her. We weren't going to let her out of our sight."

"So why did Vinnie come up here?" I said. "And why did he come alone?"

"He told me he didn't want to drag you up here again."

I tightened my grip on the steering wheel. "Yeah, he'll hear about that one later."

"Vinnie called me," he said. "He was driving right by the reserve. It was a spur of the moment thing."

That hit me in the gut. Spur of the moment or not, when Vinnie needed help, he chose one of his own people again. Not me.

Maskwa seemed to pick up on it. "It was too late to call you," he said. "He needed help and I was right here."

I didn't say anything. I kept driving. I turned onto the road to Calstock, passing the sawmill and the power plant, then the spot in the woods where we had found the Suburban. The crime scene tape was gone now. There was no trace of what had happened here.

We drove past the sign welcoming us to the Constance Lake Reserve. The lake appeared on our left, and then the road to Maskwa's house. Vinnie's truck was parked outside.

When we pulled in, Guy and his mother both came out of their house next door. It was a cold and bitter day and they were walking with their heads down, Guy's mother in a housecoat with her arms wrapped around her chest, and Guy in his baseball jacket. They joined us in Maskwa's living room, all six of us in that one small room. Maskwa threw some more wood into his stove.

"How did it go?" Vinnie asked. He was sitting in the back corner, farthest away from the fire. Helen was on the couch, watching the fire through the glass door on the stove.

"We got through it," I said. "They want to know where you and Helen are."

"I imagine."

"We told them we didn't know."

"Thank you."

I was just about to ask when the explanations would begin, but then I found a measure of patience for the first time in my life. I kept my mouth shut and sat down.

Maskwa made coffee, and the rest of us sat there in silence. Finally, Vinnie took out a folded piece of paper from his pocket and gave it to me. Helen didn't look at me. She didn't move.

I unfolded the paper and read it. It was a reprint from the *Detroit News,* dated January 21, 1985. The headline read "Death Toll in Hotel Fire Grows to 27."

I glanced up at Helen. She had her hands clasped tight together in her lap.

The picture. It showed the burned-out remains of a building, a hotel on Warren Avenue, near Wayne State University. It was a grainy black-and-white photo, made even grainier in the reprint. It looked like something from a hundred years ago.

The story itself started out with two more people dying at the hospital, plus another person who had not been included in the initial count. Most of the dead were Canadians. A junior high school class had come down from Sudbury to take part in a choral concert at the college. Nineteen of the dead were students.

I looked up at Helen again. She kept staring at the fire. Something came to me then, something she had said to me at the lodge.

No kids. None of them had kids. Helen, Hank, Ron, and Millie—it was what they all had in common. The strange gloom that was hanging over the lodge when we got there—it occurred to me now that it wasn't just because they were closing down the business. There was a much bigger reason.

I went back to the article. The fire had started next door, in a dry cleaner's. It had spread into the hotel. There was some question about the sprinkler system in the old hotel, and the fire exits. An investigation was underway.

I looked at the date on the article again. I thought back to January of 1985. That was right in the middle of my lost year, the year after my partner and I were gunned down in that apartment building on Woodward, the year after my marriage ended and I left the police force. I remembered the fire, but only vaguely. It was just something on the front page of the newspaper.

The last paragraph was a long list, each name followed by an age and a home town. I scanned through the names. I found Stephanie Gannon, 13, Sudbury. I found Melissa St. Jean, 13, Sudbury. I found Brett Trembley, 13, Sudbury, and Barry Trembley, 13, Sudbury.

This time when I looked up at Helen she cleared her throat and spoke. "Now you know," she said. She didn't look at me.

Maskwa handed me a hot cup of coffee. He sat down next to Guy's mother. Guy was sitting on the floor next to Vinnie. They were all watching the flames in the wood stove.

"I wasn't there," she said. "Hank wasn't there. Ron and Millie weren't there. The kids wanted to go by themselves. Just their friends and a couple of chaperones. They were so excited."

She looked down at the cup in her hands. She didn't drink from it.

"Melissa and Stephanie were best friends. They were in that room together. They were planning on going to college together. They were going to be bridesmaids for each other."

She swallowed hard.

"At least they were together when they died," she said. "They had that much."

There was silence in the room for a while.

"They say the smoke gets you first," she finally said. "They say you never feel the fire itself. You don't even wake up. But it started at midnight. That's the thing. In a hotel room by themselves for the first time, there's no way those two kids would have been sleeping at midnight."

A single tear ran down her cheek.

"Afterward, we'd all get together once a week. All the parents. Sort of like a support group. We'd try to help each other. After about a year, people started to drop out of the group. It was time to move on, they said. It was time to stop dwelling on it. That's what one woman said to me. It's not healthy, she said. You've got to let go."

Another long silence. The wood crackled in the stove.

"She had another child. That's why she said that. She had somebody else. We didn't. We had nobody. Maybe it was unhealthy, holding on to each other like that. All these years. But we were all we had. Nobody else could understand. I couldn't be with somebody else, somebody who didn't know how it felt. So we stayed together."

She wiped her nose with her hand.

"Claude tried to look after us," she said. It took me a second to realize who she was talking about now. "As much as he was grieving himself, losing his daughter, I think he felt responsible for us."

Claude. I looked back down at the article, scanned the list of names. I didn't see anyone named DeMers.

"Her name was Olivia Markel," Helen said. "That was her married name. She was the music teacher."

I found the name. Olivia Markel, 27, Sudbury.

"Claude found out about the investigation," she said. "He had a friend, a detective down in Detroit."

I skimmed through the article again. "The hotel," I said. "The sprinklers and the fire exits."

"No," she said. "That's not what I'm talking about."

"No?"

"The dry cleaner's next door," she said. "They were trying to put an arson case together. I guess it's a hard thing to do. Especially a place like that, with all the chemicals . . . It's not enough to prove that it was set intentionally. You have to prove that the owners did it themselves, or paid somebody else to do it."

"The owners—"

"Red Albright. And his little gang. There were five of them. They owned a lot of businesses back then. The dry cleaner's wasn't doing so well, so they burned it down. That's what happened. The police couldn't prove it. But that's what happened."

"I'm not getting some of this," I said. "I'm sorry. How did they get up here, all these years later?"

She shook her head. "Claude shouldn't have told us about the investigation. I know he regretted it ever since. The way it just kept eating at us ... Especially Hank. It was driving him crazy. He was going to go after them himself, he said. For a while, it was all he ever thought about. When we all bought the lodge together, he used to sit there by the fireplace ... This was the fireplace you saw, the one he never let anybody build a fire in."

I saw the empty fireplace in my mind. I heard the moaning sound it made when the wind rushed over the chimney.

"He'd sit there," she said, "and try to come up with the best way to get those men, every one of them. He knew he could find them. He knew he could go down there and ring their doorbells and see their faces. It was just ... what to do next. I thought I finally convinced him, he'd just ruin his life, what was left of it. Or whatever life we might be able to have together. I thought he was getting over it. Finally, I thought maybe he had let it go. And then they called us, just like that. Albright himself. This man. This voice on the phone. Back when our phone was working. He called us."

"Of all the places to go hunting in Canada," I said, "they called you?"

"They got tired of hunting deer and they wanted to try something bigger. They heard there were some good moose lakes up here, and there aren't that many lodges left. Ours just happened to be the one they chose. After all these years, just when I thought Hank was getting to be himself again . . . He told me it was just a twist of fate. But that maybe it was supposed to work out that way. Like God sent them up here. He actually said that. Like we were finally being given the chance to see the men who killed our children."

I knew it wasn't that simple. They may have burned down their business, whether they had been charged for it or not. The fire spread into the hotel, which may or may not have been up to fire codes. It was a whole chain of events that might have turned out a hundred different ways. But I wasn't going to say that to her.

"I know what you must be thinking. I know how it sounds. But you can't understand what it feels like until it happens to you. I'd have dreams about my daughter. About the fire. I couldn't get to her."

Her voice was ragged now.

"I can't make you understand," she said. "The dreams—"

We heard the rumble of a car passing by outside. The sound got farther and farther away, and then it was quiet again.

"When those men got here, I wasn't sure what to expect. I was afraid to even look at them. But Hank, my God, he was out there shaking their hands, looking each one of them in the eyes. If I had done that—"

She stopped. She looked back at Vinnie.

"If I had done that, I might have seen your brother. I might have known he wasn't one of them. I might have seen that he didn't belong."

Vinnie didn't say anything. The light from the fire was reflected in his eyes.

Five men. That's all Hank had seen. Albright and his business associates.

Five men.

"Hank flew them out to Lake Agawaatese. It's the farthest away. There aren't even many moose up there. Just bears."

She kept looking at Vinnie.

"I didn't know, Vinnie." She said it like she was still trying to convince him. "I didn't know what he was going to do."

"You knew he was going to kill them," Vinnie said.

"Vinnie—"

"How could you not know? All of you."

"Ron knew. He was there with Hank, out at the lake. He and Hank ... They were there. They did it together. And then Ron and Hank took the Suburban out that morning, the morning they were supposed to have flown back. They took the Suburban and Hank's truck, I mean, and left the Suburban in the woods. I didn't know at the time. I wasn't there. Hank told us to go away, me and Millie. We came back that Saturday. The Suburban was gone. At first I thought—"

"What?"

"I thought the men were gone. I thought maybe ... I· don't know ... maybe they didn't do anything. Maybe they flew them back. Then Hank told me. It's done, he said. That's what he said to me. It's done."

"You knew, Helen."

She picked her hands up out of her lap. She held them up for a moment and then let them drop again.

"Yes," she said, in a voice so low I could barely hear her. "Yes, I knew."

"What about DeMers?"

"He didn't even know those men were up here. Not until after. They came out to the lodge, Claude and his partner—what was her name?"

"Reynaud," I said. "Natalie Reynaud."

"They came out here that morning, when the call came up from Detroit about the missing men. That's when Hank took him

295

aside and told him what had happened. I thought Claude would strangle him."

"What was he going to do about it?" I said. "He was a police officer."

"Yes, and he had taken an oath. He said that to Hank. He had to turn us in. All of us. But then—"

"What?"

"He didn't. He just didn't."

I thought about DeMers, about the way he had treated us. The hot and cold act, and everything he had said and done to convince us to go home and to stay there. It all made sense now. It was tearing him up. And the two of us digging around up here was the last thing in the world he had wanted.

"What about later?" I said. "When he flew up there with Hank?"

"I was there when Claude came over. He didn't have his partner this time. He said that you and Vinnie had flown up to the lake, and that you were still up there. Hank got his rifle and tried to put it in the plane, and Claude asked him what the hell he was doing. Hank said he'd have to take care of things if you and Vinnie had found out what he and Ron had done. Claude told him that wasn't going to happen. They were going to fly up and bring the two of you back. And if you had found out, then we'd all just have to deal with it."

She looked back at Vinnie again.

"Claude said there was already one innocent man dead. He wasn't going to let it happen to two more."

Vinnie nodded his head once.

"I swear to God," Helen said. "I thought that was going to be the end of it. I thought Claude would take care of it and it would all be over. But Hank must have sneaked that rifle onto the plane somehow. They flew up there . . . And Hank, he must have—"

She started crying.

"He was protecting us," she said. "That goddamned fool. He didn't want any of this to touch us. Now he's gone. Claude is gone. Ron and Millie are gone. Everybody's gone except me."

Maskwa got up from his chair and went to her. He stood over her and gently placed one hand to the side of her face. Vinnie stayed in the corner. He was looking up at the ceiling now, blinking away the tears.

"You weren't coming up here for revenge," Maskwa said. "You came up here to help them."

"I had my friend at the *News* run their names," Vinnie said. "It was so easy to find that article. I knew it would be just as easy for anybody else. Alex was there when Albright's brother stopped us. He saw the look in his eyes. And the way they both seemed to think about it, like they had some idea . . . I knew they'd find them sooner or later."

"Would you have done the same for Ron?" I said. "If you had gotten to him in time?"

He closed his eyes. "It has to stop somewhere, Alex. Okay? Those kids died in that fire. Hank and Ron, they killed Albright and those other men. And my brother with them. They burned them up. So Albright's brother came up to kill some more. More fire. More goddamned fire, Alex. What am I supposed to do? Go burn some more of them?"

Maskwa kept his hand on Helen's face. Vinnie opened his eyes again and watched the two of them.

"No more," Vinnie said. "This is where it ends. Helen has to go away. She has to go somewhere where they won't find her."

"I know where we can go," Maskwa said. "I can get the plane ready."

I didn't have to ask what they were talking about. I knew there were a dozen places they could take her, like maybe Moosonee, on James Bay. Once she was there, she could either go to one of the other reserves on the Ontario side of James Bay, or take the ferry over to Quebec.

Nobody would ever find her. Not the police. Not the men from Detroit.

I knew Vinnie had done this once before. A woman was in trouble and he took her into his family, a family that extended for thousands of miles, across all borders. And he made her disappear. Now I was seeing it firsthand.

"No," Helen said. She took Maskwa's hand away from her head. "You're not taking me anywhere."

"Helen, you have to—"

"No, Vinnie. I waited until Alex and Maskwa got here, so they could hear the whole story. Now it's time for you and me to go to the police."

"I don't think you want to do that," Vinnie said.

"I'm not going to run away," she said. "I'm going to tell them everything that happened." She hesitated. "Everything except Claude. There's no reason to pull him into this. He died a hero. Let him stay a hero."

"They'll find out eventually."

"Maybe, maybe not," she said. "But I don't have to tell them."

"Helen . . ." Vinnie said. He tried to find some words but couldn't.

"Let's go," she said. "Let's go do this right now."

They tried to talk her out of it, but it was obvious her mind was made up. A few minutes later, we were standing outside in the cold dead yard, watching Vinnie and Helen drive away. Helen looked at us through her window, then lifted her hand and put it flat against the glass.

I said my own goodbyes to Maskwa, this incredible man, and to Guy and his mother. I got in my truck and started down the road. There were snowflakes in the air. I drove down the empty highway, all the way to the station in Hearst, and parked next to Vinnie's truck. I knew it would be a long wait, so I settled in and went to sleep.

A couple hours later, I picked my head up and saw Vinnie coming out of the station. He was alone, and he looked as tired and miserable as any man I had ever seen.

He gave me a nod and got in his truck, and then I followed him all the way home.

Chapter Twenty-Seven

That winter came in as if it wasn't really sure of its mission. It would snow a few inches, then stop. We never got buried. It would go down to zero at night, but we didn't have any of those thirty-below nights where you worry about your pipes freezing.

I spent Thanksgiving with Jackie and his son, the three of us alone in the Glasgow. The place was open that night, but nobody else came in until after nine o'clock. I left the place and drove over to Vinnie's mother's house and finished up my Thanksgiving night with my new adopted family.

We had one big snow in early December, but aside from that the winter stayed mild and some of the snowmobilers even canceled their reservations. That meant a little less noise and fewer drunken fools running into each other. Somehow I adjusted.

When Christmas came, I had my busiest holiday in years. I started out over at Vinnie's mother's house again, had lunch with Jackie, and then I headed over to Leon's house for dinner. I gave toys to his kids and a bottle of wine to Eleanor, and they actually seemed to enjoy having me around this time. It helped that I wasn't asking Leon to do any private eye work.

Until after dinner.

Eleanor was putting the kids to bed when I told him what I was thinking about. I had seen what Vinnie had done for Helen. I was thinking maybe I could do something for somebody, too.

"And maybe a little bit for yourself?" Leon said.

"Okay, maybe. Just a little bit."

He called me a couple of days later. I sat on the whole idea for a couple more days. Maybe I was trying to talk myself out of it. I woke up on New Year's Eve day convinced that it was a bad idea.

Sometime late that afternoon, I changed my mind.

I had a bottle of champagne in my fridge. I had been saving it for God knows what, for drinking by myself again on another New Year's Eve. This year I might have shared it with Vinnie and his family. Or Jackie and Leon. I had more family now than ever.

But that wasn't enough. For some reason, after what I had been through, I felt like I needed something more.

I put the bottle of champagne in the truck, drove out into the cold day. I had the plow on the front of the truck, the cinder blocks in the back for traction. Even with no snow on the ground, I was ready. That's the way I am.

I drove over the bridge. The man in the customs booth looked my truck over and asked me if I had heard something about a snowstorm. I told him no, but the minute I took the plow off we'd get dumped on. He thought that was funny. He wished me a Happy New Year and sent me on my way.

I had the directions on the seat next to me, courtesy of Leon. It wasn't that far away, that was the crazy thing. I figured I'd have to drive all day again. But the address was in Blind River, a little town on the North Channel, maybe an hour and a half east of Sault Ste. Marie.

I took the Queen's Highway out of the Soo and followed it through all the small towns on the coast. I had come down this same road on the way to Sudbury, when I was looking for Vinnie. This time there was a lot less at stake. So why did I feel so nervous?

The sun was going down when I hit Blind River, the days so damned short now. I found the intersection in the middle of town, took a left and headed north. The town gave way to wetlands and empty fields spotted with thin traces of snow. I went over a little bridge and found the farmhouse on the right, set back from the road. I pulled up the gravel driveway and stopped. There was a car pulled up in front of a small barn, but the house looked dark.

I got out and went to the front porch. There was a Christmas wreath hanging on the door. I rang the bell and waited. Twenty seconds passed. I rang the bell again.

The door opened. Natalie Reynaud stood there in the light of the doorway. She was wearing jeans and a white cotton shirt, and she looked at me like I was the last person she ever expected to see standing on her porch. Which I suppose I was.

"McKnight?"

"Good evening."

"What are you ... What is this?"

"I'm here to give you something. May I come in?"

She didn't move. "What are you talking about?" She looked down at the bottle in my hand. "Did you come here to give me a bottle of champagne?"

"No," I said. "Something else. The champagne is just ..." I ran out of words. At that moment, I started to feel like an idiot and I might have left if she hadn't opened the door all the way for me.

"Come on in," she said. "You're letting the warm out."

"My father used to say that," I said as I stepped inside. "You're letting the warm out."

She stood in front of me with her arms folded. "I'm not on the job right now," she said. "I took a leave."

"I know," I said. "I mean, I don't know, but I'm not surprised. I did the same thing myself."

She kept one arm folded around her and ran the other through her hair. "McKnight, I don't know how you found me, or why you came all the way out here, but—"

"Here," I said. I gave her the piece of paper.

She took it from me. She held it for a moment like she was unsure what to do with it. Then she unfolded it and read the article. She read it quickly and then she looked up at me. "What's this about?"

"Can we sit down?"

"Over here," she said. She led me to her dining room table. It was an antique oak table with ornate claw feet, and it matched the rest of the room perfectly. There was a hutch with china plates displayed in rows, and an old pie cabinet with the air holes in the metal panels. A chandelier hung from the ceiling with five crystal bowls.

"It's a nice house," I said.

"It's my grandparents' house."

I looked out into the next room. "I hope I'm not disturbing them."

"I doubt it. They're both dead."

I sat down at the table. My collar felt hot around my neck.

"Look," she said, "are you going to tell me what this article means?"

"Please sit down," I said.

She let out a long breath and sat down across from me. I couldn't help but notice what the antique light did to her eyes.

And for the first time I saw a hint of red in her hair.

"Read the names again," I said.

She looked at the article. The expression on her face changed. "Gannon. St. Jean. Trembley." She looked at me. "Where did you get this?"

"Someone at the newspaper ran a search with those names. It was easy."

"I know what happened up at that lodge," she said. "I read your statement. Was that the way it really went?"

"I thought you said you were on leave."

"I'm getting a little concerned here. Maybe you should go."

"There's another name in that list," I said. "Olivia Markel."

She looked at it again. "I see it. What about her?"

"Her father was your partner."

It took a few seconds for that to sink in. "Claude had a daughter? He never said anything about her."

"It was a long time ago. Before you even knew him, I'm sure."

"I don't get it. What does this have to do . . . with anything?"

"They were all together," I said. "Those people at the lodge, and Claude. They've been together ever since that fire in Detroit."

"But Gannon—" She thought hard about it. "Gannon was the one who killed him."

"In the end, yes. When Vinnie and I found out what they had done to those men, Claude apparently wanted Gannon to come clean."

"How do you know this?"

"I assume you have something like the Fifth Amendment up here in Canada?"

"Just tell me."

"I have to know I can trust you."

She looked at me forever. Somewhere in the house, a grandfather clock chimed nine times.

"Tell me," she said.

I told her about Helen, and what Vinnie and Maskwa had done for her. And my own part in it. I told her the whole story. When I was done, she sat back in her chair and closed her eyes.

"They'll find out eventually," she said. "Someone else will make the connection."

"Someday," I said. "Maybe. But it doesn't have to come from you."

"So is that why you came here? To tell me the truth about Claude? Is that going to change anything?"

"Yes," I said. "It changes everything. He left you behind for a reason. You don't have to blame yourself anymore."

She shook her head.

"Did you hear me?"

"Yes," she said. "I understand what you're trying to tell me. But—"

"Why are you here?" I said.

"What do you mean?"

"In this house. It looks like it hasn't changed in fifty years."

"When I took the leave," she said. "I came back here." She looked up at the ceiling, like she could see through it to the far-thest corners of the house. "This place means a lot to me, but I'm wondering if maybe it's time to do something with it."

"Just like me," I said. "For me, it was my father's cabins."

She put her elbows on the table. She leaned forward and looked at me close. "I'll give you one thing," she said. "You were right about the people at work. Nobody would even look me in the eye anymore."

That was all I needed, just the way she had moved toward me. It was a little thing, just a few inches. But it was enough. I was building another bridge over another chasm, this one maybe the biggest of all. Another bridge, another connection. Another step for me on my way back into the human race.

Outside, a northern wind picked up. It was cold out there. It was cold and dark.

"You've been through it," she said. "You know how it feels."

"Yes," I said. "But I had to do it alone."

She kept looking at me. "What am I supposed to do now?"

"It's New Year's Eve," I said. "You feel like making a toast?"

"Depends on what kind of champagne you brought. Is it any good?"

"Hell if I know."

"I'll get the glasses," she said. "Don't go away."

I didn't. And that's how it began.

Happy New Year.